"TONIGHT WAS MAGNIFICENT."

Jeremy hesitated before he added, " But Chicago is another matter. We will need to add acts . . . animals . . . crew. Chicago will cost us money before we have ample opportunity to accumulate money and if we are not fully prepared, we may never again have the occasion to play a venue on that scale."

"On the other hand, if we could be successful there . . ." She said the words aloud but more to herself than to him.

"Yes, but it's a risk, Lucy—one we'd better all be prepared to face."

She smiled up at him. "You don't know circus folk, Jeremy. We're in the business of taking risks."

He smiled and lifted his glass to her in a toast. 'I'll talk it over with Harry and with Adam back in New York."

"You're going back to New York?" she blurted without thinking.

His smiled broadened. "Why, Miss Conroy, would you miss me if I did?"

She felt the heat rise to her cheeks. "I . . . of course not—that is . . ." He laughed and she did as well. "The truth is that we have gotten used to having you around—purely for entertainment, you understand." *Lord above, she was flirting with the man.*

Dear Romance Readers,

In July 2000, we launched the Ballad line for four new series, and each month since then we've presented both new and continuing stories set everywhere from medieval England to the American West—the kind of passionate, romantic stories you love best, written by the most gifted authors. At the back of each book, we'll tell you when you can find subsequent books in the series that have captured your heart.

this month, Willa Hix offers the second and last installment in her highly romantic *Golden Door* series. What happens when a British rake forced into the circus business meets a high-wire artist who acts as if *she's* running the show? In **Gone Courting**, you'll find out! Next, the always talented Sylvia McDaniel returns to the sultry heat of New Orleans with **The Price of Moonlight**, the second in her steamy *Cuvier Widows* series. Is the handsome man who happens onto the plantation of a stunned widow the answer to her prayers—or a temptation she can't resist?

The fabulous Tracy Cozzens continues her *American Heiresses* series with **White Tiger's Fancy**, as an impulsive young woman schemes her way into a big game hunt in India—and finds the daring hunter has captured her heart. Finally, reader favorite Suzanne McMinn concludes her sweeping *The Sword and the Ring* series with a tale of childhood love and grown-up decisions in **My Lady Knight**. Enjoy them all!

Kate Duffy
Editorial Director

The Golden Door

GONE COURTING

Willa Hix

ZEBRA BOOKS
Kensington Publishing Corp.
http://www.kensingtonbooks.com

One

Lucy Conroy could not catch a break. Just when it had seemed that she might actually be about to settle into a normal life—marriage, children, a real home—Reginald Dunworthy had up and left her. She should have known better than to trust a lion tamer—arrogant breed, both beast and man. Not to mention the fact that he was also an ungrateful bastard. Her father had made him what he was, taught him every trick of the trade, provided the finest animals available.

As if his leaving her weren't enough, he'd added insult to injury by electing to run off with the bane of Lucy's professional existence—the famous Eleanore Wilson, star of the Parnelli Brothers Circus. Eleanore had been the first woman to publicly perform the feat of hanging from the trapeze by her ankles at the very apex of the big top—a trick she and Lucy had learned together when the two had been friends and performing together in The Conroy Circus Cavalcade Extraordinaire. Eleanore had used that and her feminine wiles to worm her way into the Parnelli operation. Well, they'd find out soon enough that she was a one-trick wonder.

But the real capper had come when Lucy realized that Reggie must have taken the savings that she had been carefully accumulating for their future. He was the only one who knew about her dream of settling down one day to a normal life. He was the only one who knew about the money—and where she kept it.

One more season and there would have been enough for a down payment on a place like the small farm on the shores of Lake Michigan she'd seen when the circus traveled through northern Wisconsin. How she had chattered on about her dream life as she and Reggie walked that land together. Reggie would build an addition onto the house. They would have children—at least half a dozen. Lucy would have a garden filled with flowers. The children would . . .

Stop it, she ordered herself as she swung out high over the practice ring below. *He's not worth your tears.*

But, the tears came nevertheless. She stood on the flybar and pumped more vigorously until she was swinging so high that she was almost parallel to the ground far below her.

"Lucy!"

She slowed the trapeze a little and glanced down. Her brother, Ian, stood looking up at her.

"Harry wants to meet with us up at the house." From the day they'd been adopted by Harry and Shirley Conroy, Lucy and Ian had called their parents by their given names whenever the conversation had anything to do with the family business. That had been Shirley's idea of a way to show the others that there would be no special consideration for the children.

"Coming," Lucy replied and went from standing to a sitting position as if she were simply taking a seat on the living room sofa. Then she launched herself into a free fall to the net below. One bounce . . . two, and then she lay there a moment watching the now empty trapeze continue to swing above her.

"You okay?" Ian asked.

"I will be," she said with determination as she grasped the edge of the net and somersaulted out.

"'Cause the man ain't worth your tears, Luce."

She tossed her hair back and wrapped herself in a cape. The tears came again, silent but undeniable. "I loved him," she croaked.

Ian wrapped his arm around her shoulder and pulled her close. "Honey, you loved the *idea* of loving him. He's been gone nearly a month now—time to move on. Besides, Reggie never shared your dreams—not if you think about it honestly. Reggie only cares about one thing—Reggie."

"But . . ."

"You know I'm right, Luce," was all Ian would say as he walked with her toward the house.

And she did. She'd always known that Reggie was merely indulging her flights of fancy, but like the fool she was, she had thought she could change him. The truth was that he would do almost anything for a few stolen kisses and the hope they might lead to something far more intimate. He'd have promised anything if he'd thought it would get her into his bed. That's what had kept him with her—the challenge of taming her. He'd said it himself—jokingly, but with the ring of truth. Apparently, Eleanore had been easier to tame.

"But he stole from me," she said through gritted teeth, "and that I won't forget."

"You're not likely to be able to prove that, Luce." They had reached the back door of the old farmhouse that served as the winter headquarters for the company and the family home when they weren't on tour living out of a train. "Either way, I think there's something going on that's a mite more troubling for all of us, judging by Harry's tone when he asked me to round everybody up." He opened the door for her, and together they entered the kitchen as the warm air from the ancient cookstove mingled with the cold they'd let in with them.

"Grab yourselves a cup of coffee," Shirley Conroy urged. "They're gathering in there." She nodded toward the front of the house, where the two front rooms had long ago been converted into one large meeting room for occasions such as this.

Harry Conroy leaned one arthritic hip against the edge of the battered desk he used to work on the books and plan the season's itinerary. He looked tired, and a persistent cough racked his small, wiry body. He was sixty years old but looked older, and Lucy had to admit to herself that she'd been so wrapped up in her own problems that she hadn't really seen the toll that the long, hard winter and repeated illness had taken on her father.

Lucy glanced at her mother and caught her watching her husband. Shirley's face was lined with worry—about the bills, about the coming season, and most of all, about her beloved Harry. Shirley was Harry's second wife and she was fifteen years younger than her husband. It was clear to anyone who saw them that the two were devoted to each other and to the unwanted children they had adopted.

How fortunate was Lucy that these wonderful people had taken her into their lives? They were the only parents she'd ever known. They'd plucked her from the orphanage, along with Ian, to make their family once they'd realized that Shirley wouldn't be able to bear children. They'd given them love and a home and a career. And they had given them the childhood they had all but given up as a lost cause after years spent living in the orphanage. Lucy went back to the kitchen and got a cup of coffee for her mother. Shirley smiled wearily and accepted the offering.

The room was packed with members of the company, although Lucy was the only one in rehearsal garb. The others looked quite ordinary, dressed as they were in regular work clothes. They might have been the employees of any business gathering for a company meeting, if one didn't count Ida, the snake charmer, who never went anywhere without either a reptile or a colorful feather boa draped around her throat. Today she had selected a fuchsia boa of ostrich feathers. Then there were the identical Rawley triplets, contortionists who were almost never seen without their siblings.

Several people glanced up as Lucy entered the room, and then busied themselves with quiet conversation, blowing on their steaming coffee or finding something of sudden interest outside the window. She knew that they were thinking as much about Reggie's leaving her as about his leaving the company. She noticed the way conversations would suddenly stop or become too animated when she passed by. Everyone felt bad for her, and Lucy hated that. She'd had enough pity when she was living at the orphanage to last her a lifetime.

Harry pushed himself up from the desk and smiled as he held up one hand for quiet. "Morning, folks."

"Morning," was the mumbled reply. It was clear that everyone was nervous. In some ways, they'd been waiting for—and dreading—this meeting for weeks.

"Folks, I'm not gonna sugarcoat this thing," Harry said, his voice steady. "We had ourselves some serious setbacks these last couple of years. The virus in the elephant herd, folks leaving for better-paying jobs, others leaving the business for good . . ." His voice trailed off and he slumped back against the desk. Shirley took a step forward as if to go to him, but he pulled himself up and faced his employees. "The good news is that our major investor, the Porterfield Fund of New York, is sending us some help to help us put things right. Shirley and I have agreed that it's time to put the business of running this thing into the hands of a businessman. Adam Porterfield has selected one of his best men to come out here and take charge of things for a while."

An immediate buzz raced through the room. Everyone was talking at once: some voices protesting the idea of an outsider coming from New York; others simply wondering what it all meant.

"Now, folks, Adam is the late Clayton Porterfield's son. Clay was my dearest friend, and Adam's taken over the business now. I would trust my life to Adam—he's that much like his father." The protests and grumbling stopped. "The new man is from England and they do some good work over there with circus companies. In fact, that's where the whole thing got started. Might interest you to know that this guy's got himself a title and everything: *Sir* Jeremy Barrington."

The suppressed tension among those gathered in the small room ignited into protests of outrage. Harry held up both hands. "Stop your bellyaching. If Adam says this Barrington fellow can be of help, then we'll give him a chance. We're already three weeks late starting our season. Do you want jobs or not?"

The room settled back into a tense silence. Harry paused, glanced at Lucy, and then hooked his thumbs into his suspenders. "There's some more good news," he said. Something about the way Harry kept glancing in her direction made Lucy pay close attention to his next words.

"As you know, Reginald Dunworthy left us about a month ago to join the Parnelli outfit." He paused and cleared his throat before continuing. "Earlier today I had a call from Nick Parnelli, and he's offering to buy Duke and King."

"No!" Lucy cried out, and everyone in the room rumbled their agreement with her protest. King and Duke were two of the three lions that Reggie had used in his act. More than that, they were the youngest and most active of the group and, therefore, the most exciting animals in his act. The remaining lion was an arthritic old-timer named Tut.

"Now, settle down, everybody. Nick is willing to pay top dollar, and it'll buy us valuable time to get back on our feet. Besides, for the time being, we don't have a lion tamer to replace Reggie, so I took the deal."

"I reckon it'll buy us a little time if they brought a good price," Ian said.

"They did," Harry assured them all.

The others settled back into their seats and waited for Harry to continue. But Harry started to cough, and the longer he coughed, the more alarmed people became.

"So, when is this Barrington fellow getting here?"

Ian asked above the general murmuring as soon as Harry had sipped some water and regained control.

"Tomorrow or the next day, I expect," Harry replied.

"What's he gonna do?" somebody called out from the back of the room.

"Yeah, can he tame lions?" somebody else asked, and everybody chuckled.

"I doubt it. He's a businessman, let's remember," Harry added. "On the other hand, Adam says the boy's got a real flare for show business, so maybe that's a good sign, huh?"

The mutters of concern began again.

"Now, let's not get our dander up," Harry said in a loud, commanding voice. "This Barrington guy is gonna need our support. He's coming in here to help us back on our feet. There may be call for some . . . changes. . . ." The grumbling erupted more loudly than before. Harry held up his hands. "I'm just saying, let's hear him out—at least until the season gets under way."

Lucy studied her father. She would trust him and Shirley with her very life, but she could see in his eyes that Harry didn't entirely believe what he was saying. He was worried about the Englishman and what he might do.

She glanced over at Shirley and saw her using the hem of her apron to dab at the corner of her eye. "A mite of soot," she said hastily when she saw Lucy watching her. Her smile did not reach her eyes. "Come on, Lucy. Help me get the noon meal out. Solly's shorthanded again."

"Coming," Lucy replied, but she turned to Ian. "What have you heard?"

"About the Englishman?" Ian shrugged. "He's

some kind of duke or lord or something. He's been working for Adam Porterfield for the last several months, and Adam told Harry that the man had a talent for managing entertainment businesses. Beyond that, all we have to go on is Adam Porterfield's assurance that this Barrington fellow has been sent to save the circus—not sell it off."

"Well, that's something," Lucy said, but she couldn't shake the uneasy feeling that such assurances didn't hold water if the company could not turn things around financially speaking—at least pay their own way. Ian knew as well as she did that Clayton Porterfield had held Harry in high esteem. But, Clayton was dead now, and the son could not be expected to hold to the same standard of loyalty.

Jeremy Barrington gazed out the club car window at the passing landscape, and his heart sank. Nothing as far as the eye could see but farmland and forests and the occasional town that was no more than a train station and a couple of stores in most cases. Ever since the train had left Chicago, this had been the view.

The layover in Chicago had caused his hopes to rise. This was a city that was every bit as exciting as New York, if not quite as cosmopolitan. He had stayed the night luxuriating in a fine hotel, enjoying a delicious multicourse meal, and treating himself to an evening at the theater. He had wired his friend and mentor, Adam Porterfield, to keep him apprised of the progress he had made in this forced journey to the outback, trying to put an enthusiastic stamp on the words. Adam had replied with the news that there would be a surprise for him, to be delivered the week following his arrival in Wisconsin. Given Adam's sense of humor, Jeremy was afraid to imagine what the surprise might be. Clearly, the financier had delighted in giving Jeremy this loathsome assignment. He was to spend the next several months out here in the wilderness trying to mold a bunch of ragtag circus performers, who had already proved their mediocrity, into a profitable business.

He had vowed to redeem himself with Adam Porterfield. After all, he had made a mistake that could be credited to overzealousness. Granted, his decision to take funds from one client in order to invest in what he had thought would be a major deal had never been outright larceny. Had that been the case, he would have kept the money for himself. And, to Jeremy's relief, Adam had admitted that he understood that Jeremy's intentions had been noble. Still, the error had been serious enough and stupid enough that Adam had decided to teach him a lesson.

Jeremy lit a fresh cigar and accepted the brandy the porter brought on a small silver tray. The service on the train had been first-rate through most of the journey, but it was clear that once he left Chicago, he was traveling with a far less sophisticated crew.

He turned his attention to the portfolio of papers and reports he had brought with him. In the weeks before Jeremy had left New York, Adam had seen to it that he was well briefed on the circus business in general, and the history of the Conroy company in particular. The reports before him showed records from the past several seasons of the Conroy Circus Cavalcade. Five years earlier, the company had appeared to be on its way to major growth and success. Then, two years ago, the owner and manager had begun to show signs of poor health. That, coupled with bad weather and a general economic downturn across the Midwest, had resulted in falling ticket sales and the flight of some of the more prominent acts to more profitable companies.

The group had begun losing money, and the free fall had continued and showed no evidence of abating. Over the winter, some sort of virus had rampaged through the prize elephant herd—the company's single claim to fame in the circus world—reducing the herd by half, so that they could no longer claim "the largest herd of pachyderms in the land."

Jeremy unfolded some of the lithograph posters from past seasons. The quality of the design and printing had declined right along with the balance sheet. The long list of attractions on a five-year-old poster had dwindled to a list of three major attractions in the past year. They included Regal Reginald Dunworthy and his Kings of the Jungle, the previously noted Largest Pachyderm Herd in the Land, and Lady Lucinda Conroy, Angel of the Big Top. Second billing was given to Trixie LaMott and her Wonder Horse, Bucko; the Flying Jacoby Brothers, Tumblers, Acrobats, and High-Wire Artists Extraordinaire; and Babbo, a clown who, judging by the illustration, made his entrance by riding a bicycle that was several sizes too small for him.

Jeremy lingered over the illustration of Lucinda Conroy. She appeared petite and fragile in her white sequined costume, yet there was something of defiance and supreme self-confidence in the tilt of her chin. He wondered if that could be attributed to artistic license or if it was a true portrait of the performer. According to the most recent report he'd received from Adam, the lion tamer had left the company, and with the elephant herd decimated, it would appear that Miss Conroy was now the sole featured performer. She was also the owner's daughter. Jeremy wondered if she was up to the challenge of carrying an entire season on those narrow shoulders.

Jeremy refolded the poster and put it away, then leaned back to stare out the window, no longer registering the unremitting boredom of the scenery. He thought of New York and of Olivia, his stepsister and greatest supporter. It was Olivia who had stood up for him, hocking her late mother's jewels to pay his debt, seeing him off at the train station, and assuring him that she had every faith in his ability to succeed in this venture. At the moment, he wished that he could share in that confidence. The truth was, he felt like a fish out of water. What did he know of circuses and such? What did he know of the kinds of people who might patronize such a business out here in the backwaters of the country?

He took a deep draw on his cigar and forced his attention back to the reports and research before him. Specifically, he focused on the reports about the competition. Who were these companies that had succeeded where Conroy had faltered? How had they achieved that success, for surely they, too, must have weathered setbacks every bit as traumatic as those the Conroy concern had suffered? More to the point, how was he going to turn things around for them? His future depended upon his ability to do just that.

His reverie was interrupted as the train pulled into a station . . . his station. He gathered his belongings and stepped out onto the station platform and looked around. Surely, he was still on board and dreaming. It was impossible that he was actually witnessing a string of camels, mounted by several comely young ladies and herded by a large bearded man in coveralls and a bowler, strolling through town. Furthermore, shopkeepers and others along what he assumed was Main Street seemed completely unmoved by the strange sight.

"Need a lift, mister?"

Jeremy looked down into the upturned and quite dirty face of a young boy. The boy jerked his head toward a wagon that looked as if it might disintegrate if required to make one more run. "Could you direct me to the establishment of Mr. Harry Conroy?"

The kid studied him for a minute. "You sure don't talk like folks from around here." Then he grinned. "But then, you just stepped off the train, so you ain't from around here, are you?"

"The Conroy establishment?"

"I'll take you, but it's just over there—you can walk it easy." He pointed toward a cluster of buildings on the other side of the small bridge, where the camels were now crossing in stately single file as their riders chatted amiably with each other and the man in charge.

"Thank you, my good man," Jeremy said as he flipped the boy a coin and set off resolutely in the direction the boy had indicated.

"Thank *you*, " the kid shouted, clearly impressed by the tip. "I'll get your luggage and bring everything on over for you. Don't you worry about a thing, mister."

Jeremy turned. "Please, don't bother." He started to say that he would be staying at the hotel, but the boy had disappeared. *Never mind,* he thought. There would be time to deal with that later. For now, he was anxious to see exactly what Adam Porterfield had considered a fitting punishment for his transgression.

Lucy hooked her knees over the padded bar and flopped backward, causing the trapeze to swing gently as she hung there in midair. She had just run through her routine high above the floor of the winter practice facility. The late May morning was unseasonably warm, and the doors to the barn were open. She closed her eyes as she swung slowly back and forth, calming herself after the exertion of her practice session. She did some of her best thinking suspended upside down in midair, surrounded by the familiar sounds and smells of a circus stirring itself for another season.

After the first shock of Reggie's leaving had abated, she had concentrated all of her energies on her act. She was determined to top whatever Eleanore Wilson might attempt. Lucinda Conroy would be not only the star of the Conroy Circus, but the unparalleled champion of her craft. As Ian and her parents had reminded her, she had no proof at all that Reggie had taken her money. Even if he had, he could declare that he had saved from his own earnings. Certainly, Harry had paid his top performers well. Over the past season, he had even sweetened the pot by offering bonuses to those who stayed the entire season. Besides, there were no bank records or receipts to show deposits made. As easily as she could argue that Reggie spent every dime on drinking and gambling, he could argue that her fancy costumes did not come cheap. There wasn't a judge in the land who wouldn't assume that the man was the greater contributor to any money they might have been putting away for their wedding.

"Well, Reggie Dunworthy, you'll have your day of reckoning," she muttered through clenched teeth as she pumped hard and set the trapeze in motion preparatory to executing another stunt. When the trapeze came back to the lowest point of the arc, she released her grip and allowed her body to slide down until she was hanging only by her ankles.

"Easy, girl," Ian coached from his spotter's position far below on the ground. "Just get the feel of that for a minute."

Lucy arched and pulled herself back to a sitting position. "How did that look?" she called and, without waiting for his answer, provided her own. "It felt a little awkward and clumsy. I'll try again."

She executed a flawless cat-in-the-cradle move and hooked her knees over the bar. She hung there a moment, concentrating on the stunt as she viewed the world below, upside down. She closed her eyes, imagining the movement that would give the stunt the grace and agility for which she was known. She heard the familiar braying of Babbo's donkeys across the yard, interspersed with the occasional trumpeting of an elephant. Probably Cora—the star of the herd could rarely keep from expressing her opinion. Lucy heard the quiet conversation and occasional laughter of her fellow performers and crew members as they went about their business. Almost everyone was in residence now that the group was only weeks away from the start of a new season.

She frowned slightly and opened her eyes when she heard a very unfamiliar voice out in the yard, and by the sound of it, the owner was on his way to the practice barn. She let the trapeze slow to a stop as she watched the door and waited for the stranger to enter the barn. She was still hanging by her knees high above the practice ring when she spotted Sir Jeremy Barrington out in the yard.

There was no mistaking who he was. He wore a three-piece casual suit the color of a lion's coat. The color of the fabric emphasized the rich chestnut hair revealed beneath the narrow brim of his bowler. In the breast pocket was the precisely positioned tri-corner fold of a white handkerchief, and his wingback collar was highlighted by the fat knot of a gold silk tie. Across his chest, under the flaps of the open suitcoat and lying against the buttoned vest, she spotted the gold chain of his pocket watch. She shielded her eyes from the bright light outside the dim practice barn and permitted her gaze to roam the length of him, having the luxury of being unobserved herself. He was tall and broad-shouldered, and clean-shaven—which came as a bit of a surprise given the fashion for mustaches and even well-trimmed beards.

The clothes would have been a dead giveaway, even if everyone in residence hadn't been watching for the arrival of the Englishman from New York who was coming supposedly to save the day. Lucy certainly wasn't the only one watching the stranger. With only two weeks to go before they started on tour, the barn and yard were busier than usual as performers rehearsed their acts and animal handlers worked with their charges. There wasn't one among them who didn't turn to give a silent nod of acknowledgment to the stranger as he strode across the muddy yard.

Lucy viewed the man's approach with a mixture of hope and dread. She had no illusions: this could well be the company's last season. Although Harry had made light of it to the rest of the company since his announcement in the meeting two days earlier, everyone had agreed that the stranger was coming for only one of two reasons: he would either save the day or shut them down for good.

Harry had finally been forced to face the fact that he wasn't up to the grueling job of managing the company for the coming season, and to seek help. Lucy hated the idea, but even she could not deny that they were already woefully behind in bookings, not to mention that their competitors had already been on tour for nearly a month. She studied the man coming through the large double doors of the barn. She noticed his shoes—muddy now from his walk across the yard, but unmistakably the shoes of a city boy. They matched the color of his suit perfectly. They were lace-ups with pointed toes and toecaps that contrasted with the rest of the shoe. He sniffed the air and made a face, then glanced around with obvious disdain.

"First of May coming," she muttered to Ian, who glanced over his shoulder and then turned back to his work. She was certain that even if the approaching man overheard her, he'd never understand the reference. "First of May" was circus talk. It meant a greenhorn—an amateur—and anyone labeled "First of May" was considered fair game for ridicule.

"Now, Luce," Ian said softly, "you know what Dad said."

Lucy resumed her slow swing and ignored her brother's warning. Her long, wavy black hair fanned the air. She was barely aware of the rhythm of her action as she continued to consider the man who had been sent to redeem the financially floundering

Conroy Circus. "If that man is Adam Porterfield's idea of a rescuer, heaven help us all," she said, more to herself than to Ian.

"Good afternoon, my good man." The man approached Ian and touched a gloved finger to his bowler. There was not an ounce of warmth in his greeting. Clearly, he would prefer to be anywhere on earth than standing in this barn.

Lucy rolled her eyes and stilled her swinging. He advanced a step farther into the barn and glanced around before deciding it would be all right to proceed. "I wonder, ol' chap, would you be so kind as to direct me . . . ?"

And that's when it happened. In the blink of an eye, the young dandy was flying through the air without benefit of a trampoline or rigged cannon. He landed unceremoniously on his backside, near the pile of elephant dung that had caused his fall.

"Best to watch your step around the circus," Ian said tonelessly as he ambled across the makeshift ring and offered the man a hand up.

Lucy stifled a laugh, pulled herself up until she could grab the bar with both hands, and then did an effortless back flip into the net below. She loved making an entrance.

"Hello," she said as she came to rest on the edge of the net, almost nose to nose with the newcomer. As she had suspected, he had been unaware of her presence high above him, and her tumble to the net had startled him. He took a step backward, and before Lucy could utter a warning, he hit the same pile of dung and fell again.

"Have we no shovels with which to remove this?" the man demanded irritably. He struggled to his feet and pulled himself to his full height. He brought his angry gaze to rest on Ian as he removed the pristine handkerchief and tried without success to repair the worst of the damage.

"I'll take care of it, sir," Ian said and hurried off to the far corner of the barn.

"And you are . . . ?" The man turned his attention to Lucy.

"Well, now, we sure know who you are," she replied as she ignored his rudeness and somersaulted off the net. She turned and met his gaze, even though she had to tilt her head back to do so. Then, without pausing for further conversation, she brushed past him with a haughty toss of her waist-length hair for effect. On her way out the open double doors of the barn, she whipped her jersey shawl off of a chair, tying it snugly around her waist to form a skirt, before continuing on her way without a backward look.

She headed directly for the house. As she passed the corral where Cora, a large floppy-eared Indian elephant, serenely bathed herself with dust and bits of loose straw, Lucy gave the pachyderm a wink and a grin. "You gave him a real old-fashioned circus welcome, huh, girl?"

Cora paused and flapped her enormous ears slowly, as if considering Lucy's words. Then she drew back her trunk and let out a bellow of agreement. Lucy laughed and immediately felt better. She stretched her arms behind her and locked her fingers as she looked up at the cloudless blue sky. She spun slowly in a circle, catching the flash of pink and white cherry blossoms and the deep rose of crab apple flowers as she moved, letting the colors mingle and blend as she considered them through squinted eyes. Now that she'd seen him in person, her mood lightened considerably. She'd stake her entire reputation on the bet that this English dandy would be gone by the end of the week.

As she climbed the back stairs of the ramshackle house, she could see Harry and Shirley through the window. They were sitting at the kitchen table, organizing yet another stack of bills and ledgers. It seemed to her that they'd spent every waking hour organizing records ever since they'd heard that the Englishman was on his way. Lucy opened the screen door without registering the familiar squeal of the hinge. She walked to the stove and poured herself a cup of coffee before speaking. "Well, he's here," she said finally.

Harry and Shirley looked first at each other and then at her. "Then I'd best go introduce myself and show him around," Harry said, pushing his chair back from the table. He sounded as if he'd sooner shovel manure with a teaspoon.

"He may want to start by changing his fancy duds," Lucy said, blowing gently on her coffee to cool it. "He fell—twice." She took a swallow of her coffee, trying to appear nonchalant. "Slipped in Cora's stuff—twice."

Shirley started to smile, then pressed her fist to her mouth to stifle the giggles that fought valiantly to escape and finally succeeded. Lucy blew the coffee out in a spray of laughter.

"Ladies," Harry reprimanded them both with a look, but his tired eyes crinkled at the corners and he turned toward the door a little too quickly. "Looks like he's headed this way. Shirley, you might want to get a wet cloth ready. He just tried to brush off the seat of his pants, and now seems like his hand . . . well, he'll be needing that wet cloth."

This time both Shirley and Lucy sprayed coffee out as they erupted into shouts of laughter.

"Sh-h-h," Harry whispered urgently. "He's coming up the steps." Harry fanned his hand at them as he reached to open the screen for the man. "Sir Jeremy? I'm Harry Conroy. Adam sent word that you'd be arriving today, but we thought you'd be on the afternoon train."

He stood aside and allowed the younger man to enter the kitchen. When standing next to the diminutive Harry, Jeremy Barrington was even taller than Lucy had first realized. A person would think that someone so athletically built would be a mite less clumsy, she thought.

"Coffee's hot," Harry added with a nod to Shirley to hand the man the dampened cloth.

"Or maybe you'd prefer tea?" Shirley asked with a smile.

"Sir Jeremy, this is my wife, Shirley. And I believe you and Lucy have already met."

"We were not yet formally introduced," Barrington replied, pinning Lucy with his eyes.

"Oh, this is our daughter, Lucy. Why, she's the star of the show," Shirley assured him. "Everybody comes to see Lucy."

"Indeed," Jeremy said and raised one eyebrow skeptically as he considered her. His examination left little doubt of his opinion.

Lucy bristled. "Indeed," she said flatly and picked up the coffeepot from the stove. "The coffee's made," she added, filling a cup and handing it to him. "Tea's not."

He finished wiping his hands and then exchanged the soiled cloth for the coffee by handing it to her as he turned his attention back to Harry. "I left my trunk at the station. A youth has taken charge of it, I fear. Perhaps you would be so kind as to have someone intercept it and have it delivered to the hotel?"

Shirley and Harry exchanged a look.

"The hotel in town is closed for renovation," Lucy said. "My parents have set you up with a room here."

This statement gained her a glimpse of the first real crack in his aloof demeanor, and she hid her smile of triumph by taking another sip of her coffee.

"Here?" His voice actually cracked slightly, and then he recovered himself. After all, weren't the English famous for their manners? Lucy thought. "I really couldn't impose . . ." He began.

"Nonsense," Shirley assured him. "It's no imposition at all. Why, with you upstairs there and Harry's office just down the hall here, you'll have everything you need at your fingertips."

"I see."

Lucy watched him carefully and saw that he could come up with no good reason why he shouldn't accept the arrangement. "Perhaps, then, you would have someone intercept the young man and have my things brought here?"

"I'll see to it right away," Harry assured him.

Lucy seethed. How dare he treat Harry like some common servant? Why didn't he see to his own luggage like any normal man would?

"We have your room all ready," Shirley rushed to add. "It's on the front upstairs—faces away from the yard and the barn. Not so much aroma, if you get my drift."

Lucy saw a look of near-horror pass over the man's face. He turned his attention back to Harry. "I assume that there is an office for my use?"

"We set you up with a desk and good lighting right

there in your room," Harry said. "You'll be wanting a look at the books, of course."

"That would be these?" Barrington indicated the ledgers spread over the table.

"That's the current . . ."

Barrington set down his barely touched cup of coffee and began to close the ledgers and stack the papers. He gathered them into his arms. "If you would be so kind, Mr. Conroy, as to show me the way to my room, I'll review these while I wait for my trunk to arrive."

"*I'll* show you to your room," Lucy announced, appalled that the man had failed to take note of Harry's arthritis, which made it hard for him to hobble across the room, much less climb stairs. "I believe you've already assigned my father the task of collecting your luggage."

He stepped aside and let her go ahead of him. She wished she had changed out of her leotard, or at least covered herself beyond the thin clinging fabric of the shawl around her waist. She could feel him watching her as they both climbed the stairs. She lifted her chin and straightened her spine. *Let him look.*

"Shirley's given you the best room, of course."

"As opposed to what?"

"As opposed to the smaller rooms on this floor, or the dormitory out behind the barn where everyone else sleeps." She opened the door to reveal his spacious bedroom. The bed was large and made up with a handmade quilt and several pillows. There was a sitting area near the fireplace and a desk near the windows with a view of the woods and river. "You'll share the bathroom down the hall there with the rest

of the family." Lucy took a moment's pleasure in seeing his horror at this idea.

"I see." He wandered over to the desk and looked
out the window. For a moment Lucy noticed a look
on his face that approached abject depression. She
realized that the man looked completely miserable—not displeased, but miserable, like a prisoner
who had just discovered that the jail he'd been
dreading was in fact a reality. She actually felt a little sorry for him.

"I'll leave you, then," she said softly and pulled the
door closed behind her. She thought about that instant of undisguised vulnerability that she had
observed. How on earth had Jeremy Barrington
ended up out here in the backcountry of western
Wisconsin, living with a bunch of circus folk? Clearly,
he would rather be almost anywhere else in the
world.

Before heading back downstairs, she stopped by
her own room just down the hall from his to freshen
up and change her clothes. The next time she came
face to face with Sir Jeremy Barrington, she intended
to be properly clothed.

TWO

Once the circus owner's daughter had left him, Jeremy stood staring out at the disheartening countryside for several minutes. Fields, freshly plowed, stretched beyond his view. Occasionally, a fruit tree blossomed in a riot of pink or white color, and unbelievably, there were still small piles of snow in the shadows of the land. His walk from town had taken him past some sights he was still trying to register.

Outside the blacksmith's shop, he'd seen an assortment of gaily colored wagons, their sides bearing carved wood tableaux of Mother Goose tales or historical characters such as Joan of Arc and George Washington. Some of the wagons were quite tall, and he could see places on top of one for several people to sit—the bandwagon, no doubt.

A little farther on he had passed sheds where a variety of activities seemed in progress. He saw several women gathered around a large table as if at a quilting bee, but their project appeared to be a plain piece of thick canvas. He had passed stockyards and barns occupied by the aforementioned camels, plus a menagerie the likes of which he had never seen. There were elephants, hyenas, lions, two gorgeous Bengal tigers, ostriches, zebras, an assortment of chimps and monkeys, and a very large hippopotamus bathing himself in a small, shallow pond.

As he entered the yard, he'd caught the cloying scent of fried food mingling with the stench of animal droppings and sawdust. His mood had blackened with each step, and in that single moment he rued the day that he had thought he could get away with tricking Adam Porterfield.

Jeremy's head pounded with the events of the morning. The setting had been distressing enough, but then he had made that unfortunate entrance into the barn. Thankfully, only the girl and the young man with her had been witness to his fall—falls. Once the girl had stalked out, the young man had introduced himself as Ian Conroy, son of the owner. He seemed a decent enough fellow, and he'd certainly been more concerned about Jeremy's well-being than haughty little Miss Conroy had been.

He pulled out his pocket watch and checked it. Not yet noon, proving his fear that every hour of his sentence in this place was destined to be interminable. Jeremy looked at the ledgers that he'd piled on the nondescript desk. This, then, was the lesson that Adam intended to teach him. He was to take over management of this failing circus and make it into a profitable operation. The question, of course, was, *how?* Jeremy sank into the desk chair and buried his face in his hands. From what he had seen so far, putting this ragtag operation in the black would take years.

There was a knock at the door.

"Yes?"

"Your trunk's here, mister."

Jeremy opened the door to find a massively muscular man waiting, the trunk thrown over his back like a schoolboy's book satchel. Jeremy stood aside to let the man pass.

In a single fluid motion that was fascinating to watch, the man deposited the trunk next to the armoire and turned, offering his hand in greeting. "Bruno Jacoby of the Jacoby Brothers."

"Jeremy Barrington," Jeremy replied and cautiously extended his own hand to be shaken.

Bruno's grip was surprisingly gentle. "What do you and your brothers do in the performance?" Jeremy asked.

The man shrugged and wiped his hands on his trousers. "A little of this and that: tumbling, human pyramid, some juggling, clowning when Babbo has had a bit—when I'm needed to help with the clown act."

"Babbo?"

"Oh, Babbo is our head clown. He's a legend."

"And am I to understand that Babbo imbibes?"

Bruno looked startled and cornered. "Well, now, sir, from time to time we all . . ."

"Yes, well, Mr. Jacoby, I look forward to seeing your act and meeting the others in your family. Thank you for collecting my trunk." He walked the man to the open door and waited for him to take his leave.

"We're pleased to have you here, sir." The man practically bowed his way out of the room.

Jeremy actually felt the beginning of a smile— something he had had little occasion to use recently. He glanced up and saw Lucy Conroy standing near the top of the stairway, watching Bruno take his leave. She had changed her clothes and put up her hair. The change made her look older and almost prim and reminded him that he could do with a change of clothes himself.

"Miss Conroy," he called to her as she started down the stairs. She paused and turned back to him. "I wonder when I might have the pleasure of viewing your performance. After all, if you are our star, then I should very much like to see your act."

"I need to help Shirley get out the noon meal," she replied. "Two people on our kitchen staff quit last week, and the cook's shorthanded."

"That doesn't answer my query. You appear to be developing the habit of not answering my queries."

"Ian and I usually rehearse in the morning. The Jacoby Brothers use the space in the afternoons."

"And, the evenings?"

"The evenings?"

"There are twenty-four hours in the day, Miss Conroy. Surely only a few are needed for sleep and sustenance. The rest is available for improving the show, would you not agree?"

"I . . . we . . ."

Jeremy took a kind of special pleasure in seeing her struggle for words. Her eyes flashed. Earlier he had observed how their color—an unusually deep midnight blue—complemented the highlights of her black hair. "Perhaps you would be so kind as to inform the troupe that I would like to meet with them in the rehearsal facility this evening. Shall we say, seven?" He started to turn and then turned back. "Oh, and I believe that I shall join the cast and crew for lunch, if you would be so kind as to let Mrs. Conroy know."

"Will that be all?" There was no hint of submissiveness in the question. On the contrary, it was delivered with a tone of barely concealed sarcasm.

"For now," he said and closed the door.

* * *

Lucy stood staring at the door for a long moment, her mouth open, the words wedged in the back of her throat. "For now," she muttered, mocking his tone as she turned and stormed down the stairs and out to the cookhouse and company dining room. Without a word to Shirley, she began taking down the dishes and setting the table for the noon meal.

"Honey, you might want to go a little easy there," Shirley chided her. "Else we'll be eating out of the serving bowls." She continued stirring the stew without looking at her daughter. "Is there something you've got to say?" she asked when the clattering of the dishes had lessened.

"That man," Lucy sputtered through gritted teeth. "He . . . that man is . . ." She pursed her lips tightly and shook her head furiously. "What we need here is a little commiseration—a little understanding. It's not like we brought this on ourselves."

Shirley shrugged as she ladled the stew into two large tureens. "Maybe we did—at least to some degree."

"How can you even think that?" Lucy demanded.

Shirley used her apron to cover the handles as she carried one steaming tureen to the table and set it at one end. Lucy followed suit with the other tureen at the opposite end while Shirley sliced loaves of freshly baked bread. "Really, Ma, what else could we have done? We tried everything."

"We could have admitted that we were in trouble a little sooner," Harry Conroy said as he hobbled into the room. "I was too proud to admit the need for help, Luce, and my pride hurt us all."

There was not an ounce of self-pity in his statement. Lucy paused in her preparations of the table and looked at him. "You could never hurt anyone," she said tenderly.

Harry smiled and touched the tip of her nose with his finger. "Nevertheless, little girl, you had better find a way to get used to having Sir Jeremy around. He's our last hope, I'm afraid, and the quicker you come to grips with that, the smoother things will go for you."

Lucy frowned, but she nodded. "I'll try." She caught a glimpse of Shirley before she turned back to the stove. Her mother was smiling. "I'll go ring the dinner bell," Lucy said as she hurried from the room. She had never in her life won a debate with Shirley.

The company filed into the large dining hall and took their places at the long planked tables. One chair remained empty. Everyone waited. Occasionally, somebody made small talk or glanced toward the house, but after a while they all settled into silence as the food got cold.

"I say we eat," Ian said in a low, calm voice. "I got chores."

There was general agreement from the others. After they had all served themselves and relaxed into a more normal exchange of conversation and laughter, Lucy looked up and saw the Englishman standing just inside the door. She fell silent—a fact that the others noticed immediately as everyone's gaze followed hers to the man by the door.

He had changed into a fresh suit—double-breasted coat of deep-brown tweed over matching creased and cuffed trousers. He had also cleaned the worst of the dirt off his shoes and replaced the soiled handkerchief with a fresh one. He looked every inch the successful and wealthy businessman. Lucy saw several of the men squirm uncomfortably as they focused their attention on their plates. The women, on the other hand, simply stared. Justine Bowman was practically drooling over the man. He wasn't *that* handsome, Lucy thought as she forced her attention back to her food.

Ever the perfect host, her father rose and indicated the empty place. "Come, Sir Jeremy."

"Yes, please," Shirley added as she scurried to fill his glass with milk and gave Ian an impatient nudge to indicate that her son should pass the tureen to their guest.

"You're most kind," the man murmured as he took his place directly across the table from Lucy. "Hello, everyone," he added. "Please, continue with your meal, and I believe we can dispense with my title. I am in America now, after all, am I not?"

"The very heart of it," Harry agreed. "Still, best not put that title away permanently. Something like that might come in handy for selling more tickets."

"You have a point," Jeremy replied. "It just might be a useful tactic to explain our late start on the season. 'Direct from England' and all."

Harry grinned. "You catch on quick."

Gradually, conversation resumed. It was subdued and a bit forced, but it was preferable to silence. When it appeared that everyone had finished eating, Jeremy Barrington stood, and again there was immediate silence. It was as if everyone had been waiting for him to make some statement.

"In just a few weeks, we will begin this new season," he began. "This gives us precious little time to make the changes and improvements that will be necessary to overcome the losses of this last year, both in livestock and in performers—and, of course, revenues. I will expect a great deal of you in the weeks to come. You shall be required to prove your value or take your leave."

There was a low murmur of protest from one end of the room. Lucy saw Barrington turn toward the sound. "Should you disagree with these terms, you may take your leave immediately," he said quietly, and the murmuring stopped. "Please be prepared to demonstrate your performance tonight in the ring at seven o'clock. Thank you. That will be all."

That will be all? Lucy looked down the table at her father. Harry appeared as stunned as everyone else, but he made no move to interfere. Lucy was dumbfounded. He wasn't really going to tolerate this clown just sashaying into their lives and taking over, was he?

Apparently, he was.

As the others slowly left the dining hall, Lucy stood and began clearing away the dishes. She did her best to ignore the Englishman who calmly continued to eat his dinner.

"Sir Jeremy—I mean *Mr.* Barrington . . ." Harry began.

"Please, Harry, the two of us can certainly be on a first-name basis, don't you think?"

Harry smiled. "Well now, Jeremy, that's just what I was about to suggest. First names might soften a bit of the uneasiness the folks are feeling with your coming here."

Lucy began to take more time with the clearing of the tables closest to the main table, where Harry and Jeremy sat. This was a conversation she wanted to hear. Clearly, she had underestimated her father. All of a sudden, Jeremy Barrington looked as if he might choke on his food.

"You cannot be seriously suggesting, sir, that—that *everyone* in the company refer to me—to you, for that matter—by our given names?" he finally managed to say.

"Now you're getting it. You see, son, you may know a good deal about managing the numbers and such, but I know people." Harry stood and looked directly at Jeremy. "I especially know circus folk. The thing about circus folk is that when we go home at the end of the workday, we go home to each other. We are both coworkers and family."

"Therein may lie the problem, sir," Jeremy protested. "It seems to me that what is wanted here is a bit of discipline—a bit of . . ."

Harry stopped him with a shake of his head. "No, Jeremy, we have one chance at this, and we both know that. Let's work from our strengths."

Now, what on earth did that mean? Lucy wondered.

"Lucy, honey, I could use a little help in here," Shirley called from the kitchen.

Both Harry and Jeremy Barrington looked up at her as if they had forgotten she was still in the room.

"I'll just go help . . . I'll just . . . go," she stammered as she picked up a pile of scraped plates and opened the swinging door with one hip.

Jeremy spent the afternoon sequestered in his room. He was sure that everyone thought he was going over the ledgers, but in truth he was trying to devise some strategy for saving this business. Prior to his arrival, he had simply assumed that once on site, he would come up with some plan. Adam Porterfield had done far more than supply him with numerous reports and research material on successful management of a circus. He had also introduced him to experts who had worked with the best in the business—the Ringling brothers ran an extraordinarily successful operation just a few miles away in Baraboo. Jeremy had tried without effect to argue with Adam that these companies had a huge advantage. They were already successful, and everything they had done for the past several seasons had only added to that success. The Conroy Circus had just begun to taste success when everything had begun to fall apart at the same time. Now they were two weeks away from opening the season, and, in his opinion, two months or more away from being properly prepared.

He did not join the others for supper, requesting instead that a tray be brought to his room. The truth of the matter was, he had envisioned a task far less demanding. Surely, Adam did not seriously intend to entrust him with actually designing some plan to salvage this business. Surely, there had to be some clue in all of this that he was missing—something that Adam expected but would not put into words.

Jeremy turned his attention back to the more immediate matter of once again coming face to face with his employees later that evening. What had he been thinking, demanding that they all perform for him? What could he possibly say if he found the performance uninspired and hopelessly amateurish? Here he was, living under Harry Conroy's roof, eating his food prepared by his wife. The man had talked about *family*. Jeremy certainly had not anticipated the need for such close personal and daily association with his employees. He was well aware that they watched him with a mixture of skepticism and hope. It was not just important that *he* succeed if he was ever going to get back to New York. Now, over a hundred men and women—not to mention several children—were looking to him for *their* success as well.

He glanced out the window and saw the performers and animal handlers crossing the yard to the dining hall. They seemed more subdued than they had earlier in the day, and Jeremy wondered if a part of that was because now that they had met him, they had seen for themselves that he was not up to the challenge.

He was still sitting by the window when he saw Lucy Conroy leave the dining hall and round the corner of the house. Several of those passing by spoke to her, but she did not respond to her colleagues, so intent was she on her mission. Curious, and knowing he was alone in the house, Jeremy crossed the upstairs hall seeking a room that would give him a view of the other side of the yard, where she was obviously headed.

He pushed open one door without thinking and realized he had entered her room. Hesitating for only a moment, he decided that his purpose was only to get a view, not to trespass. As if to prove his point to himself, he left the door ajar and crossed the room to her bedroom window. Lucy Conroy strode purposefully across the yard and into the practice facility. She had changed back into her rehearsal clothes and draped herself in a long cape as the setting sun brought with it cooler breezes.

He saw her brother, Ian, leave the barn with a parting comment and a worried frown. Ian paused for a moment, turned back toward the barn, said something more, then threw up his hands in resignation and headed for the dining hall. Once he had disappeared around the corner of the house, the yard was deserted and Jeremy could see nothing more.

He waited for a few minutes, keeping watch on the entrance to the barnlike building, but she did not reappear. What could she be doing in there? He turned away from the window and headed for the door, but a collection of programs stacked on a bookcase near her dressing table caught his eye. He took down the first and then another, and another. He sat in the low chintz-covered chair next to the bookcase and began to study each program in turn.

She had preserved every program from every performance of the past ten years. Starting with the earliest, he saw that she had gained her first billing as "Little Lucinda, the Tiny Tumbler." The following season, she had been part of the "Flying Conroys," three seasons later she had been featured, and then three years after that, she had achieved top billing— star of the show: the "Amazing Lady Lucinda, Angel of the Big Top."

Tucked in among the programs he found several photographs. In one, a much younger and more vigorous Harry balanced a much younger Lucy high above his head with one hand. Jeremy could not help but notice that she had been a beautiful child who had grown into a stunning and desirable woman. He smiled as he realized that he had not been immune to her physical charm—the sway of her hips as she had mounted the stairs in front of him, the way her practice costume hugged every curve of her petite body. At least not all was lost if he had retained his notorious eye for the ladies.

There were other photos as well. Several were of her with the lion tamer, Reginald Dunworthy, and there was one incongruous one of a small cottage sitting on high ground overlooking a very large body of water. Jeremy turned his attention back to the programs, studying them more carefully. He realized that variety was one of the themes—every season brought a new program of acts, most likely with the same lineup of performers but got up in new costumes with new music and ever more dangerous and thrilling stunts.

"It's a spectacle," he muttered to himself, struggling to bring to light the beginning of an idea. "A perpetual assault on the senses so that . . ."

"Exactly what do you think you're doing?"

Jeremy hadn't heard her enter the house or come up the stairs. He glanced down and saw that she wore ballet slippers, which explained her ability to move without being heard. Or perhaps he had been that engrossed in the programs and photographs—in the ideas that were beginning to come, and in the barest hint of excitement at how they just might save this business.

He stood and smiled down at her. She gave one the sense that while she might appear delicate, she was anything but fragile. He could not help but notice that even in such a small package, she certainly was a vision with her riotous black hair, her flashing eyes of darkest blue, her compact but quite appealing figure. Again he savored a welcome spark of the carefree rogue he had been back in New York, when money was no object and his career was something to amuse more than something to achieve. There was no question that Lucy Conroy was every inch a woman, regardless of her stature.

"Let's get one thing straight, Mr. Barrington," she said, her chin lifted in exactly the same pose he had observed on the poster. "You and Adam Porterfield

may control my father's business for the moment,
but these are my private quarters. I expect you to
respect that. Do we understand each other?"

Jeremy indulged himself in the sudden spark of
mischief and flirtation that she inspired. "And is
there a threat in there somewhere, Miss Conroy?"

"I . . . what?" she demanded, clearly unprepared
for him to take a lighthearted tone with her.

"I am asking if there is an 'or else' in your charming little dissertation. Either I stay out of your
personal things, or else . . . ?"

She hesitated for an instant. "Or else, *Sir* Jeremy,
I shall be forced to go with one of the several companies that have approached me to join them this
season."

He did not miss the fact that her voice trembled a
little, and he knew that hers was an empty threat.
She would never leave her family. Still, he decided to
appear to take her seriously. "Indeed," he said and
turned away from her toward the window. "Then I
will have to add planning for such a contingency to
the long list of tasks already before me."

A moment passed, during which he stared out the
window and said nothing.

"Are you just going to stand there?" she said finally, her tone laced with exasperation.

"Certainly not. There is work to be done, is there
not, Miss Conroy?" He carefully stored the programs
on the shelf and nodded to her as he returned to his
own room and closed the door.

Lucy doubled both fists and raised her face to the
ceiling as she pantomimed a silent scream. The man
had not been here twenty-four hours yet, and already he was driving her insane.

"Nosy, overbearing, snooping . . ." she muttered to

herself as she rummaged through the bottom of her wardrobe, searching for the slippers she had come up to the house to get. She sat back suddenly on her heels as she recalled the scene just played out between them. Had the man actually been flirting with her? Impossible. She resumed her rummaging, found one slipper, then sat back on her heels again.

Still, there could be no denying the way his soft green eyes had sparkled when he'd challenged her threat. She had been prepared for a flash of anger or a cold warning, but his eyes had flickered with interest and his lips had twitched to hide a smile; she was certain of it.

"Oh, my stars," she mumbled. "He thinks he can get around me with charm." She spotted the mate to the slipper under the bed and reached for it. "Well, we'll just see who charms who, Sir Jeremy," she muttered with mock sweetness.

"Indeed," he replied, and she turned to find him leaning against the door frame, observing her, one ankle crossed over the other and his arms folded across his chest. He had been studying her bottom— she was sure of it. *Of all the . . .*

"Excuse me," she said in a barely controlled tone as she got to her feet and brushed past him. "I have to prepare for your command performance."

"Then you may want this," he called as she reached the top of the stairs. She turned and he tossed her the slipper she had dropped in her haste to get out of the room.

The company had gathered as requested by the time Jeremy walked across the yard and into the large practice facility—a barn converted to accommodate all of the equipment necessary to stage a three-ring circus. They all studied him warily as he moved to the center of the ring and cleared his throat.

"Good evening, ladies and gentlemen. In just two weeks we will begin our twenty-first season. During those two weeks we will no doubt need to make a great many adjustments in our program due to recent unfortunate happenings in our midst. I shall anticipate your full and unquestioning cooperation. If you feel unable to give me that, then as I suggested earlier, you should be gone by morning. You owe it to your fellow performers to make your choice tonight and leave those who stay the best opportunity for success."

Lucy glanced around at the other performers. She saw a range of emotions from anger to fear to resignation. The man was clearly out of his mind, because he had now delivered this ultimatum not once but twice in the same day. Didn't he understand? The last thing they needed was more people leaving the company.

Or maybe that's the plan, Lucy thought, her heart sinking.

"Let me be quite clear on one matter, ladies and gentlemen," the Englishman from New York continued. Once again he had their undivided attention.

"I may not be specifically schooled in the circus life. However, I know a great deal about running a business. And I am something of an expert at entertainment. If you ask my employer, he might say a bit *too* much of an expert." He paused for the smiles and titters of amusement that did not come. "I know people and what they will and will not put forth their hard-earned money to see. There can be absolutely no questioning of my tactics, some of which may seem quite unorthodox to you."

He stopped speaking and waited. Some of the others squirmed uncomfortably, but no one said a word. Finally, Harry Conroy stepped forward.

"Do you mind if I add a word or two, son?" he asked, and Jeremy nodded and stepped aside, giving the company's founder center stage.

"We've come a long road together, folks, and Shirley and I can't say how touched we are that you've stayed with us through my sickness and all of this last year's troubles. We've got a ways to go before we see light, but I want you to know that there never was a better businessman or finer friend than Mr. Adam Porterfield's father or Adam himself. If Adam has sent us Jeremy here to give a hand, then I put my trust in the fact that he sent the best. I say we give him our full support."

There was one thing that Jeremy knew about Adam Porterfield. He was a good man and a loyal friend. The Conroys had been dear friends of the family for years. For the first time since Adam had told Jeremy of his assignment to the bedraggled circus, Jeremy understood that regardless of how angry Adam was with him, he would not jeopardize the business and future of friends like the Conroys. Adam must have felt that indeed Jeremy could make a difference here. Realizing that, Jeremy stood a bit taller and surveyed the group.

"That's all I've got to say, folks," Harry said. "From now on, you'll take your lead from Jeremy."

There was silence pierced only by the restless chatter of circus animals gathered in their cages and corrals outside the barn and awaiting their chance to show their acts. Then Ian started to clap his hands together, and others followed suit, and soon everyone was applauding as Harry smiled and nodded to Jeremy. It was a clear passing of the mantle of leadership, and Jeremy was strangely moved by the older man's act.

"Thank you, Harry. Thank you, all. And now, I should like very much to see the performance." He left the ring and pulled a single straight chair into the shadows opposite the door of the barn.

At the same time, everyone else scattered in all directions as the animal trainers hurried outside to calm their charges while the high wire performers checked the guy lines and rigging and the clowns attended to their props. The band moved into position and waited for their signal to strike up the opening music—music that would cover the continuous drone of the generator providing power for the lights.

Harry stood just next to Jeremy and said quietly, "If you don't mind, Jeremy, I'll serve as ringmaster for this rehearsal."

Jeremy raised a questioning eyebrow. "We've no ringmaster?"

"'Fraid not."

Jeremy could not stifle a weary sigh. *What next?* he wondered. "Very well," he agreed, and Harry headed for the ring as Jeremy added yet another note to a growing list of needs to fill and problems to be solved.

As act after act entered the ring, performed, and left, his silence was conspicuous. Jeremy Barrington made no comment at all. Lucy noticed that he occasionally made a note in the leather-bound notebook that she'd seen him with earlier when Bruno had delivered his trunk. She eased her way around the perimeter of the barn in order to study him more closely. She told herself that she was just trying to gauge his reaction to the program being played out before him.

He occupied the chair as he did everything—as if he owned it. One leg crossed over the other, ankle resting on knee. He had removed his suit coat and draped it over the back of the chair, and the carbon-arc lamps on the edge of the circus ring highlighted the white of his shirt. His hair was thick and straight and had a habit of falling over his forehead. The color reminded her of Shirley's strong coffee laced with cream, just the way she liked it.

He wasn't thin in the gaunt sense that Ian was. Even though he appeared relaxed, lounging nonchalantly in the chair, she had a sense that he could move with sudden swiftness if something were to upset him or catch his attention. As he shifted in the chair and rocked it back on two legs, Lucy became aware that she was observing far more detail than she would ordinarily need to size up a potential opponent. The way his shirt clung to his chest when he leaned back and stretched his arms above his head. The golden skin of his forearms where he had unfastened the sleeves and pushed them back. The way he would occasionally run his long fingers through his hair in frustration and then bend to make another note. Lucy forced her attention back to his face. He was watching the current act through eyes squinted against the smoke of the cigar he'd just lit. The scent wafted across the space that separated them, as if he might have sent it purposefully to draw her out of hiding.

"Are you prepared to perform tonight, Miss Conroy?" he asked without turning when the clowns had cleared the ring for the entrance of the elephants.

"My act follows the Jacoby Brothers," she replied, stepping forward so that she was next to him.

He scribbled a note.

"What do you think of the performance so far?" She could not contain her curiosity. "You seem to be taking quite a few notes."

His eyes never left the ring as Hamlet and Cora and the other elephants were put through their paces, but he snapped the book shut when she took a step closer. "Ideas," he said with a nonchalant shrug.

"The sequence of the acts does have some rationale, you know."

"I'm sure that it does, Miss Conroy."

"Then forgive me, but why do I have the sense that you may be thinking of rearranging that sequence?"

"Nothing is accomplished in theater without the occasional surprise, Miss Conroy," he replied with an enigmatic smile. He directed his attention away from the ring to where Norma Cox single-handedly rolled the heavy platforms used by the elephants out of the ring and into a nearby stall, then emerged carrying the heavy net that would be stretched out to catch Lucinda should she fall.

"Who is that woman?" Jeremy asked.

"Norma Cox. Her husband is Arnie Cox, the elephant handler."

He nodded and entered another note in his book. "Are you not next, Miss Conroy?" he asked softly as he continued to write.

For the next several minutes, Jeremy wrote nothing in his notebook. His eyes were riveted on the small figure above him. He understood within the first two minutes of her act why she was billed as the "angel." She flew and darted and soared, each movement so smoothly integrated into the next that he had to concentrate to see the actual mechanics she used to achieve such fluidity in motion. The band—which, he had already noted with great relief, was quite excellent—accompanied her with a romantic sonata. The music seemed perfectly matched to her seamless performance.

The act was not without its heart-stopping moments, and Jeremy had to clear his throat more than once to cover a gasp as she fell effortlessly from a sitting position to suspending herself seventy feet above the ground by one ankle. As the music reached its climax, she caught a cable that Ian had lowered from the ceiling. With the grace of a ballerina, she swung out over the ring, holding only the single cable. The trapeze was caught and secured by another member of the troupe.

Jeremy watched carefully, determined to discover her finale before she could spring it on him. And then she released the cable. But instead of freefalling to the net below, she hung there by her neck, her legs and arms elegantly positioned as if she were a figure in a music box, spinning in synchronicity with the closing strains of the music. Her hair concealed the strap she had obviously placed around her neck without his seeing her do it. His heart hammered, as much because of her sheer grace and beauty as her daring.

To his surprise, her fellow performers burst into cheers and applause. Ian slowly lowered her to the net, where she whipped off the neck strap with a flourish and a wide smile and then tumbled expertly out of the net and onto the ground to take her bow. The cheers and whistles of her peers continued, and several of them moved forward to embrace her and pump Ian's hand in congratulations.

Jeremy stood and walked toward the group, aware of the thin veil of perspiration on his forehead in spite of the chill in the barn. His heart had skipped a beat when she had dropped into that spin. Of course, the net was there to break her fall, but still . . .

"That was most impressive," he said, his eyes on her even though she paid him no mind and seemed engrossed in fastening the oriental frog closure of her cape.

"Thank you," she said quietly. Then she looked directly at him. "Ian and I are working on an apparatus that will allow me to do the same stunt, only spinning, by holding the strap with my teeth."

"Now, Luce," Ian protested, "you know how I feel about—"

"Of course, it needs work and will take some time to perfect," she continued as if her brother had not spoken, "but, so far, no other performer has perfected the neck spin, so we have claim to that for the time being."

"We'll discuss it," Jeremy replied, meeting her gaze until she looked away.

"Lucinda," Harry called to his daughter and Jeremy noticed that she colored slightly. Harry had remained at the edge of the ring, and Jeremy now realized that the man had neither applauded nor joined in the congratulations once she was safely on the ground.

"Yes, Papa," she replied meekly and went to him.

"You took quite a risk," Jeremy heard the older

man begin as he drew his daughter under one protective arm and walked with her out to the yard.

"I know, Papa, but . . ." Her voice was eager, like a child's who has accomplished something spectacular. It was the first time Jeremy had heard her call Harry by anything other than his given name.

Harry raised one finger to stop her excited chatter, then continued talking to her as they walked away. Jeremy could not hear his words, but he knew that the man had been as frightened as he had been.

"Well," he said as he turned back to the others, "I believe there are only two acts yet to review?" They nodded and several moved off to prepare for the last two acts. "I think we can run through these without benefit of a ringmaster's introduction."

When the final two acts had performed, Jeremy addressed the entire company with the exception of Lucy and Harry, who had not returned to the barn. "Thank you all for your efforts tonight. I can see that while there is work to be done, there is also talent for doing it. Please assemble here tomorrow morning at nine and we shall begin. Until then, good evening."

Slowly the performers filed out of the barn. Several crew members stayed behind to put everything back in place, ready for another day of rehearsal. As Jeremy walked across the yard, taking care to step on solid ground, he was aware of activity in the yard as the handlers settled the menagerie of animals for the night.

"Mrs. Cox," he called out to the large woman he had observed earlier in the barn.

"Yes, sir?"

The woman stood to her full height, which was close to his own six feet. She placed her hands on her wide hips and stood with feet planted firmly as she waited for him to speak.

"Have you considered putting together an act of your own?" he asked.

Norma Cox stared at him for a long moment. He could see a mixture of expressions play across her face as she stood in the light from the barn. The one she selected to express surprised him. She burst out laughing—great guffaws of knee-slapping laughter that had her doubled over. "Oh, that's a good one, sir," she exclaimed. "Arnie, come over here. Mr. Barrington has just—"

"I'm quite serious," Jeremy declared, acknowledging the woman's husband as he joined them.

Norma stopped laughing and looked utterly confused. "You are?"

"Exactly what kind of act might Norma be doing, sir?" Arnie asked.

"It occurs to me—that is, I don't wish to offend the lady," Jeremy began, addressing his remarks to Arnie. "Your wife appears to be quite strong, sir."

Arnie grinned. "That she is. She can lift me if I get in her way, that's for sure."

Jeremy considered the man, who was a good six inches shorter than his wife. "Really?"

"That's a fact," Norma said proudly.

"Well, you see, most of our competitors have a strongman act or sideshow. . . ."

"You want me to dress up like a man?" Norma asked.

"I want you to dress as a woman and become Miss Norma, the World's Strongest Woman," he replied.

Arnie and Norma looked first at him, then at each other, then back at him.

"It might just work, Norma," Arnie said slowly. "You could—"

"I could," Norma agreed excitedly without giving him a chance to finish his thought. Then she looked at Jeremy and grinned broadly. "Oh, thank you, Mr. Barrington," she squealed as she caught him in a bear hug and nearly swung him off his feet in her excitement. "I just don't know how to thank you. Hey, Trixie . . ." she bellowed at the trick rider who was headed for the dormitory. "Guess what?" She started after her friend but then turned and placed one large hand on either side of Jeremy's face and gave him a loud, smacking kiss on his forehead.

When Jeremy had recovered, he turned to find Arnie standing there, grinning up at him. "She's always wanted to perform," he explained and took Jeremy's hand between his own callused ones. "Thank you, sir."

"You're welcome," Jeremy replied as the man took off after his wife to share the news. Jeremy let the feeling that he had done something truly wonderful wash over him. It had been a long time since he'd felt this good. As he continued across the yard and up the creaking, warped steps to the back door of the farmhouse, he was whistling softly. *"A day that begins badly is still a fine day if it ends well,"* his mother used to say.

Lucy watched from her bedroom window as the man crossed the yard after stopping to have what must have been quite an amiable conversation with Arnie and Norma. If Norma's reaction was any indication, he had made her quite happy indeed. Perhaps he had thanked her for her efforts behind the scenes. Lucy considered that this seemed out of character for the man, but then, he appeared to take some pleasure in surprising others.

In terms of the evening's surprises, her own unveiling of the trick she had been working on for weeks had come as an unpleasant surprise to her parents. Harry had gently reprimanded her for taking such a risk without discussing it first with him and her mother.

In her day, Shirley had been a star in her own right. She had pioneered many of the stunts considered common to any trapeze act in this day and age. Lucy had always relied on her for advice and coaching, but for this stunt, she had worked alone, drawing only the reluctant Ian into her confidence. The moment she had heard Harry call her 'Lucinda," she had known she was in for one of his quiet lectures. She had tried disarming him by calling him "Papa," but it hadn't worked.

"Do you know what could have happened up there tonight?" he had asked as he led her from the barn and back up to the house.

"But . . ."

"No 'buts,' young lady. Wait until your mother hears of this. How many times has she warned you about trying to do things up there without thoroughly working them through?"

"But . . ."

"Lucinda, I know why you're doing this, and I will not permit it. Jeremy Barrington is here now and he has his orders direct from the son of Clay Porterfield. *They* will see that we are all right; do you understand me?"

His voice had shaken slightly with the intensity of his warning. She knew that it was his love for her that caused him to be so upset. "All right, Papa," she had replied, and then she had hugged him hard. "But Papa, wasn't it a wonderful trick?"

Harry had been unable to stifle a low chuckle. "It was magnificent, Lucy. Never saw anything like it in all my born days."

In the end, when they reached the house, he had told her mother that Lucy had come up with a new ending for the act that was going to need Shirley's help to perfect. Shirley had listened intently as Lucy described the stunt, asking questions now and then as she thought through the steps that led to the surprise of it. Shirley had been almost as excited as Lucy had been when devising the trick in the first place, and Lucy had promised to show her mother the actual trick the following morning.

Now she stood at her window, watching Jeremy Barrington as he first talked to Arnie and Norma and then continued across the yard and up to the house. She heard the back door open and close, heard the clank of the coffeepot being lifted and set back onto the stove, heard his tread through the hall and up the stairs. And then, she heard him pause. Was he standing outside her door—the first he would reach at the top of the stairs? Was he considering knocking?

She heard him move on down the hall and into his room. When she heard the click of his door closing, she let out her breath and realized that she'd been holding it from the moment he had started up the stairs.

"You are behaving like some ridiculous child," she admonished her reflection in the pedestal mirror as she brushed her long hair vigorously. "What on earth would make you think that this man would have the slightest interest in stopping by your room?"

Because when our eyes met after I had completed my performance, I saw something more than professional interest.

"Nonsense. Do you learn nothing from the mistakes of the past? This man is cut from the same self-centered cloth as Reggie, and you flatter yourself to think for one moment that any interest he might show goes beyond the purely carnal."

He was afraid for me.

"He was afraid for his own economic future. He's no fool, and he knows very well that at the moment, you are his star—his very bread and butter."

But . . .

"Oh, for heavens sake," Lucy chastised her dreamy-eyed reflection, "go to bed. You have weeks in which to make a fool of yourself if you're so determined to do so."

Three

For the remainder of the time before beginning their season's tour, they rehearsed morning and night. In between these full-scale rehearsals, each act was assigned a precise rehearsal time in the practice ring, and specific things to work on during rehearsal. In addition, Jeremy gave every single person at least a triple role to play if they did not already have one. Shirley would not only manage the costumes, she would also play the bell calliope in the parade—and, of course, manage the ticket booth for each performance. Norma would not only serve as her husband's crew for his act with the elephants, but would don an especially feminine costume and ride in the parade displaying her strength by lifting various types of weights, including several children at one time. During her sideshow performance, she would draw them in with the promise to see a woman lift a full-grown man over her head—which she would fulfill by lifting Arnie.

Three days before they were to board the train and leave on tour, they invited the entire population of the town and surrounding area to preview their performance. There was nothing unusual in this. What was different and caught the attention and delight of the townspeople and farm families in the area was the fact that Jeremy had insisted that the event include a fully staged parade through town, and not one but two performances—just as they would have on tour. On top of that, he permitted people to pay their admission in foodstuffs that could be stored and used on tour. Children were admitted for free, provided they agreed to help with the chores of setup and cleanup after each performance.

The response was overwhelming, coming as it did from a community used to circus folks. Indeed, it seemed as if every single person living within ten miles had come out to watch the parade. In spite of their grumbling at the long hours and demands of Barrington, the members of the company had to give him a grudging respect as they paraded through downtown and received the thrill of cheering throngs greeting them from both sides of the street. Jeremy had even ordered the setup of the big top on the outskirts of town, and somehow he had managed to get a reporter from the *Milwaukee Sentinel* to travel clear across the state to see the show.

"Miss Conroy." Jeremy stopped Lucy as she crossed the yard, headed for the costume wagon.

Lucy turned and waited for him to catch up to her. They had not had a direct conversation since that first night in the barn. She had been aware of him watching her through every rehearsal, but he always left before she reached the ground after her act, and however many notes he gave the others, he never seemed to have any for her.

"I want you to leave out the neck twirl," he said when he reached her.

"You're joking," she replied, but she could see that he wasn't. "But why?"

"It's far too risky."

She had performed it perfectly in every rehearsal but one. During their final rehearsal on the day before, she had been distracted and overtired. She had made a mistake in locking the strap to the rigging, and the strap had not held. She had plummeted to the net below, upset with herself for not focusing on her work. When she had swung herself down from the net and stalked over to the rope to go back up to try again, she had come face to face with Jeremy. He had looked at her for a long moment and then turned and left the barn.

"If you're worried about what happened yesterday, that was my fault. It won't happen again."

"No, it won't, because you will not be attempting the trick again unless I give you permission. Is that understood?"

"But . . ."

"You should move along to wardrobe, Miss Conroy. The first performance is less than an hour away."

He walked away and left her standing there. For an instant, she found herself considering the attractive possibility of perhaps learning Zepati's knife-throwing act. It would give her enormous pleasure to sling a six-inch blade somewhere in the very close vicinity of Jeremy Barrington's left ear. Instead, she turned on her heel and headed for the wardrobe wagon.

She did as she was told—not for the Englishman but because she did not want to cause further problems for her parents. There would be time enough to put the stunt in once they were on the road. In the afternoon performance, she ran through her roster of daring acts flawlessly, ending with what the posters heralded as her death-defying slide, during which only the angels themselves could assure her safety. Effortlessly she fell back from the bar and caught herself by her toes as the trapeze swung back and forth. The audience gasped as one, and she saw Jeremy smile. Then, she released one foothold and hung there by one foot for what seemed an eternity. The audience went wild, cheering and stomping in thunderous approval when she let go of the bar and tumbled gracefully into the net below.

She took several sweeping bows, her smile brilliant as she turned to each side of the ring to accept the accolades that were her due. But as she left the ring, the smile that had been as fake as Babbo's red nose disappeared as she brushed past Jeremy without a word.

"Miss Conroy . . . Lucy!" he called.

She did not break stride until she had reached her dressing tent, where he knew full well that she had a quick change in order to be ready for the finale. He did not follow her.

Between performances, Lucy reset and checked her equipment, pressed her costume, and then went up to the house to get some rest before eating a light supper. For the next five months, she would repeat the routine practically every day, except she would rest in her compartment on the train.

As she walked through the kitchen, she heard voices from her father's office. When she realized that one of the voices belonged to Jeremy Barrington, she moved a little closer to the doorway.

". . . wine and dine local dignitaries," Jeremy was saying.

"That'll take some funds that we don't have right now," Harry reminded him.

"I've wired Adam to ask for an advance."

"You want to be careful about that sort of thing," Harry said. "Asking for more from Adam, I mean."

There was a long, heavy sigh, and then Jeremy said, "I must do whatever it takes to make a go of this, Harry." His voice was low and intense.

"I don't suppose you'd be willing to tell me what landed you with this assignment in the first place, would you, son?"

The silence stretched on for a long moment, and Lucy assumed that Jeremy had simply shaken his head in the negative. She could not see either man without being seen herself, so she prepared to tiptoe away from the door and then pretend she had just entered the house. Just then, she heard Jeremy's reply.

"I'll tell you this much, sir" it was either take this assignment or go to jail."

"I see," Harry said slowly.

Lucy heard the sound of cup on saucer and knew that her father had set his ever-present cup of coffee back on his desk.

"Well, son, I thank you for your honesty."

"I assure you that there was no criminal intent— you can ask Adam yourself. I intend to succeed in this. I am quite determined to prove myself—both to Adam and to you, sir."

Harry chuckled. "Let me tell you something about Adam Porterfield. You would not be here if he did not sincerely believe in your ability to help us out. And if he believes in you, then that's enough for me."

"Thank you, sir."

"Now, about those local dignitaries—might be just the ticket after all," Harry said thoughtfully. "Did I ever tell you about the time that . . . ?"

Lucy edged away from the door and crossed the kitchen to the back door. She opened and closed it firmly, and the reaction was exactly as she had expected.

"Shirl?" Harry called. "Is that you?"

"No, Papa. She's still over packing up wardrobe." Lucy stood in the doorway to the office, ignoring Jeremy as she spoke directly to her father. "I'm just going to lie down for a bit."

"Jeremy here says you had a good show today, darling," Harry said.

"Are you going to be in the ring tonight?"

Harry had begged off serving as ringmaster for the afternoon performance, citing the need to get things from the office in order for the tour. The eldest son of Norma and Arnie had filled in for him. "I'll be there," he promised.

Lucy kissed him on the cheek and nodded to Jeremy before leaving the room.

The afternoon performance had brought in a fairly good crowd, but it was standing room only that evening. Jeremy stood at the performers' entrance to the huge tent and watched the people file in and take their seats. Sales of popcorn and cotton candy had been brisk, and everyone seemed to be in a festive mood. Jeremy recognized several people who had been present for the afternoon performance and had obviously returned. Surely, that was a good sign. The tins and bags of food had piled up throughout the afternoon and into the evening. At least they would be able to eat during the first weeks of the tour, and the sale of the lions would pay salaries until they could do a few performances and, hopefully, rebuild the coffers.

"Well, Sir Jeremy, shall I get this thing rolling?" Harry Conroy was dressed in his ringmaster costume of bright red tailcoat over black riding pants tucked into knee-high polished black boots. His top hat was covered in red satin, with a wide black grosgrain band.

"Why, Harry, I do believe you've grown an inch or two since last we met," Jeremy said with a mock frown as he considered the man.

Harry grinned. "Two-inch heels and an inch-thick sole does wonders for a short man's ego," he said with a wink. "Gives me a certain presence, don't you think?"

Jeremy laughed. "I do indeed. Shall we get on with the show?"

He watched as Harry signaled the director of the band, who struck up a fanfare as Harry strode confidently to the center of the ring. "La-a-adies and gentlemen!" he exclaimed, and the crowd gave him their full attention.

Jeremy stepped aside as all the performers lined up for the grand entrance that started the show. He could see Lucy toward the back of the assembly. She stood on a trapeze mounted on the back of a small flatbed wagon pulled by two matched ponies. She was dressed in a sapphire blue harem costume in keeping with the "Arabian Nights" theme of the grand entrance parade. As she passed him, she looked down and their eyes met for a brief instant. Jeremy saw the flicker of something in her gaze, but he could not have said whether it was interest or ire—either seemed possible with the impossible Miss Lucinda Conroy.

The show ran without a hitch through the first three-quarters of the performance. Everyone seemed to acquire an extra bit of energy from what was essentially a dress rehearsal in front of a live audience. Acts that Jeremy had thought questionable sparkled with excitement. Clown stunts that he had found tiresome in rehearsal suddenly seemed fresh and innovative when accompanied by the squeals of the children's laughter. Jeremy leaned against one of the support poles and permitted himself to relax and to consider the possibility that he might actually enjoy rebuilding the profits of the company—assuming it didn't take him away from New York for too long.

Earlier Harry had told him of some excellent performers whose companies had recently merged with larger companies or had shut down for lack of business. In Jeremy's experience in business, such employees were often ripe for a new venue. Over the past week, he had put out some feelers to those companies that had gone out of business, to see about acquiring animals to bolster the menagerie, as well as wagons and other equipment. Already he had begun to receive some positive response. Now, all he had to do was come up with the money to pay the bills.

"Ladies and gentlemen, boys and girls of all ages, please direct your attention now to the top of the center ring as the Angel of the Big Top, Lady Lucinda, flies among the stars."

Jeremy looked up. The canvas at the very top of the tent was painted a deep midnight blue and dotted with small white sequined stars. The lights positioned on the center pole lit the makeshift sky as the paste stars appeared to come alive. And suddenly, she was there, flying into view in a white-sequined gossamer costume that made her indeed appear angelic. Her long hair was braided and intertwined with sequins and fake pearls. She wore white tights and white ballet slippers with white satin ribbons that laced to her knees. The sleeves of her costume flowed like butterfly wings, and the skirt ended in a handkerchief hem that flared around her calves. The audience gasped and then cheered as she made her first transfer from one swing to another and then landed on a narrow aerial perch that made it appear as if she were suspended in midair.

The power of her act lay not only in her beauty and grace, but in the continuous flow of movement. She transferred effortlessly from one stunt to the next, hardly allowing the audience to catch their breath before delivering the next thrill. Jeremy saw that she was almost ready for the finale—the place where she dropped to the position of suspending herself by her ankles and then released one foot. He smiled as he looked around the ring at the upturned faces. If they thought they had seen something up to now . . .

The audience caught their breath as one, and then they began to applaud and cheer and whistle. Jeremy looked up, and there, high above him, was Miss Lucinda Conroy, doing precisely what he had strictly forbidden her to do. She was spinning around and around seventy feet above the ground, held there by nothing more than a simple strap around her long, elegant neck. Her arms were widespread so that the sleeves and skirt of her costume fanned out and she indeed looked more than ever like an angel in flight.

After what seemed a lifetime to Jeremy, she slowed

her spin and accepted the trapeze that Ian had sailed her way. She pulled off the neck strap after catching the trapeze; then, grasping the bar with both hands, she swung out and back, pumping hard to gather speed. Then, at the bottom arc of her swing, she released the bar and fell to the net below. The audience was on their feet instantly, applauding and cheering as she gracefully maneuvered her way to the edge of the net and somersaulted to the ground to take her bows.

The roar of the crowd was deafening as Harry walked out and took his daughter's hand and led her around the ring, pausing every few yards so that she could take yet another sweeping bow. Harry's eyes gleamed with pride, and Jeremy knew that the man had no idea that Lucy had disobeyed Jeremy's direct order. He moved to the exit, knowing she would have to pass him on her way out.

"Miss Conroy," he said with a tightlipped smile as she turned and blew a kiss to the audience, once again garnering their explosive applause. Jeremy moved to her side, smiling into the lights as he took her hand as if to escort her to her dressing room. Since they were still in full view of much of the audience, he knew that she would not resist—at least until she was certain that she wouldn't make a scene. "I believe you and I need to have a little talk," he said as he tightened his grip on her hand and placed his other arm around her waist.

"I have to prepare for the finale," she said, trying to pull away.

"The finale can do without you tonight." He led her away from the tent and out of the light.

"I'm cold," she complained, not looking at him.

He removed his coat and put it around her. "Now,

then, there is one thing we will get straightened out tonight."

She shot him a look, and her eyes flashed with contention.

"Whether you like it or not, I am in charge here. In order for me to be effective in helping your father to save this little venture, I must have the complete cooperation of every member of the company. That includes you, Miss Conroy."

"You know nothing about circus people or—"

"This is not a subject that is up for debate, Lucy. You will either adhere to my instructions or you will not perform."

Her eyes widened and then she laughed. "You're joking."

"I assure you, I am not."

Her smile faltered. "But . . ."

"There is no question that you are indeed the star of the show, Lucy, but you are not the entire show. I think that even you must agree that those people in there came to see a variety of acts tonight, and no matter how magnificent your performance was, it alone would not have been enough."

He watched as her eyes filled with tears.

"Ah, I see that you do understand," he said. "Then we shall not speak of it again, and until I say otherwise, you will leave the neck-spinning out of your act, as well as any other daredevil stunt you may be considering."

She looked at him again, and he saw that he had misjudged her tears. They were not tears of remorse, but rather the expression of her outrage. "You may have many people—including my parents—convinced that you have our best interests at heart, *Sir* Jeremy. However, I believe that you have come here against your will, to do a job in which you have not the slightest interest other than the selfish one of earning your way back into the good graces of your employer. I don't trust you any further than I can throw you, Jeremy Barrington. I will do whatever it takes to be sure that you don't destroy this company with your bumbling inexperience and your arrogance, and I would suggest that *you* consider *that*." She flung off his coat, not caring whether it fell to the ground, and walked resolutely back toward the spotlight just in time to take her place in the grand finale.

Four

The Conroy circus train consisted of two obsolescent day cars refitted with bunks for most of the performers, plus two additional cars divided into compartments to house the lead performers. There was a dining car, a car where lithographers turned out posters and paste to advertise the show at each stop, and something called a pie car, which, Jeremy came to learn, was a sort of club car where performers could gather for cards, snacks, and reading. As Jeremy had expected, there were boxcars for animals and equipment, even older cars renovated as dormitories for the crew of roustabouts, and flatcars for loading the wagons. For conducting the business of keeping to the schedule and storing the receipts and ledgers, there was a car outfitted with a safe and office space. Finally, there was a private car used by Harry and Shirley and Lucy in past seasons. Ian preferred to sleep with the crew. Harry had insisted that Jeremy must take their car for his own.

"We can take over Reggie's old stateroom and Lucy can bunk with Trixie. You'll be needing to entertain some of the local dignitaries," Harry said, then added with a wink, "and of course, a young fella like you must occasionally have need for the company of a lady from time to time."

It was the only time in his adult life that Jeremy could recall anyone saying anything that caused him to blush. He had protested only slightly and then accepted Harry's offer, not so much because of the old man's reasoning, but more because he was so relieved to think that there would be some semblance of a refuge to which he might escape.

Lucy barely noticed the interior of the train anymore. To her the cars were not the crudely outfitted overhauls of their originals. To her, their furnishings were well used, not shabby. For Lucy and many of the others in the company, the train was home on the road. Pulldown cots above each seat in the dormitory cars doubled the sleeping space, since each seat also converted into a cot. At night, each sleeping berth had curtains for privacy. The dining car was far from elegant as the company ate in shifts and a crew made up of the wives and older daughters of the roustabouts prepared the meals. Food was simple but abundant. It was one thing that Harry had insisted must not be shortchanged, and thanks to Jeremy's idea of requesting food as admission, the larder was very well stocked.

But that morning when the train was pulled onto the sidetrack to load the equipment and animals, the entire company got a surprise. A car had been added to the back of the train—a fairly new and freshly painted and outfitted Pullman, and along with it was a steward hired specifically to serve the needs of Jeremy Barrington.

"Mr. Porterfield sent that," Harry told them at lunch. "It's for Jeremy to use as he wines and dines the bigwigs along the way. He won't be needing our car after all. Gives us some class, don't you think?"

It was clear that Jeremy would travel in style while

the rest of them were packed into close quarters, but Harry was not about to allow anything like a fancy railroad car cause friction in his company. "Besides," he added without looking at them as he slurped his soup, "Jeremy isn't like the rest of us. He's not circus folk, even though his heart's in the right place and he wants more than anything for us to have a successful season. Still, the boy is accustomed to the good life. He comes from high society back there in London—his daddy holds a seat in Parliament and has some big castle out in the country, according to what I hear. Might be interesting to see how folks out and about react when they hear we're being managed by a real, live English duke."

His comments had the desired effect. Instead of being upset, everyone agreed that the car was an asset and the perfect place for Jeremy to maintain his residence and office during the tour. At Shirley's suggestion, Jeremy further secured their support by inviting everyone on board for a party the night before they were to leave on the first leg of the season's tour.

The party was a lively and raucous event. Jeremy had hired Molly Briscoe, who ran the local diner in town, to provide the food and servers, and he had also brought in a couple of local musicians to play and sing as entertainment. Everyone was already having a wonderful time by the time Lucy arrived with her parents.

Harry had not looked good at supper, and both Lucy and Shirley had tried to persuade him to forego the party, but he had insisted.

"The boy needs all the support we can give," he told Shirley. "You know that."

"Why?" Lucy asked. "Why are you taking such care to make sure that he is accepted?"

"Because, Lucy dear, he's our savior. We succeed or fail with him. We surely fail without him."

"I don't believe that. All we need is—"

"Now, see here," Shirley said sternly, "your father knows best. It's about time you came down off that high horse and accepted what's what. The man is here to do a job. He's on our side, and you would do well to stop fighting that."

"He doesn't know the first thing about the circus," Lucy argued.

"He knows business," Harry replied wearily, "and at the moment, that's what counts. Now, go get yourself dressed and let's get to this party."

Lucy was on the verge of bringing up the comment she had overheard Jeremy make about either coming to Wisconsin or going to jail, but realized in the knick of time that her parents would know she'd been eavesdropping. Resigned to her fate, she trudged up to her room and started to change.

She hated arguing with her parents, but why couldn't Adam Porterfield have simply given Harry and Shirley the money and the railway car? Surely, her father was better qualified than Jeremy Barrington to put things right again.

"Luce?" Shirley knocked lightly at her door.

"Almost ready," Lucy replied.

Shirley came in and sat on the bed. "Honey . . ."

"Ma, I know what you're going to say, and ordinarily I would agree. We need help—I know that, but . . ."

"No, honey, not 'but.' Jeremy Barrington is our help. Your father trusts him. Why can't you?" She stood behind Lucy and arranged her daughter's hair into an elegant upsweep with two fat curls left to fall over her shoulder.

Lucy stared at her mother's reflection in the mirror. "It's not something I can explain. It's just this feeling that he's . . . I don't know . . . irresponsible."

"He has a stake in this, too."

Lucy turned to face Shirley. "That's the other thing—"

Shirley held up her hand. "I'm going to ask you once to put aside your reservations and accept that you may not know the whole story. Now, your father is waiting."

"I'm ready," Lucy replied. Then she looked at her mother for a long moment. Shirley held out her arms to her.

"It's going to be all right, child. Everything will be all right," she promised, and Lucy very much wanted to believe her.

After they had been at the party for about an hour, Lucy saw Harry and Jeremy talking. They stood apart from the other guests, and unlike the others, who were laughing and enjoying themselves, their expressions were solemn. Harry was doing most of the talking. Shirley hovered nearby. Jeremy nodded several times, then reached out and gripped the older man's shoulder in a gesture of consolation. The two men shook hands and Harry turned to Shirley, who seemed relieved to take his arm and head back across the room toward the exit.

Lucy made her way through the crowded room to intercept them.

"Is everything all right?" she asked and noticed that her father looked positively gray.

"I'm just a little tired," he replied with a weak smile. "You go on and enjoy yourself."

Lucy felt her heart pounding. Something wasn't right here. She'd been so busy rehearsing and working the past two weeks that she had barely had time to see her parents. Each night when she returned after the last rehearsal, they had already retired. Also, it occurred to her that Harry and Shirley had both stopped coming to the rehearsals after that first week.

"Papa," she said softly and reached out to touch him.

Harry smiled again and then slumped against Shirley. "Get me out of here," he begged.

Lucy grabbed his other arm in an attempt to help her mother support him. "Ian!" she screamed, and suddenly the room went quiet as everyone turned in their direction.

Immediately, there was a murmur of concern, and Jeremy Barrington stepped out of the crowd. "Let me take him," he said as he lifted Harry in his arms and headed for the door. "Ian, go for the doctor," he instructed.

"In here," Shirley said as soon as they reached the house. She led the way to the first-floor bedroom.

Jeremy placed Harry carefully in the center of the bed and began to help Shirley undress him. "The doctor will be here soon," he assured her quietly.

Shirley nodded. Lucy stood just inside the door, her eyes refusing to accept the picture before her. Her father looked like a frail old man lying there. He was unconscious now and not moving.

Shirley glanced over at her. "Lucy, go and get me another blanket from the chest."

Numbly Lucy did as she was told. Her mind raced as she tried to make sense of what had just happened. Of course, she knew that her father had had some health problems. That's why he'd sent Adam Porterfield that letter asking for help in the first place. But the doctor had assured them that Harry would get better—that it was just a bronchial condition that would get better with some rest and warmer weather.

Even so, the cough had hung on. She recalled now, night after night, hearing him long after they'd all gone to bed. She thought about the dark circles and lines of worry that marred Shirley's beautiful face. Lucy couldn't believe that she had been so wrapped up in her own concerns that she had failed to see how really sick her father was.

"Pneumonia," the doctor diagnosed an hour later. "He needs to stay put if he wants to get better anytime soon." He looked up at Shirley, Ian, and Lucy as they stood around the bed. "That means stay put right here, not on some drafty circus train."

Shirley nodded. Lucy looked at Harry, who had regained consciousness and was lying in bed, weak and listless, as the doctor spelled out his treatment. Her father met her gaze. "The boy will be fine," he said weakly as if reading her mind.

Lucy smiled encouragingly. "Sure, he will, Papa," she said and sat on the edge of the bed as she took his hand between hers and stroked it. "Ian and I will make sure that he has everyone's support, won't we, Ian?"

Ian nodded and swallowed hard. "You just rest," he said in a raspy voice that betrayed his deep emotion. He put his own hands on his mother's thin shoulders, and she turned her face to his chest for comfort.

"Go get Jeremy," Harry ordered, looking at Lucy.

"I'll get him," the doctor replied. "He's been waiting out there in the office since I got here." He closed up his bag and stood. "Now, Harry Conroy, we both know that you're a stubborn man, but I'm telling you: either follow my orders to the letter or I won't be responsible for the consequences."

"He'll stay put," Shirley said before Harry could reply. "I'll be right here to make sure of that," she added, giving her husband a look that left him no room to argue.

Harry smiled. "Looks like I'm outnumbered."

"I'll be by in the morning." He nodded at Shirley, who followed him out into the other room.

Seconds later Jeremy appeared at the door.

"Come in, son," Harry said, beckoning to the younger man.

Jeremy stood on the opposite side of the bed from where Lucy sat. Ian had left with Shirley so he could drive the doctor back to town. Harry patted the bed beside him, indicating that Jeremy should sit. When he had, Harry took his hand, still holding on to Lucy's as well. "Now, the two of you listen to me," he said. "I am counting on both of you to see this through. You'll be needing each other to make a go of this, and"—he shifted his gaze to Lucy—"you'll need to find ways of getting along. Is that understood?"

Lucy nodded.

"Out loud, Luce," he prompted.

"Yes, Papa," she murmured, not daring to look at Jeremy.

"Okay, then." Harry drew a deep, ragged breath. "I can rest easy, then. You'll stay in touch?"

"Yes, sir," Jeremy replied.

Harry patted Jeremy's hand as he released it. "You've got some good ideas, son—unusual, but then, in our business the unorthodox is often what wins the day."

Lucy looked up at Jeremy and saw that he was as concerned about Harry as anyone. Her heart softened a little in that moment, and she promised herself that she would try harder to see the potential that her father obviously saw in this Englishman whom she and her brother had dubbed a "first of May" rookie that first day.

She recalled the conversation she had overheard between Jeremy and her father. It was clear that he needed to succeed every bit as much as the family's business did. Whatever had happened back in New York, he had been given one chance to redeem himself. Of course, that didn't necessarily mean that he would have her family's best interests at heart. After all, in the business world the definition of success was the profit line.

"Everything is going to be just fine, sir," Jeremy was saying. "How can I possibly fail when I have the 'Angel of the Big Top' as my leading act?"

It took most of the following day to finish loading the menagerie and the last of the supplies and equipment. By late afternoon it was time to leave. The company would travel through the night to their first destination. Lucy boarded the train and went straight to the compartment that would be her home for the next several months. It seemed strange to be pulling away and still see her parents and their private car sitting there. Harry had assured her that they were keeping the car with them so they'd have a way to join up with the company later, when he was feeling better.

Lucy waved and blew kisses to Harry and Shirley, who had come as far as the back porch to see them off. Harry looked pale and exhausted but he was smiling at her. She could not help but wonder if she would ever see him again. Suddenly, she realized that she had just assumed they would all be together—always.

As the train chugged and huffed its way out of town, she settled in. She had become an expert at making the most of her compact quarters. But this felt different. Was it because Harry and Shirley weren't there? Because this was the first season in three years without Reggie and being part of a couple? Because . . . ?

"Oh, for Pete's sake," she chastised herself, "you're being ridiculous." But, as the train rounded the first bend and she realized she had truly left Shirley and Harry behind, she could not help but cry.

"Hey, Luce," Trixie LaMott called from the doorway, "come join us. Ian is warming up his banjo."

"In a minute," Lucy replied, swiping the back of her hand at her tears.

Instead of leaving, Trixie put her arms around Lucy and drew her close. "Your pa is gonna be just fine, Lucy. You know that there's nothing that can bring down that old man—he's too stubborn, like his little girl here." She hugged Lucy tight, all of which served to set off a fresh burst of tears. "Now, come along, before little Miss Jacoby gets her claws into that handsome brother of yours."

Lucy laughed at that. It was no secret that Trixie adored Ian and that he was far too shy to make a move to take their friendship to the next level. Polly Jacoby was also attracted to Ian, but unlike Trixie, Lucy suspected that for Polly the fun was in the hunt.

If she ever captured Ian's heart, she would simply move on to her next conquest.

When they entered the pie car—a kind of town square—Lucy felt instantly at home. Several of the men were smoking and playing cards. Ian had attracted his usual crowd of friends and admirers as he sat on a bench near the row of windows and tuned his banjo.

If Lucy were casting a play about Ichabod Crane, there was not a doubt in her mind that her brother would be perfect in the title role. He was tall and bony and his facial features could best be described as birdlike. His eyes were small and close-set, but they crinkled with humor and delight at the antics of those surrounding him. His large nose hooked over a small mouth, and his dark hair that matched the color of her own emphasized his pale skin. He wasn't handsome in any traditional sense of the word—certainly not in the way that Jeremy Barrington was.

Lucy shook off the thought. Why would she even begin to compare the Englishman to her brother?

She turned her attention to the voluptuous, cupid-mouthed Polly Jacoby. "Better watch out," Lucy said softly to Trixie. "She's practically salivating."

Trixie crossed the narrow width of the car in three steps and plopped down on the bench right next to Ian. "Play that new ragtime thing, Ian," she said. "Lucy, come sit here with us and sing." She indicated the spot on the other side of Ian. Lucy grinned and joined them, leaving Polly no recourse but to move away.

An hour later, the car was crowded with members of the company, and everyone was singing. Norma was playing the old, battered upright piano in harmony with Ian and his banjo. Several members of

the band also got out their instruments and joined
in. The car was fairly swaying with the lively music
and singing, and Lucy suddenly felt as if it might not
be a terrible season after all.

Just then, she saw that Jeremy Barrington had entered the car. As always, the reaction to his
appearance was mixed. Lucy could see that for some
he was still not a man they felt they could completely
trust, while others seemed to have warmed to him
over the past two weeks. Then there were the old-
timers, who had seen a dozen or more like him
come and go. To them he was just another member
of the company.

Lucy had just been persuaded to sing a solo when
Jeremy entered the car. "Please, don't stop on my account," he said. He looked directly at Lucy. "I should
very much enjoy hearing you sing, Lucy."

He sat down in the chair closest to where she
stood next to Norma at the piano. He stretched his
long legs out in front of him and crossed them at the
ankles. Then he removed a cigar from his coat
pocket and bit off the tip. Someone hurried to offer
a light, and he nodded his appreciation. "Anytime
you're ready," he said softly.

Norma played a little arpeggio to give her the key.
Lucy considered refusing but then looked around
and saw that the others expected her to sing—for
them, not him. She smiled at the others and
launched into the song.

Toward the end of the ballad, she worked up the
nerve to face him directly. He was watching her intently, and she found that she could not look away.
She wanted to, but it was as if he held her there phys-
ically. She closed her eyes and held the last note, and

then opened them immediately when she heard his applause.

With a smile that was devastating in its power to captivate and charm, he stood and moved toward her. Then, to her utter amazement, he swept into the most dramatic curtain call bow she had ever witnessed.

"I bow to your talent, milady."

Lord help me, he is gorgeous, she thought. It occurred to her that his kind of elegant good looks often came in a man who was weak or soft, the kind of man she'd never really liked. There was something about Jeremy Barrington that gave that elegance dimension and strength, and that made him a man that she'd be wise to keep at a distance. *It's the accent,* she told herself firmly.

By midnight everyone had returned to the sleeping cars. It was always hard getting to sleep that first night of the tour. There was weary laughter and quiet talk as Lucy and Trixie undressed and prepared for bed. Throughout the train, Lucy knew that some performers lay awake and mentally ran through their routines again. Others dreamed about the crowds and the applause and the excited faces of the children as for the very first time they saw an elephant or lion, or a woman flying through the air.

Lucy had undressed down to her chemise. The window in the cramped compartment was stuck. She lay down on the bunk, knowing that she at least needed to rest, even if she didn't sleep. She tossed and turned until Trixie complained. She lay on her back and crossed her arms over her chest. It was like lying in a coffin. Her stomach growled loudly. She began to picture a tall glass of milk and a thick hunk of homemade bread smothered in Shirley's strawberry jam. She flopped over on her stomach.

"Oh, for Pete's sake, Luce," Trixie complained, "go to sleep."

Apparently, she wasn't having as much trouble settling in. It seemed as if the rhythm of the train wheels rumbling against the tracks had worked their magic. Lucy stared up at the ceiling of the car as she listened to Trixie's deep breathing, mumbled dream words, and definite snoring.

She sat up and waited. Satisfied that she would not wake Trixie, she refastened the waist of her petticoat and wrapped her shawl around her bare shoulders. Then she eased herself out the door of the compartment and moved on silent bare feet through the car.

First, some air. She carefully opened the door that led to the platform. In past seasons, the family car had been the last car in line. Now it was the fancy Pullman occupied by Jeremy Barrington. Lucy sighed and walked to the edge of the opening between the two cars, determined to make the best of her opportunity to enjoy the refreshingly cool night air. The rush of the early summer breeze was like deliverance. She lifted her face to it, drinking it in eagerly. Her shawl slipped from her shoulders, exposing her arms and neck. She felt the wind lift her hair. It was going to be all right, she decided. It had to be.

Jeremy stretched and pushed himself away from the large, ornately carved desk that dominated one spacious compartment of the custom-built private car. It was late and he was tired, but he knew that sleep wasn't likely to come easily. There was still a great deal of work to be done, and now with the illness of Harry Conroy, they were more shorthanded than ever—not to mention that they desperately needed a ringmaster.

He paced the length of the luxurious car, barely registering the inlaid walnut panels, gilded mirrors, and polished brass fittings. In the drawing salon hung not one but two small crystal-and-bronze chandeliers. Those alone would have been the envy of many a socialite back in New York.

New York. How he missed it—the theater, the people, the sheer energy of the place. He sat for a moment on a tufted brown velvet ottoman and ran his fingers through his hair. He fingered one of the pale gold silk tasseled pillows. Tomorrow they would arrive in Higginsville for their first performance. In spite of what he had seen at the dress rehearsal, they weren't ready. They weren't nearly ready. He stood up and flung the pillow across the room.

He forced himself to focus on how he might handle himself when they arrived in Higginsville. He had counted on Harry's being there as a sort of buffer, not to mention someone he could look to for advice and counsel. In the short time he had known the man, he had come to respect him enormously.

"Let me whittle this down to a manageable size for you, son," Harry had said just that morning between fits of racking coughing. "You only need to concentrate on delivering the best possible show; the rest will take care of itself."

"But, it's a bit like managing a small town," Jeremy protested. "Between the crew and the performers and the staff and the—"

"The crew and staff—they know their stuff, Jeremy. The worst thing you can do there is to try and tell them what to do or change how they do it. Like any worker who toils behind the scenes, they want one thing from you—your respect for a job well done."

As he recalled the circus man's advice, Jeremy found that he was feeling a bit less anxious. Pushing aside the heavy embroidered velvet curtains that led to a short corridor and his stateroom, he shrugged out of his coat and sat on the edge of the large bed that his steward, Ezra, had turned down for the night, to remove his shoes. He stood again, opening his vest and discarding the stiff collar of his shirt as he stared out the window at the silhouetted landscape speeding past in the dark night. But he was not seeing the countryside of Wisconsin. He was remembering his father and how he had conducted their family business.

Lord Barrington had been a stern taskmaster and a snob when it came to class hierarchy. It would never have occurred to Jeremy's father to show respect for a laborer's efforts any more than he would have seriously considered withholding Jeremy's salary when he failed to complete an assignment. Jeremy was his son, and his failings were chalked up to boyish caprice. His father had been born and bred to a strict class system. He didn't know any other way to manage.

When Jeremy had come to New York to work for Adam Porterfield, he had learned the hard way that there would be consequences for failure to perform. Adam was a fair man, but he had not maintained the wealth and success his father had accumulated by playing the fool. Jeremy intended to emulate that style of management. He would be fair, and he would be firm, and he would take Harry Conroy's advice and concentrate his energy on putting together the best possible show while trusting his managers and crew bosses to handle their jobs.

The land they traveled tonight was mostly flat— endlessly stretching toward the horizon, beyond which lay the next town. He faced months of this— one day in Higginsville, then on to the next town and the next and the next. He would need to find new talent, add new surprises to the program. He would have to stay one step ahead of his competitors. The stateroom seemed oppressive. He opened a window and leaned against the sill. A shift in the train's cadence as it rounded a curve caused him to shift his balance. Perhaps a breath of the night air would calm him.

He paused at his desk and selected a cigar from the humidor. Adam had included the humidor monogrammed with Jeremy's initials as a gift along with the private car. It was as clear a signal as anything that his boss and mentor believed in his ability to deliver on the challenge he had been given. He closed the humidor and moved to the fully stocked bar, where he splashed amber liquid into one of the crystal snifters, then wrapped his hands around the bowl of the glass to warm the brandy.

At the far end of the car was a dramatic observation room with windows on three sides to provide a panoramic view of the countryside. Even at night, one could sit in the darkened salon and witness the passing scene. But Jeremy chose the nearest exit and stepped out onto the platform at the front of his car where it attached to the rest of the train. The car in front of his was dark. He imagined they were all dark now. He took a long swallow of his brandy and leaned against the cool, smooth varnished wall of the car as he bit off the tip of his cigar but left it unlit.

It was from this position in the shadows that he observed Lucy slip through the narrow opening of the car beyond his. She was only a few feet from where he stood, yet she was completely unaware of his presence. Jeremy took full advantage of the opportunity to observe her.

She was barefoot and not properly dressed. Her hair was free as if she'd brushed it out before going to bed. It was as black as the night sky. She lifted her face to the moonlight, and in that movement there was something regal and yet primitive about her. He felt a desire that he had promised himself he would not permit—at least with any member of the company. He needed to concentrate on his work, and the last thing he could tolerate was more complications. There would be women in the towns—there always were. And those women could be safely left behind.

The train shifted again and the shawl fell from her shoulders and caught in the crooks of her elbows. Jeremy remained perfectly still, watching her. When she had come down from performing the very stunt he had forbidden her to do in the preview performance, there had been something about the way her eyes had sparkled as she took her bows that night. He had known that look. It was a look that spoke of longings and dreams and, at the same time, determination and fearlessness. He knew now that it was those eyes that had filled his thoughts. He knew that look because he had seen it a thousand times looking at his own reflection. But what he had seen in her dark eyes was something more: strength and self-assurance.

He focused on the pale smoothness of her exposed shoulders. His eyes traveled the length of her throat to the tilt of her chin, to her slightly parted lips, poised to receive the kiss of the night air. His hand tightened involuntarily on the brandy snifter, clinking it against the brass railing. Immediately, she spun around and gathered the shawl to cover herself.

"Forgive me for startling you," he said, moving the single step from his platform to hers and blocking any intention she might have of going back inside. "I, too, came out to get some air," he added in a pleasant conversational tone, hoping that she would believe that he had just now stepped outside and had not been watching her for several minutes.

"It's . . . that is . . . I couldn't sleep." Lucy readjusted her shawl to better cover herself, then realized that she was standing before him in her undergarments. *Well, he's seen you in less,* she reminded herself, but immediately wondered how much he had seen—how long he had really been standing there.

"I enjoyed your singing earlier," he said.

She could not deny that he was being a perfect gentleman, making polite conversation, standing slightly away from her, not pressing forward. She permitted herself to relax slightly. "Thank you."

He rested one hip on the railing, which brought him a step closer. The smoke from his cigar circled lazily between them. He sipped his brandy. "I'm surprised that you couldn't sleep. I would anticipate nerves from a newcomer, but you are hardly that, Lucy."

She smiled. "No. I've been performing since I was

ten, but I still can't sleep on the first night of the tour. There's little use in going to bed." Heavens to Hannah, what was it about this man that had her discussing intimate matters such as sleep and going to bed? Surely, ladies that he knew would never discuss such topics openly.

"I couldn't sleep either," he said. Then he smiled that devastatingly handsome smile of his. "I assure you that in all my life, I have never had trouble sleeping. It must either be something in the air . . . or perhaps . . ." He looked at her for a long moment, as if considering whether or not to continue.

"Perhaps what?" she asked.

"Perhaps, like you, I care very much about what will happen tomorrow and the day after that. Perhaps I want very much for us all to be a success."

His voice was low and soft and she leaned toward him to catch the words. Lucy was intensely aware of him—of them sharing the small confined space of the narrow platform. If she reached out, she could touch him . . . he could touch her. His shirt had been pulled free of his trousers and it was open enough that she could see his bare chest. His hair was not the perfectly groomed coif she had come to expect, but rather it was tousled as if he had run his hands through it.

"I like traveling at night," he said, looking out at the passing scenery. "It's a bit like traveling through time and space, don't you think?"

"I never considered, but yes, it is . . . different than traveling during the daylight." She followed his gaze and became equally mesmerized by the panorama moving rapidly past them.

"And exciting?" He had leaned forward so that his face was close.

"Yes," she replied breathlessly. There didn't seem to be anything else to say, so she stood very still, feeling the nearness of him.

"Aren't your feet getting cold?" he asked in a very normal voice a moment later. "I know mine are, and I have on my stockings."

"Why, Sir Jeremy," she teased, "a proper Englishman like you outside without his slippers?"

He laughed, and she found that she liked the sound of it, enjoyed a feeling of power at her ability to make him laugh. Then, he reached over and traced the pad of his thumb across her cheek, and any idea that she had of having power over him vanished.

"I have to go in," she said, but seemed incapable of moving an inch.

He nodded, then brought his other hand up to cup her face.

Lord help her, he was going to kiss her, and—more to the point—she wanted that kiss.

"You'd better go in," he repeated softly as he skimmed his thumb lightly across her lips.

She only had to make her move and she knew that he would step aside and let her pass. He was, after all, a gentleman. It was up to her, though, for he would not make the first move to release her. He would not stop her from going, but he wouldn't make it easy for her, either.

Then her stomach growled—roared, actually, for it was certainly loud enough for both of them to hear it above the rhythm of the train clacking against the tracks. Jeremy grinned. "Was that coming from you, Miss Conroy?"

She blushed and was thankful for the dark.

"You aren't one of those silly women who starve themselves for the sake of their figure, are you?" He dropped his hands from her face to his hips as he demanded information.

"I eat," she replied petulantly.

"But not today. You were worried about Harry all day, and then you were still in the club car while others went for supper." He took her arm and started toward his car.

"Unhand me," she demanded, but his grip was firm.

"Not until I feed you," he insisted. "You are far too important to the success of this venture for me to permit you to starve yourself." He gave her a gentle push that sent her through the open door and into the splendid coach.

"This is not at all proper," she fumed, pulling free of his grip the moment he had led her halfway through the car to the salon.

"Sit down," he ordered as he pulled out a chair at the small dining table.

She sat, but as soon as he turned his back, she was up again. His hands came down firmly on her shoulders. "Sit down," he repeated with quiet authority. "Nothing improper is going to happen here. We are going to have something to eat. If it's your reputation you're concerned about, no one will ever know you were here."

She almost laughed at that. He clearly did not know a thing about the total lack of privacy on the road. "Everyone will know," she groused. "More to the point, *I'll* know, and I won't have you thinking that just because I am a performer . . . in the entertainment business . . . that you can—that I am some kind of . . ."

"Floozy?" he said as he set out plates and glasses.

She shut her lips tightly and glared at him.

"I assure you, Lucy, I am not in the habit of having to force myself on women. I do quite nicely all on my own." He placed a linen napkin across her lap. "And you are no floozy. Now, what would you like to eat?"

"I'm not hungry," she insisted stubbornly as her stomach betrayed her with yet another loud growl.

"And I'm Queen Victoria. How about a glass of milk?"

Cool, frosty milk. Lucy's mouth watered at the thought of it. On the other hand, there was milk to be had in the company's kitchen—milk she could get on her own.

"Miss Conroy?" Jeremy stood waiting for her answer, and judging by the expression on his face, he knew that she wanted that milk.

"Milk would be lovely," she replied, folding her hands primly in her lap and looking up at him with her curtain call smile.

He considered her with some skepticism but seemed satisfied that she would at least stay put for the milk. "I'll just be a minute," he said, glancing at her twice over his shoulder before disappearing behind fringed brocade draperies that separated the elegant room from a tiny galley kitchen.

Lucy waited only a few seconds, until she heard sounds of him getting the milk, before heading for the door. She did not miss how the thick Oriental rug caressed her bare feet or how the door had smooth polished brass handles unlike the worn nickel-plated hardware in the rest of the train. Once outside, she wasted no time traversing the platform. Safely inside her sleeping car, she glanced up to see Jeremy Barrington standing at the door to his Pullman, holding a glass of milk and scowling at her.

Five

It was still pitch dark when the train pulled onto the siding in Higginsville, but the roustabouts were immediately out and engaged in the unloading of wagons and animals. Overnight the lithographers had printed the posters announcing the parade and two performances that they would stage that very day. Young boys who had somehow got wind of the train's impending arrival stood around blowing on their hands in the chill of the morning, waiting for the posters as well as paste buckets they would need to paste the colorful artistry on any available surface.

Jeremy had barely fallen into a fitful sleep when he heard the commotion. Men yelling and whistling through their teeth to stir the animals into action. Others unloading the canvas and poles that would soon be raised on the large open space at the edge of town. He was surprised to realize that, far from feeling annoyance at being awakened so abruptly and early, he was anxious to be out in the midst of the action. He dressed quickly and hurried outside.

Someone handed him a tin cup of strong black coffee as he strode along the length of the train, watching the activity. People came to him with information—the bandleader was going to divide the musicians into three sections to ride on wagons spaced over the entire parade route. In Shirley's absence, Arnie and Norma's son was willing to take on the job of playing the calliope as it brought up the rear of the parade, but then, who did he want to serve as ringmaster?

"I'll do it," he said without stopping to consider what he was saying.

"You, sir?" Norma asked, bushy eyebrows raised in disbelief.

Jeremy smiled at her. "Why not? How hard can it be to walk down a street and blow a whistle from time to time?"

"That's the spirit," she said, giving him a hearty slap on the back before letting out a piercing whistle of her own and heading off to scold three roustabouts who were doing something that obviously displeased her.

"I have the lineup right here, sir. Would you care to see it?" The nervous little man whose name Jeremy could never seem to recall, but who, Harry had assured him, was a master advance man, held a single sheet of paper.

Jeremy scanned it quickly, using the light from the cookhouse car. "I don't see the names of our top acts," he said, running over the list again. "Miss Conroy . . . Trixie LaMott . . . the Jacoby Brothers . . ."

"But sir, the stars never parade," the man assured him.

"Mr. . . . ."

"Carson, sir. Constantin Carson. Please call me Con."

"Well, Con, please let everyone know that in this company, *everyone* parades—even me . . . even you, Constantin Carson."

"Me, sir?" the little man squeaked.

Jeremy walked around him, sizing him up. "Yes. I do believe that you would be an excellent clown."

"A clown, sir? But . . ."

"Go and tell everyone that they are to be ready to parade, and then report to Babbo and tell him I said you were to accompany him and that I hold him responsible for seeing that you are properly costumed and appropriately made-up." He smiled at Con and nodded encouragingly, then something caught his eye and he moved on down the tracks. "You, there, have a care with that wagon," he shouted.

"Well, well, well," Trixie said to Lucy as the two of them stood on the platform. She blew on her coffee and studied Jeremy. "Looks like somebody or something lit a fire under his tight little bun."

"Trixie!" Lucy exclaimed and then giggled. "He is quite . . . active this morning, isn't he?"

"Positively brimming with fervor," Trixie replied. "Looks good on him, I'll give him that. Not that he isn't already just about the most gorgeous hunk of male I've ever laid eyes on."

"Why, Trixie!" Lucy feigned a shocked expression. "What if Ian hears you?"

Trixie laughed. "Never can tell. Might be just the thing to light a fire under *his* cute little bun," she replied with a wink as she dumped the remains of her coffee over the railing and went back inside to finish dressing.

Lucy stood sipping her coffee and watching Jeremy Barrington. She noticed that he was talking to the roustabouts and they were smiling and throwing comments back at him. She couldn't hear what was being said, but she knew from their posture and the sounds of occasional raucous laughter that drifted back her way that they were enjoying their interlude with the boss. After a few minutes of what appeared to be lighthearted banter, she saw Jeremy take off his coat and roll back his sleeves.

She leaned out over the railing for a better view, shielding her eyes against the rising sun. She could not believe what she was seeing. Jeremy Barrington had joined a row of men to help with the unloading of the huge support poles for the tent. His English accent was clearly distinguishable from the comments of the others. There was no doubt that he had been totally accepted by these established cynics.

When the poles and canvas had been unloaded, she heard one of the men farther down the line call out to him, "Hey, Jeremy, we could use a hand unloading these here lions," the man shouted, and everyone—including Jeremy—laughed.

Lucy had been around the rough types who made up the crew all her life. She had never ever seen them like this. With Harry, they were respectful but silent—even morose sometimes. They would mutter under their breaths, argue with each other over who was not pulling his fair share of the work, and go about their work with a sullen, irritated expression. Harry usually kept his distance as long as they did the work.

Jeremy Barrington had somehow walked into the thick of them and charmed them the way Reggie used to charm his lions. She frowned. One more reason to watch herself around the man. If his actions started to remind her of Reggie, she should take that as fair warning. They were two of a kind—not that she had the slightest interest in Jeremy from any sort of romantic point of view.

He waved his hand at the crew as if to say, "Carry on," before continuing on his way. Lucy studied him for a long moment. Trixie had a point. Never in all her born days had she seen a man who looked every bit as good from the backside as he did from the front. The man had a way of moving that made a woman take notice—no matter her intentions not to do so.

Jeremy walked the length of the lineup for the parade, greeting the performers and teamsters as he checked both wagons and animals to be sure that they were clean and thoroughly decked out in their finest trappings. He had been discouraged when he'd gone to wardrobe to be fitted for the costume of a ringmaster and realized just how faded and shopworn many of the costumes appeared. The wardrobe mistress had assured him that under the lights everything still looked great, but he was worried about how those same costumes would appear in the harsh light of day.

He saw now that he needn't have worried. In most cases, the performers were positioned high atop colorful wagons that had been freshly painted before the start of the season. Details of their costumes were not visible to most, and the sunlight often caught a bead or sequin or bit of braid and reflected off it to give it an illusion of sparkle. The wagons garnered their own share of attention. He began to relax as he made his way toward the front of the lineup.

Lucy was positioned atop her parade swing. She was laughing at something her driver had just said. Her hair shone in the sunlight and she was again wearing the bright-blue harem costume.

"Good morning," he said, looking at the driver first and then up at her. He had to shield his eyes from the sun to see her. "It would appear to be a fine day for a parade."

"Yessir," the driver said with a grin. "A fine day indeed."

Lucy remained silent.

"Miss Conroy, I wondered if you might have any advice for me," he said, addressing her directly now as he moved alongside the small flatbed wagon and looked up at her.

"Don't look back," she replied.

"I beg you pardon?"

"Don't look back once you take the lead and the parade starts," she repeated. "It's bad luck."

"I see. Well, we wouldn't want that for our first outing, would we? Are there any other superstitions I should learn?"

"Not at the moment," she replied and smiled.

He could not decide if she was making up the silly harbinger or not. He would not put it past her to be teasing him, trying to make him look the fool. He replaced his hat and quickened his step toward the front of the assembly. There, he took his place in a small chariot pulled by two ostriches, blew a long blast on his whistle, and began his first parade.

It was really quite thrilling to make his way down the main street of the small town and see crowds of people gathered along the sides, cheering and smiling. Small children had been boosted to sit atop their father's shoulders. Older children clung to trees and lampposts they had climbed for a better view. Others ran alongside, determined to follow the parade all the way back to the circus grounds. Shopkeepers had closed up their shops and joined the rest of the citizenry in watching the parade. Jeremy saw several young ladies eyeing him with interest, and he tipped his hat and gave them a broad smile, which caused them to blush and cover their mouths with gloved hands.

As the parade made the turn at the end of the street and headed out of town to the open space where they would stage the day's performances, Jeremy's heart skipped a beat when he saw the pointed spires of the tent in the distance. Small, colorful flags whipped in the brisk spring breeze, beckoning patrons to come, put down their money, and enjoy the show. As they drew nearer, he could smell the fragrance of popcorn and sawdust. He saw that the ticket wagon had been rolled out and positioned just in front of the smaller tents that housed the sideshow exhibits.

He leaped down from the small cart designed to resemble a Roman chariot, and headed for the main tent. Inside, the rings were in place and surrounded by rows of bleachers that he sincerely hoped would soon be filled with paying customers. Harry had been right. The crew had done their work and done it with excellence. He needn't have worried about them. Now, if only the performers would do as well.

"You the man in charge?"

Jeremy turned and found himself looking down at a very small, heavyset young boy with the face of an elderly man. "May I help you?"

"Name's Wally—Walter Wiggins. I'd like to join your show."

"I see. And what, exactly, is it that you do, Mr. Wiggins?"

"I'm a human cannonball," Wiggins announced.

"How old are you?"

"Forty years old."

"Forty?" Jeremy could not help the shocked tone.

"All right, forty-two, but I can still be shot out of a cannon right to the top of the tent and down again into the net. You work with a net, don't you?" he asked as he pulled the stub of a cigar from one pocket and stuck it in his mouth without lighting it.

"We have a net for certain acts," Jeremy assured him. "Are you a citizen of Higginsville, sir?" He was still trying to determine if this person who was no more than four feet in height could possibly be a boy trying to pull his leg.

"I've been staying here ever since the Parnelli Brothers came through here last year and gave me the ax," Wiggins replied bitterly.

"And, do you mind if I ask why you were dismissed?"

"I drink," was the unapologetic reply. "Once in a while I drink too much. One night I drank a little too much before my act, and when I flew out of the cannon, I upchucked all over the place . . . stuff flying through the—"

"All right, Mr. Wiggins, I grasp the details. Precisely, why should I hire you?"

The man looked up at him and squinted. "Because you got no cannonball act," he replied slowly as if Jeremy might be a bit thickheaded.

"Wally?"

Lucy's wagon had just reached the circus grounds, and she had swung herself down and jumped off before the driver could fully halt the horses. "Wally!" she shrieked joyously and ran to the little man.

The two of them clasped hands and grinned and started talking at once. "I can't believe . . ." "I heard that . . ."

Jeremy cleared his throat to get their attention.

"Oh, sorry," Wiggins said, still holding Lucy's hand as he turned his attention back to Jeremy. "The mister and me was just discussing terms," he explained to Lucy.

"I don't believe that we had come quite that far, sir," Jeremy said.

"Oh, but you must hire Wally," Lucy insisted. "He's simply incredible. Harry always wanted to have him join us, but the Parnellis would never release him from his contract." She turned back to Wally. "Why on earth didn't you come to us this winter?"

Wally actually blushed. "I was ashamed to come. Never been fired in my whole life."

Jeremy stared at the man. His shame was for being sacked, not for the fact that he'd . . .

"It's all worked for the best," Lucy said as she put her arm around the little man and looked up at Jeremy. "Isn't that right, Jeremy?"

"I . . . that is . . ."

"Harry would leap at the chance to add Wally's name to our roster. He can start tonight, right?"

"I—we have no cannon," Jeremy said, suddenly grasping the escape he needed.

"I own my equipment, sir," Wally replied. "If you can let me have a couple of the boys and a wagon, we can get the thing loaded and set up by tonight's performance."

"Costumes?" Jeremy asked.

"Got those, too. Guy like me is a mite hard to fit," he said with a wink.

Jeremy felt cornered. Lucy was still looking up at him with those huge deep-blue eyes of hers. The little guy was still looking up at him, chewing on that unlit stub of a cigar and with his thumbs hooked under his suspenders.

"Mr. Wiggins, I really do need to attend to this afternoon's performance. Perhaps if you would be so kind as to stop by my office around five o'clock, we could—"

Wally stuck out his hand and shook Jeremy's with surprising firmness. "You got yourself a deal, mister. I'll get my stuff loaded up and over here and be there at five."

Before Jeremy could say another word, Wally Wiggins was trotting across the grounds, calling to one of the roustabouts, who hailed him with the same enthusiasm with which Lucy had greeted him earlier.

"Is there anyone that man doesn't know?" Jeremy muttered.

"Everybody loves Wally," Lucy replied with a grin. "Thanks," she added. "I know you might have some reservations, but I assure you that Wally is truly the best. He'll be a wonderful addition to the company."

"As long as he doesn't drink," Jeremy said.

"At least not before a performance," she agreed and laughed. "Well, I've got to change. Thanks again. Harry will be really pleased about this." She waved and ran toward the dressing tent to change and warm up for her performance.

The afternoon show went off without a hitch, and while the local populace appeared to enjoy themselves, Jeremy was discouraged. He knew that in the larger towns, where people had more access to a variety of entertainment, more would be expected. He had heard some of the patrons comparing acts to other circuses they had seen. Apparently, the Parnelli Brothers featured a trapeze artist who rivaled Lucy's act in daring and skill. Knowing that everyone would be grabbing a bite to eat before the next performance, he headed over to the cookhouse.

Lucy was sitting at a table with Trixie and Ian. Jeremy filled a plate and approached their table. "May I join you?"

"Sure," Ian said, getting up. "Take my place. I'm finished and I want to recheck that rigging before tonight's show.

"Me, too," Trixie added, standing as well. "That is, I want to check—that is, I have things to do," she finished in a rush as she glanced at Ian. "Wait up, Ian, and I'll walk over with you."

Jeremy sat on the hard bench and placed a napkin on his lap. Lucy continued to eat. "Do I detect a bit of a romance there?" Jeremy asked, nodding toward the exit, where Ian was holding the door for Trixie.

Lucy smiled. "It's a strange romance. He's crazy about her but too shy to do anything about it. She's crazy about him, and if she were any more obvious in her adoration, we'd have to erect a shrine."

They ate in comfortable silence for a few minutes. "I wanted to discuss something with you—get your opinion, if you don't mind," he said finally.

"I'm flattered," she replied and continued to concentrate on her food.

"In observing this afternoon's performance, it occurred to me that . . . well, that is . . ."

"We need some bang," she said bluntly, nodding. "Wally's cannonball act will help," she added.

"No doubt. I was wondering if you have ever heard of a performer by the name of Eleanore something-or-other? I believe she is with the Parnelli outfit."

Lucy's fork was halfway from her plate to her mouth. Slowly she put it back on the plate. "What about her?"

"You know of her, then," Jeremy said and rushed to continue. "I overheard one of the patrons this afternoon speaking about the act that she performed here last season. It seems that . . ." He stopped speaking when he saw her looking at him, her cheeks flushed, her eyes glittering with what he could only describe as fury.

"Eleanore used to live with us. Shirley taught her everything she knows. There is nothing—*nothing* that she does in her act that she didn't learn from Shirley or steal from me. If you are suggesting for one minute . . ."

He held up his hands to ward off her anger. "I was not suggesting anything, Lucy. I simply wanted to discuss . . ."

She stood. "I do not *discuss* that woman . . . I do not even permit her name to be spoken in my presence. *If* you are so concerned about adding a spark of excitement to our performance, then stop forbidding me to do the finale of my act. I worked all winter to perfect that, and I can assure you that the Parnelli Brothers have never seen that one, nor has anyone in any town we will visit this season."

She gathered her dishes and left him sitting there.

"Our Lucy," Wally Wiggins commented as he eased himself onto the bench next to Jeremy, "she's a spitfire, that one. You might want to avoid discussing Eleanore Wilson with her. Some bad blood there."

"So I gathered," Jeremy said and pushed his plate away. He wanted to know more but was reluctant to ask Wally for further details.

"The boys and me got the cannon over here, tested it out and all. You want me to have a go at it tonight?"

"Higginsville might not be the proper venue, Mr. Wiggins, given the unfortunate circumstances of your last performance before these citizens."

Wally grinned and ducked his head. "You got me there, sir." He did not seem inclined to leave.

"Was there something else you wished to discuss?"

"Well, Norma was telling me how you'd given her this sideshow job. Now, Norma, she can lift her Arnie clear off the ground."

"We've worked that into her act," Jeremy said.

"Well, you see, Mr. Barrington, she can lift me with one hand—might be interesting, don't you know?"

It was *brilliant.* Jeremy smiled at the man. "Mr. Wiggins, I believe that you may be performing this evening after all. Come with me."

That evening the grounds surrounding the big top and side tents swarmed with people. Several families who had attended the afternoon performance had succumbed to the pleas of their children to stay for the evening performance as well. It was a good sign, Lucy thought as she checked the rigging for her act. Wally had stopped by to see if she knew where he could find Norma, and had told her about Jeremy's accepting his idea to join Norma's sideshow act. Lucy had to admit that she would not have thought that Jeremy's ego would stand for accepting ideas from a man like Wally. Perhaps that meant that she could find a way to persuade him to let her take some license with her act as well.

"Ian, what do you think about abandoning the net?" she asked, hearing a step behind her and assuming it was her brother.

"I think, Lady Lucinda, that it would be taking quite a risk," Jeremy replied in a calm, even tone.

Lucy turned. Her instinct was to argue the point, but she caught herself. She considered him for a long moment, thinking about the kind of women he was probably used to being with. They were, no doubt, refined society ladies—the kind of women who used feminine wiles to work their will. Lucy knew that such tactics would be as foreign to her as it would be for those high society types to swing by their ankles sixty or seventy feet in the air. Still, there was no harm in trying.

"Well, of course," she replied sweetly and saw a flicker of wariness in his eyes at her change in tactics. "But then, risk is as necessary as lights, costumes, and music if one is to continue to build surprise and excitement to its proper climax, is it not?"

Jeremy smiled and moved a step closer to her. "Why, Miss Conroy, are you suggesting that there is an element of seduction in our work?"

Lucy felt the color rise to her cheeks. She had suggested no such thing, but she did not back away. Instead, it was she who took half a step nearer to him, making it necessary to tilt back her head and look up at him with wide eyes as she spoke to him in almost a whisper. "Think of it, Jeremy. I am up there and they are down here. Their hearts are already pounding; their breath has quickened; they hold tight to their seats, anticipating the next thrilling move."

It was his turn to color. She saw in his eyes that he was beyond thinking of the act and was now thinking only of the fantasy her words created.

"If we removed the net at that last climatic moment . . ." she continued breathlessly. She intentionally left off there. There was a long moment when neither of them spoke. They stood there, their faces close, their eyes locked.

Finally, Jeremy blinked and cleared his throat. "It's . . . an interesting idea."

Lucy stepped back, all business now, and pressed her advantage. "It is," she agreed.

"Perhaps if we tried it with the final stunt," he mused.

Lucy was having trouble containing her excitement. He was going to let her do it! She waited for the final permission.

"Is there some way that you might have a rope nearby that you would hold on to as a backup in the event you would slip?"

"But . . ."

"Because, as much as I may agree with your theory and logic, Lucy, there is one risk I will not take, and that is the risk of having you injured . . . or worse."

She started to say something in protest, closed her mouth, and studied the ground for a moment. "Can I disguise it? The web?"

"The web?"

"The rope you want me to have coming down from the top next to the trapeze. I want to cover it to make it less visible to the audience. Can I do that?"

"Yes, as long as it is readily available for you to grasp, and that you do not release it until you are certain that you are secure in the foothold on the trapeze. Do we have a bargain?"

She nodded once, still not looking at him.

He placed his index finger under her chin and lifted her face to his. "Do we?"

His eyes searched her for the truth.

"Yes, we have a bargain."

He did not release his gentle hold on her chin, nor did she move the half step away from him that would have been all that was necessary to end the contact. He was definitely going to kiss her. She was sure of it. She felt her eyelids flutter, for she was going to let him kiss her.

Are you out of your mind? She chastised herself and forced her eyes wide open and took the necessary step away from him.

He was smiling, and she knew that he had read her mind and knew that for an instant she had actually fallen under the spell of his charm. *Cocky rascal.*

"I have to find Ian. We have work to do."

He waited until she was all the way across the ring and then called to her. "Miss Conroy?"

She turned.

"Do not try to get round me in this. Do it my way or there will be no subsequent discussion of any further changes to your act. Is that quite clear?"

He was every inch the person in charge, where just seconds before he had played the seducer. She realized that she had set out to seduce him and he had turned the tables on her. *Damn the man.*

"Miss Conroy?"

She had quickly learned that when he meant to assert his power over her career, it was "Miss Conroy." When he wanted something from her, it was "Lucy."

"Crystal clear, Your Highness," she replied with a deep, mocking curtsy.

Six

The first two weeks of performances came off without a hitch. Jeremy began to feel as if they might actually be able to make a success of the entire season. Lucy's mood, on the other hand, seemed to grow blacker with every performance. She could not shake the feeling that things were going *too* well.

"What are you so worried about?" Trixie asked one night as the two of them lay in their berths. "The man has already brought three new acts on board. He's found a terrific ringmaster. I mean, Otto must have been touched by the ringmaster angel—he's that good and you know it. *And* you know as well as I do that no circus veteran would have given the guy a chance, but Jeremy saw something and took him on, and look at how wonderful he is!"

"I know, but—"

"But, nothing. I know you, Lucy Conroy, and what's eating at you is that you were so sure that he wasn't gonna fit in or help or make a difference. You can't stand being wrong—never could. Besides, I think there's something else that's got you stewing."

Lucy could not see Trixie in the dark, but she knew her friend was smiling that Cheshire cat smile of hers. "And what might that be?"

"You like the guy. More than like him. You're every

bit as charmed and attracted to him as every other
woman on this train is. There's one major difference."

"And I am sure that you'll enlighten me," Lucy
replied.

"He feels the same attraction for you."

"Go to sleep, Trixie." Lucy turned her face to the
wall and pretended disinterest.

"Open your eyes, honey. You could have Sir Jeremy Barrington eating out of your hand and not
even have to work at it. Wish Ian was that easy." She
yawned and shifted in her berth. "Night, honey."

They were only a month into the season, and
somehow Jeremy had wangled them a chance to perform for three days over Independence Day in
Springfield, the state capital of Illinois. There was to
be a special performance for the governor himself
and several hundred invited guests. The Conroy outfit had never played any town as large as that, and
the only dignitaries they'd attracted were small-town
mayors or county judges. Lucy just didn't think they
were ready for such a test so early in a season when
they had started off shorthanded—not to mention
late—from the start.

"I think it's going to be just grand," Trixie gushed
one night when several of them had gathered in the
pie car after supper.

Wally shifted his unlit cigar stub to the other side
of his mouth. "I have to admit that when I first laid
eyes on that English fella, I never in a million years
would have expected that he could pull off something like this."

Ian grunted his agreement while Lucy stared at

the three of them in complete disbelief. They had been playing cards to pass the time, and Trixie had been babbling for several hands about how wonderful it was going to be, meeting all those important people and having the chance to perform for them.

"Am I the only sane one in this group?" Lucy asked, snapping down a card with unnecessary emphasis. The others looked at her. "We aren't ready for such a big show," she said as if talking to a bunch of two-year-olds. "If you consider any other company that travels this area, would you honestly pick us as your choice to play the capital?"

"You underestimate us, Luce," Ian said and laid out his hand. "Gin."

Trixie recorded the score while Wally gathered and shuffled the cards.

"You nervous, Lucy?" Wally asked as he dealt a new hand.

"Let's just say that I would feel a lot more confident if Harry was here running things." She collected her cards and studied her hand.

"Jeremy's gonna call a company meeting tomorrow afternoon," Ian said after they had played in silence for a couple of rounds.

"He told you that?" Lucy had noticed that Jeremy had been spending more time with Ian lately. He seemed to seek her brother out, and the two of them would hold long discussions . . . if you could call Jeremy doing most of the talking and Ian occasionally nodding his head a discussion.

Ian nodded and picked up one card while discarding another. "Gin," he said quietly.

"Makes sense," Trixie said. "We only have the one performance tomorrow, and that's in the evening, so there's plenty of time for a meeting once everything is set up."

"What's the meeting about?" Lucy asked.

Ian shrugged. "He wants to talk about those three days in Springfield. He's got some ideas. He's run them past Harry and Shirley, and now he's ready to talk about them to the rest of us."

"How is Harry?" Trixie asked.

"And Harry agreed with his ideas?" Lucy asked, ignoring Trixie's question because she knew her friend was simply trying to send the conversation in a different direction.

"The man's no dummy," Wally commented as he squinted at his cards and chewed his cigar. "Think about it, Luce. This week alone, he's added elephants to the herd, found a new trick-riding act, and made a deal on fabric for new costumes. And he's got a line on a trained-bear act that Parnelli let go just last week. That's not even mentioning the fact that he had the good sense to tout my act on the posters as a main draw." Wally grinned.

"Are we to make a company, then, of Parnelli's leftovers?" Lucy protested and saw immediately how she had hurt Wally's feelings. "Oh, Wally, I didn't mean you. I'm sorry—truly. Please forgive me."

She placed her hand on Wally's and he nodded his acceptance of her apology.

"Let's hear the man out when he speaks to us tomorrow, Luce," Ian added quietly without looking at her. He laid out his hand. "Gin."

"Oh, for Pete's sake," Lucy muttered as she abandoned her cards and got up from the table. "I'm going to bed."

* * *

Everyone was in costume for the parade when they gathered in the main tent for the meeting the following afternoon. Jeremy waited for everyone to be seated in one section of the bleachers. He glanced around, checking to be sure that everyone was there. Lucy looked around as well and saw that no one had wanted to miss this. From the boys who fed and bathed the animals to the leader of the band, everyone was waiting for him to tell them his plans.

"Good afternoon, ladies and gentlemen," Jeremy began. "I suspect that you have all heard the rumor by now that we are to engage in a version of a command performance for the governor of the great state of Illinois."

There were murmurs of excitement throughout those gathered. Jeremy held up his hand and everyone gave him the attention he'd requested with that single gesture.

"It's not Her Majesty, of course," he continued with a smile, "or the president, as I might have preferred, but there will be time enough for that. We shall consider this preparation for those more majestic events." He glanced around and waited for the murmuring to cease. "Ah, I see that many of you are skeptical. I must tell you that I shall have no patience with such cynicism, and neither should any of you. Should we be successful in this unusual opportunity to perform before these dignitaries of the great state of Illinois, there is every possibility that the governor will assist us in gaining an engagement in Chicago for several days."

Now the buzz became louder and more excited.

"Of course . . ." Jeremy shouted to regain their attention. "Of course," he continued in a more normal tone once he had it, "this does not come without a price."

There was not a sound as everyone waited.

"We will have to cancel or postpone some of the stops in smaller communities along the way. I have spoken with Harry Conroy—who, by the way, continues to improve daily. He may even be able to attend our performance in Springfield if he continues to obey his doctor."

Everyone applauded and cheered.

"I have also consulted with Harry's true healer in all of this—his lovely Shirley."

There was a spattering of applause as well as some chuckles and comments of pleasure at the prospect of seeing Harry and Shirley again.

"At any rate, Harry and I feel very strongly that one does not abandon one's commitments. Should we perform in Springfield and in Chicago, our season will, of necessity, be lengthened. We will return at the end of our regular season to every single village and perform as promised. Of course, such an extension would qualify as—I believe you refer to it as 'a cherry pie job'?"

It wasn't the first time that Jeremy had used his knack for winning over even the most cynical among them with his use of circus slang. It would not be the last. In this case his reference to cherry pie had told them that the extra shows would mean extra money. As he had expected, everyone applauded this decision.

Jeremy smiled. "I may assume, then, that you are in agreement and that I can count on you to remain with the company for the additional performances." He waited a moment, pacing back and forth with his hands clasped behind his back. Once again the company grew quiet, anticipating that there was more to be said and that it might not all be good news.

"All of this good news does not come without some concerns. The fact of the matter is, ladies and gentlemen, that as talented as you are, we are not yet making the best of those talents. In addition, we are still a bit . . . lean, shall we say . . . when it comes to acts that measure up to the standard of the larger companies touring in this area. At the moment, being tapped for this particular honor has come as a result of business and financial contacts—Mr. Porterfield has been a colleague of the governor's for many years. The two of them were college classmates and have entered into a number of business dealings over the years."

He saw Lucy studying him intently. It was clear that she was one of the skeptical members of the group. He turned his attention to Ian, who nodded with encouragement.

"I have asked Mr. Ian Conroy to assist me in making certain that we are properly prepared for this engagement. As such, he will serve in a new position as the company's manager."

He paused a moment to let the reaction run its course. He saw that, as expected, it ranged from surprise to endorsement. It was exactly what he had anticipated, and he breathed a sigh of relief that, in this matter at least, he had made a wise and popular decision. He held up both hands, and once again his audience grew quiet in anticipation.

"What is needed here is a concerted effort on the part of every performer to find some way to enhance performance—to raise the bar, so to speak."

Lucy was half out of her seat to protest. Jeremy caught her movement from the corner of his eye and continued. "Among your ranks, only Miss Conroy has consistently come to me with ideas for enhancement of her act. The rest of you, I am sad to say, appear to be satisfied with the status quo. As we move to this next level, such an attitude will be unacceptable and will no doubt eventually lead to the need for you to find other employment."

Now the muttered comments were delivered with a hint of protest and outrage. Jeremy ignored them and continued.

"I have called you here today to issue a challenge—one that I have been given clearance by Mr. Porterfield himself to support with monetary enhancements where warranted." That certainly got their attention. Jeremy suppressed a smile. As he had expected, money was a common language. "I am challenging each and every one of you to devise ways that you might strengthen your performance in such a way that no other circus in this region could boast talent even approaching yours at whatever skill you have chosen to demonstrate in the ring."

As one, they sat there staring at him as if he had just suggested that each and every one of them walk on water.

"I will tell you right now that Mr. Ian Conroy and I will review your suggestions. There is one codicil to your assignment. We will tolerate nothing that endangers either the performer or a member of the crew or the audience in any way; is that clear?"

As one, they nodded.

"Then I would suggest that each of you contemplate this matter as it applies to your performance over the next day or so and be prepared to bring Ian your ideas no later than Friday night. We will review them on the train that evening and we will meet again on Sunday next. Are there any questions?"

Silence.

"Then, ladies and gentlemen, we have a parade and performance to do," he said quietly, and they understood that they had been dismissed.

As the company filed out of the tent, there were quiet conversations among one or two, but most had turned their thoughts inward. Jeremy could see that for some of them he had offered the possibility to try things they had only dreamed of being able to bring into their acts. For others, he saw that his challenge had the opposite effect. It represented not opportunity but just more work.

"Miss Conroy? I wonder if I might have a word with you."

Lucy paused before turning back to face him. "Of course."

"You know my reservations about the finale that you performed prior to the start of our season."

"You've certainly made them clear enough."

"Well, Ian has convinced me to give you the opportunity to include that in your act."

Her eyes glittered with excitement, but she maintained her composure. "You understand that Ian is not a man to suggest this without having considered it from every side? As my brother—if there were the slightest danger above what is normal for someone in my profession—he would never . . ."

Jeremy nodded. "Yes, I understand."

"So, I may add it?"

"For the governor's invitational in Springfield," Jeremy agreed. "I suspect that you can make good use of the time until then to rehearse."

"I've been rehears—that is, yes. That would be good."

Jeremy's eyes twinkled. He suspected that she had never stopped rehearsing the stunt in spite of his forbidding her to perform it. "How many revolutions can you manage?" he asked.

She seemed surprised at the question. "I don't understand."

"Do you think you might manage as many as a dozen or more?"

"A dozen!" She laughed. "Of course. The other day I—that is, I believe in time I might increase that number by quite a margin." She looked up at him, her eyes narrowing. "Of course, with our travel schedule there is so little time for rehearsal. I truly believe that adding the stunt now—purely for the purpose of being at my best for the invitational performance . . ."

"I see." He nodded as if considering a new idea. "It occurred to me that it might add to the drama if we could have the audience count as you spin around and around and around. Perhaps you have a point that starting with this evening's performance, we might actually capitalize on the anticipation as we move toward the governor's performance. What do you think?"

Her smile was dazzling, and his heart skipped a beat just knowing that something he had suggested was capable of producing such a joyous reaction.

"I think . . . why, I think . . ." She stumbled for words, and then she gave the small leap necessary to encircle his neck with her arms and plant a kiss on his cheek. "I think that Trixie and the others might be right. You might just work out after all," she said and kissed his cheek again before letting go. "Thank you," she called as she dashed off toward the exit. "Wait until I tell Ian. Thank you, Jeremy. I won't let you down," she promised.

As he watched her fairly dance across the compound, he lifted his fingers to his cheek, still warm from her lips. He had frequently contemplated the possibility of what it might be like to kiss Lucy, to hold her in his embrace—even to take her to his bed. But such musings had come in the general realm of the manner in which he instinctively assessed any attractive woman with whom he came in contact. Something about her spontaneous reaction had touched him in a way that was both confusing and enticing. Sometime in the past few weeks, he realized that his interest in Lucy Conroy had moved beyond the casual to something far more purposeful.

"You're entirely welcome, Miss Conroy," he said, even though he knew she was too far away to hear him.

That evening's performance was an unqualified success. Every act brought thunderous applause. Lucy's brought the people to their feet. Breathlessly they counted her death-defying spins, chanting the number in chorus with the rim shot of the drummer. To the delight of the crowd and the consternation of Jeremy, she actually paused after twenty-five turns, hung there for one interminable second, and then started to spin in the opposite direction. The crowd went wild, no longer counting, they were on their feet now, cheering and clapping in time to the cadence kept by the drummer. The leader of the band held his baton poised. Every musician held instrument to lips, ready to give a final triumphant fanfare when she reached her limit. All eyes were on Lucy. Jeremy saw that even her fellow performers had gathered at the entrance to watch. He had counted fifty spins.

Finally, she stopped, hanging there with her head thrown back, her arms spread wide as if poised for flight. Ian sent the trapeze sailing toward her. Effortlessly she caught it and held on as she released the neck strap. Then, grasping the flybar with both hands, she pumped and swung herself back up and onto the platform, where the light stayed on her while the audience cheered and the band played. Lucy grinned and accepted their adoration with a dramatic bow as the band struck up the music for the grand parade that was always the finale to any performance.

The lights focused again on the center ring as the entire company filed into the tent, and still the crowd stood. It was a night Jeremy knew he would never forget. It was a feeling of such triumph and joy. He wanted to feel it again and again. If this was the reward for hard work, he was very much in favor of it.

After the final exit, the performers gathered around Lucy and Ian. Everyone seemed to be talking at once. Jeremy stood to one side, observing the company for a long moment. He saw people who just days earlier had been satisfied to do the bare minimum necessary to keep their jobs. He saw people who had that night surpassed their own best expectations of their talent. He saw genuine respect for the few performers whose talent exceeded the ordinary. Trixie was without a doubt the best horsewoman Jeremy had ever seen. Wally had flown from his cannon to the very top of the acrobatic pyramid that Bruno and his brothers had constructed. Babbo had delighted the crowd with his antics and charmed the children with his sad clown face, and he had done it all without taking a drink. That, in and of itself, was a triumph.

Jeremy saw that Lucy was looking past the others, directly at him, even though she was still surrounded by cast and crew alike. She smiled and nodded her appreciation for compliments as she worked her way through the crowd toward him. The chatter of the others gradually petered out. Lucy's large, dark eyes were riveted on Jeremy as the group parted and allowed her through. He waited for her to reach him, making no move toward her.

"Thank you," she said huskily when she was standing only inches from him. Her voice was filled with emotion and so soft that he doubted anyone else had heard her. Somehow, the fact that her words were intended for his ears alone gave them all the more meaning.

Without waiting for him to speak, she took his arm and urged him to join the others. "Ladies and gentlemen and children of *all* ages," she said in her best ringmaster's voice, "I present to you *Sir* Jeremy Barrington!"

Jeremy felt a silly grin twitch and then flare to life as he allowed Lucy to lead him into the thick of the gathering. He felt people pound him on the back, grasp his shoulder, shake his hand. Trixie kissed his cheek and Norma pulled him into a bone-crushing embrace.

"Never had so much fun in all my born days," she whispered, her voice shaking with emotion.

Jeremy seemed incapable of any response. He

tried a couple of times to find appropriate words but ended up simply looking around at each of them and grinning like one of the kids he'd seen sitting in the front row.

"Speech!" Wally cried, and the others took up the chant.

Jeremy held up his hands to silence them. "It was a wonderful performance," he began and paused. "Can we do even better?"

"Yes!" they roared back.

"Very well, then," he said in his clipped accent. "You shall continue to better yourselves. I shall continue to better our bookings. Is that a fair bargain?"

"Yes!" they shouted again.

"But for tonight, since we have no performance tomorrow on the Sabbath, would you do me the honor of joining me in my car for a bit of refreshment once you've changed?"

"Yes!" they shouted once again and dispersed immediately to bed down the animals, remove their makeup, and change out of their costumes.

Lucy stood there a moment after the others had headed off to their tasks. "It truly was a very special performance, Jeremy," she said. "Harry would have loved it."

"It's still early in the season, Lucy. There is still every possibility that he will have that opportunity."

Her eyes flickered with hope. "Perhaps," she said. "Well, I should go and change."

"You'll come to the party?" he asked as she turned to go.

She glanced back at him and smiled. "I wouldn't miss it."

As Lucy walked back toward the dressing area, she

knew that he had not moved. He stood there watching her, his gaze almost tangible.

When she approached the tent, she could hear the subdued but still animated chatter of her fellow performers. The atmosphere was charged with the excitement of their success. It was almost as if everything that they had known had shifted ever so slightly. Things were the same and yet . . . better. Jeremy Barrington had found a way to take what they had done day in and day out for years, and turn it into something new and exciting. He inspired them to tap the best they had to give. These were the very same people who, only weeks earlier, had stopped believing in themselves, who fully expected that the company would fold before they could reach the next town.

She had to consider the fact that she might have judged him too quickly at the outset. For the thing that had impressed her most was that afterward, when by all rights Jeremy could have stood in their midst and taken credit for their success, he had given them their moment. He had waited outside the family circle, watching them, enjoying their euphoria with the wistful look of a small boy who watches from outside the window as others celebrate. And, when his eyes had met hers, she had been drawn to him, needed to go to him and bring him into his rightful place as a member of the group. Yes, everything had changed in one magical evening.

"Luce, what shall I wear?" Trixie moaned as she rummaged through her trunk, discarding one gown after another. "Is Ian going to come to the party? Did he say he was coming?"

"He'll be there," Lucy assured her. She selected

one of the gowns. "This one," she said, holding it out to Trixie.

"The yellow? I don't know, Luce . . ."

"Ian loves you in yellow," Lucy assured her.

"Did he tell you that?" Trixie's eyes sparkled with anticipation.

"Not in so many words, but I know my brother and I saw the way he looked at you the first time you wore this. Trust me, it's the perfect choice."

Trixie clutched the gown to her breast. "And what about you?" She spotted one of the discarded gowns and snapped it up. "This, Lucy. Wear this."

It was a red satin gown with a wide square neckline framed by broad velvet straps that would cover her shoulders. "It seems a bit . . ."

"Daring? Yeah, don't it just!" Trixie replied with a grin and burrowed into the trunk again to emerge with a pair of long white leather gloves. "Oh, my sweet friend, you are gonna ruffle those perfect English feathers of our esteemed boss tonight. Now, get a move on. I don't want to miss a minute of this party."

In spite of Trixie's urgings, Lucy took her time scrubbing off her makeup and washing off the dust and grime of the day's work. By the time she was finished, she felt relaxed and calm . . . until she tried putting on the red gown.

"Trixie," she called out to her friend, "I can't wear this. I can't even fasten it."

"Of course you can," Trixie replied. "Hold your breath."

Lucy did as she was told and Trixie closed the last fastener on the gown.

"But . . ." Lucy protested, staring at her exposed skin in the mirror.

"Oh, for heaven's sake, Lucy. It's not like the man hasn't seen your form before. Leotards have a tendency to leave very little to the imagination."

"But they cover," Lucy argued, tugging at the neckline of the dress.

Trixie brushed her hands aside and readjusted the gown. "Stop that," she ordered, cupping Lucy's breasts and pushing them up until the tops swelled just above the line of the gown. She stood back and considered her work. "It'll do," she announced.

"No, it won't," Lucy said, firmly squirming around until she had managed to raise the gown to cover just a little more.

Trixie released an exasperated sigh. "You're impossible." She pointed to her own boyish figure. "Do you think I wouldn't give my left leg to be able to show a little bosom?"

Lucy frowned, then grinned. "It would appear that I've got bosom to spare, so I'd be more than happy to lend you some."

The two friends burst into a fit of girlish giggles that was interrupted by a light tap at the post just outside the tent entrance.

"Lucy? You ready?"

"It's Ian," Trixie mouthed and turned back to the mirror as she nervously checked her hair and face and the neckline of her own gown.

"Come on in, Ian," Lucy called.

"I thought . . ." His words hung there as Trixie turned to face him. "Holy . . . !" he murmured, clearly unaware that he had made a sound. He swallowed hard and wet his lips, his eyes riveted on Trixie.

Lucy grinned. "Why don't you and Trix go on ahead? I just have to finish putting my hair up."

"If you're sure," Trixie said, taking Ian's arm. She was already halfway out the door, and Ian was her willing escort.

"Oh, don't mind me," Lucy assured them both and turned to see that she was speaking to an empty space.

Seven

With Trixie gone, Lucy gave serious consideration to changing into something more demure, but she could hear everyone else already on their way to the party. She didn't want to make a scene by arriving late. With one last look and one fruitless tug at the gown, she gave up.

"Ah, my lady fair," Wally greeted her as he and Arnie and Norma met her on their way to the party. "You are looking especially lovely this evening, my dear."

"Why, thank you, kind sir," she replied, playing along with him. "And don't you look quite debonair!"

Wally grinned and whipped the end of his silk scarf over one shoulder. "One does try," he replied. Norma and Arnie just rolled their eyes.

By the time they arrived, Jeremy's spacious car was filled to capacity with members of the company and crew. Jeremy had made sure that there was plenty to eat and drink. Several of the musicians had brought their instruments and were entertaining the group with renditions of the latest ragtime tunes. Trixie was moving to the music and Ian was watching her with barely concealed adoration.

Jeremy stood at the far end of the large drawing

room, a lit cigar in one hand, a drink in the other. He was talking to a man Lucy had noticed sitting with the mayor at the performance. When the man spotted Lucy, he permitted his eyes to roam the length of her body and back again, coming to rest briefly on her exposed neckline before returning to her face. Lucy had seen his type before—a supposed gentleman who looked upon a woman like her as a dalliance, an easy conquest. She turned away and waited for his inevitable appearance at her side. She sincerely hoped that he was not going to turn out to be someone whom she needed to pretend to like for the sake of the company. That had happened before when Harry and Shirley had entertained men who could secure a particularly desirable booking. The difference then, of course, had been the presence of Harry, her father and protector. Even the most ambitious cad restrained himself in the presence of a woman's father.

She knew the minute that the man came up behind her, and she stiffened her spine to forestall the shudder that threatened.

"Miss Conroy?"

She pasted on her stage smile and turned. "Yes?"

His gaze flickered more boldly over, her and he smiled knowingly. "Evan Gilchrist," he said. "I am a close associate of the mayor of Chicago."

"Really? Not *too* close, I hope," she replied and took pleasure in the fact that he had caught her meaning, judging by the color that rose above his collar.

He laughed without humor. "Have you ever been to Chicago, Miss Conroy?"

"Oh my, I must have been there once," she replied, playing the fool that he obviously expected her to be. "I travel so much, you see, one town begins to look like the one before."

"I should like very much to show you the sights of Chicago, Miss Conroy. It can be quite an enticing place." He moved half a step closer, and Lucy stepped away and felt the wall against her bare back.

"I'm sure. Perhaps if we ever . . ."

"Oh, forgive me," he murmured, his face so near that she could smell the whiskey on his breath. "Did I fail to mention the fact that I have just now extended an invitation to Mr. Barrington to bring his company to our fair city in September?"

Lucy bristled. "The Conroy Cavalcade belongs to my father, Mr. Gilchrist. Mr. Barrington is only—"

"Filling in for Miss Conroy's father while he is under the weather," Jeremy said as he took a position next to her, forcing Gilchrist to retreat more than the half step he had taken toward her.

"Of course," Gilchrist said, his face ruddy now as he swallowed the last of his drink and licked his thick lips.

"Norma," Jeremy called out as the large woman passed by on her way to the banquet table, "this is Mr. Gilchrist, a friend of the mayor's in Chicago. He appears to be in need of a fresh drink. Would you be so kind?"

Norma's eyes lit with excitement. "Chicago? Oh my heavens, I have *always* wanted to see Chicago. Why . . ." She took hold of Gilchrist's arm and practically carried him toward the bar.

"I apologize," Jeremy said.

Lucy shrugged. "It happens from time to time. Most of the women here have experienced something like it." She made no effort to pretend that she didn't know what he was talking about.

"You do look beautiful, Lucy."

To her surprise, she took no offense. If Evan Gilchrist had uttered those very words, she would have had to battle the urge to strike him. She glanced up at Jeremy.

"The gown belongs to Trixie and it—"

"Just accept the compliment, Lucy," he said, and he was smiling.

"Thank you," she murmured.

They stood next to each other for a moment, letting the party flow around them. "Are we truly going to Chicago?" she asked finally, more to break the silence between them than anything else.

"I need to discuss it with Harry and Shirley, but at the moment it seems promising."

He was looking out over the party, enjoying watching the others, who were clearly having an extremely good time. The idea that he needed to discuss such a major booking with Harry seemed to come as naturally to him as drawing on his cigar did. Lucy was both surprised and moved.

"I'm sure that Harry will agree," she said.

Jeremy gave her his full attention. "Do you think so? It could be quite profitable. On the other hand, the question becomes whether or not we are ready for such a prominent engagement."

"But why would you think we are not? You said yourself that tonight's performance . . ."

"Lucy, tonight was magnificent—for Springfield. Chicago is another matter. We will need to add acts . . . animals . . . crew. Chicago will cost us money, before we have ample opportunity to accumulate money and if we are not fully prepared, we may never again have the occasion to play a venue on that scale."

"On the other hand, if we could be successful there . . ." She said the words aloud but more to herself than to him.

"Yes, but it's a risk, Lucy—one we'd better all be prepared to face."

She looked up at him. "You don't know circus folk, Jeremy. We're in the business of taking risks."

He smiled and lifted his glass to her in a toast. "I'll talk it over with Harry and with Adam back in New York . . ."

"You're going back to New York?" she blurted without thinking.

His smiled broadened. "Why, Miss Conroy, would you miss me if I did?"

She felt the heat rise to her cheeks. "I . . . of course not—that is . . ." He laughed, and she did as well. "The truth is that we have gotten used to having you around—purely for entertainment, you understand." *Lord above, she was flirting with the man.*

His eyes twinkled. "Always glad to oblige a lovely lady."

"Hey, Luce, how about a song?" Wally called from across the room.

Ian had taken his place at the piano, and a couple of the musicians were also waiting for her to join them.

"Ah, your fans await," Jeremy said softly.

During the sing-along that lasted for over an hour, Lucy was aware of Jeremy's every move. For a while, he listened to the music but did not join in the singing. Once he spoke to Evan Gilchrist, and the conversation seemed quite amiable. Shortly after that, Gilchrist and two other men from the mayor's staff left the party. When the musicians struck up a ragtime tune, Norma insisted that Jeremy dance with her, which he did to the delight of everyone. He was as tall as Norma, but she outweighed him by a good fifty pounds, yet somehow he made her appear quite graceful and elegant, and the dance that had begun as a bit of tomfoolery ended with applause from all the other guests.

Lucy found herself wondering what it might be like to dance with Jeremy—to waltz with him, just the two of them. She shook off the fantasy and turned her attention back to her friends. She and Trixie teamed up to entertain the group with a raucous duet, and everyone crowded around them, clapping along in time to the music as they sang verse after verse. When the crowd of guests parted and started to leave, Jeremy was no longer in the room. Someone said that they had seen him go outside, probably for some air. The party had spilled out into the yard surrounding the train, and those inside went in search of Jeremy to say their good-nights.

Lucy and Wally helped Norma and Arnie collect drink glasses and plates of food and place them on the sideboard. Ezra, Jeremy's steward, had been given the night off—another unexpected kindness that caught Lucy's attention.

"Better check the observation room back there," Wally suggested wearily when Norma and Arnie had left. "I saw that Gilchrist guy and his cronies headed out there earlier with drinks in hand, and they came back empty-handed."

"I'll do it," Lucy said. "You look exhausted. Go on." She shooed him with a wave of her hand.

Wally grinned. "I won't argue—I don't think I can take one more step than it'll take to carry me back to my bunk. Good night, Luce."

Jeremy had not yet returned, and Lucy found herself alone in the luxurious car. She collected the glasses from the observation room at the very back of the train but did not immediately return to the drawing room. It was dark and quiet in the elegant room. The only light was moonlight. She found herself thinking about the night that Jeremy had brought her into his car to give her a glass of milk. She thought about him sitting here in this room as they traveled through the night. She imagined him stretched out on one of the large chairs, his feet propped on the ottoman, his tie undone and shirt unbuttoned, the shock of hair falling over her forehead as he studied the latest reports and ledgers. She imagined herself sitting there with him, reading or sewing sequins onto her costume. She ran her fingers lightly along the back of a chair as she played out her fantasy.

Then she shook off the images and reached for one half-filled glass.

"Lucy?"

"I was clearing the last of the glasses," Lucy said politely. "I'll just leave these on the sideboard and . . ." She started to move past him, but he stopped her with a light touch on her elbow.

"May I?" he said but did not wait for an answer before taking the glasses from her and setting them back on the side table. "Could you stay for a bit?" he asked when she took a step toward the door.

Lucy paused and heard him settle himself into one of the overstuffed chairs. "You see, I received some very good news today—news of a personal nature. I'd like to share it, and I should very much appreciate it if you would sit with me for a few minutes."

"It's very late . . . and . . ."

"You're worried what others might think?"

For reasons she didn't understand, she thought about other women in his life. Sophisticated women who would accept his invitation to sit and talk. After all, he wasn't proposing anything improper. He simply wanted to unwind a bit after a long day's work. She tried to relax, leaning against the arm of another of the high-backed observation chairs. She was still too aware of his nearness in the small room and of her attraction to him.

"I rarely consider what others may think of me," she replied with a bravado she was sure did not sound at all convincing.

He smiled. "My stepsister and Adam Porterfield have married," he said.

She wasn't sure how to respond to that. "And this pleases you?"

He grinned. "This *delights* me beyond anything I can imagine, Lucy."

"Then you are close with your stepsister."

"Well, yes, now we are close. Not so very long ago, however, Olivia would have cheerfully seen me hanged."

"I see," Lucy murmured, when she did not see at all.

"You see, I rather used Olivia to achieve my own intentions of coming to America—against my father's wishes. She had every reason to be furious with me, but in the end, it was Olivia who stood by me." His voice took on a wistful tone. "She believed in me when I didn't believe in myself."

"Perhaps she saw a side of you that you keep hidden."

He turned to her with interest. "Perhaps. Do you have such a hidden persona, Lucy? When you are up there among the stars, what are you thinking about?" His tone was light, conversational, but he watched her with an intensity that was unnerving.

"I don't think," she replied. "I just . . . fly. It's truly as close as a human can come to feeling such freedom, I think."

"I envy you that." He crossed his feet at the ankles, loosening his tie as he did so. "Tell me about yourself, Lucy."

"There isn't a great deal to tell," she said. "I never knew my parents. Harry and Shirley plucked me out of the orphanage when I was seven. The rest you saw when you discovered those programs and photographs in my room."

He smiled. "I am truly sorry for my intrusion that day. It was really quite presumptuous of me."

They were silent for a moment. She made a show of looking out the expansive windows, though there was little that she could see. She was suddenly aware of the manner in which the low light in the room added to the intimacy and tension between them.

"And what about you?" she countered, turning her attention back to him.

She had anticipated a wry smile, but he frowned and turned away for a moment. Then he shrugged. "Unlike you, I had the advantage of knowing both my parents. My mother died when I was quite young. My father remarried, bringing me a stepmother and, of course, Olivia, my stepsister. And then my stepmother died suddenly in a riding accident."

"How awful. Your father must have been devastated."

Jeremy shrugged. "Not really. I think it was the first time I realized how much his life focused only on his business and political dealings. I swore never to find myself in that position."

"What of your stepsister?"

"Olivia?" He smiled. "I got her hired on as a companion to Adam Porterfield's aging mother while I got myself a position in his business. It is Olivia who has triumphed. Not only has she wed Adam, but she has her own business as an established fashion designer in New York now."

"How marvelous for her." Lucy could not think of what else to say, assailed as she was by dozens of questions.

"As for me, I made mistakes—one rather large mistake, from which I am determined to redeem myself in the eyes of Adam Porterfield . . . and Olivia." He paused. "Am I not what you expected, Lucy?"

"I couldn't really say what I expected."

He nodded and slipped back into silent reverie. Lucy stood and began straightening the pillows on the window seat and setting the room in order.

"Red is not your best color," he said after a moment.

Where on earth had that come from? "I'm sorry you don't approve," she replied, but her tone left little doubt of the irritation she felt at his criticism. Why was it that just when she began to think he might be someone she could like, he pulled something like this?

He smiled and stood, walking around her as if analyzing her dress. "I didn't say that I did not like the gown. The fact is, I like the design of it very much. It shows off . . . it suits you."

"Then it's the color you don't like?"

"As I mentioned, my sister designs clothes. She lived with me for a time in New York, working out of my apartment. I began to appreciate certain elements of color."

"And what would you suggest?" She was determined to stand her ground, even though his nearness unnerved her terribly.

"Emerald green or perhaps a sapphire blue." His eyes roamed without inhibition over the revealing neckline of her gown, to her bare arms above the tops of the long gloves. He moved a step closer. Lucy could not control the increasingly rapid rise and fall of her partly exposed breasts. For reasons she could not have explained, having Jeremy look at her with desire was vastly different from having a man like Gilchrist do exactly the same thing.

"No. Peach," he said softly, his fingers hovering a fraction of an inch from her cheek. "With that incredible complexion and those eyes . . . a delicate blush of peach, I should think."

His voice was low, nearly a whisper. His fingers lightly skimmed her cheek, down her neck to her collarbone. She kept her eyes locked on his but felt his touch at the strap of her gown, felt the fabric move and fall from her shoulder.

"Mr. Barrington," she said nervously.

He stopped further protest by placing two fingers lightly on her lips. She closed her eyes. She felt him rearranging wisps of her hair that had escaped the carefully constructed coiffure. The torture continued as he trailed his thumb across her earlobe and down, bringing it to rest at the center of her lower lip.

She savored the nearness of him, the scent of brandy and tobacco, and the intoxicating rhythm of his thumb moving lazily back and forth across her lip. What was he thinking? Why didn't he kiss her?

What was the source of his hesitancy? Was she not desirable enough? She felt a scandalous urge to capture that finger inside her mouth.

"Lucy?" His breath was warm against her skin.

When had his other hand moved to the back of her waist, where now he pressed to draw her closer? When had her hands flattened against the lapels of his coat? And where was the common sense to rescue her when she felt his mouth a hair's breadth from her own?

"Sweet Lucy," he murmured, but still he did not kiss her.

Jeremy was confounded by his hesitancy with this woman. Something about her gave rise to protective urges that were entirely new to him. He had never been one to deny himself the pleasures a young woman might be persuaded to offer. That first night on tour, when he had brought her into his private car the first time, it had not been to take her to his bed but rather to ply her with a glass of milk, for heaven's sake. Was it possible that he was actually considering asking her permission to kiss her?

Ridiculous. Jeremy Barrington had never in his life paused to consider whether or not a woman would allow his kiss. The women he had known—regardless of their status in society—had welcomed his advances. Hell, most of them had flirted shamelessly, sending signals that were blatant in their invitation. Some of them had been so forward that *he* had been the one to back away.

But Lucy Conroy was different. Could it be his respect for her parents that was the blockade? Earlier, he had actually had to resist the urge to intervene when Evan Gilchrist had become a bit too familiar.

In that instant he had understood that he did not like it when other men looked at her with their coarse fantasies plain as day in their expressions.

And what fantasies had he entertained as he detained her in the darkness of this private place? *Hell, kiss her, you bloody fool, and get it out of your system.*

He tested the waters by moving his lips over her cheek and down the line of her jaw. She made no move to resist. Her pulse quickened as his lips brushed her throat. The beating reminded him of a captured bird, uncertain of its fate.

As he continued his course of kisses to her shoulder, where the strap had fallen, he fought the urge to push the fabric lower, to expose the alabaster of her breasts that had tantalized him from the moment she'd entered the room earlier that evening.

She flinched slightly and made a murmured protest when he pushed the strap lower. He looked up and saw that she was watching him with confusion and an expression of such sweet agony that he was lost.

"Precious Lucinda," he moaned and denied himself no longer. With one hand pressing her hips, urging her closer yet, he cupped her chin as his mouth covered hers.

She did not shrink from his kiss. Rather, she seemed to welcome it. That was unexpected—and thrilling in that he had failed to anticipate her reaction. Jeremy liked surprises, especially pleasant ones. If she had struggled, pretended to resist when he knew they both wanted this kiss, he might have been more forceful. Instead, he found that her reaction gave rise to a gentleness that he would not have thought himself capable of executing in the throes of a passion such as he felt for this woman. That tenderness was thrilling in its own subtlety. Taking the time and finesse to gauge her every response before making his next move was new to him, and he found himself caught up in the task of imparting pleasure rather than seeking to gratify himself.

He feathered light kisses across her mouth, her cheeks, her eyelids. He whispered her name and then traced the inner silhouette of her ear with his tongue. She pressed closer and moaned softly as she turned her face to his, seeking his mouth with her own.

He obliged her with a kiss designed to distract her from the movement of his hands up to her bare shoulders and then slowly down and around until he was cupping her breasts. She opened her mouth to protest or plead for more—he could not be sure which—and he took full advantage. He slid his tongue past her teeth, plunging and withdrawing as he thrilled to her instinct to open herself to him as her tongue waltzed with his and their breaths came in audible gasps of desire.

In another moment he would take her there on the floor, if necessary. His fingers ached to rip the satin gown from her, exposing the true satin of her breasts . . . her thighs . . . her . . .

"Lucy," he said raggedly, forcing himself to pull away. She looked up at him, the deep pools of her dark eyes confused and languid with pleasure. *He must be losing his grip. She was eager, willing, and yet he hesitated.*

How long did the kiss go on? Seconds? Minutes? For Lucy it seemed both an eternity and all too fleeting. Long enough that she discovered feelings and sensations that she'd never known. Brief enough that she yearned for more time to experience the passion he aroused in her.

Her first reaction was surprise at his tenderness. Had he taken her in a rough way, she might have found the will to resist. Instead, his surprising hesitancy and gentleness obliterated any resolve she might have mustered to resist. She found herself savoring the soft fullness of his lips on hers. When she finally came to her senses enough to realize that he had moved the hand that had once cupped her face to the place where the second strap of her gown barely capped her shoulder, she gave a shrug of pure reflex, assisting in the effort to fully expose her shoulders to him.

Then, his mouth was open and his tongue moved deeper into the recesses of her mouth and then withdrew. She felt an indescribable need to respond—with her mouth, her tongue, her hands clutching his shoulders, her hips pressed to his. He moved his hands over her naked shoulders . . . circling ever closer to the rise of her breasts above the décolletage of the gown and then lower until he cupped them through the taut fabric. Instead of pulling away as any lady would have, she felt an overwhelming desire to partake of everything this man might offer her. She wove her fingers deep into his hair, grasping its thickness as he drove her to a fever pitch with his open mouth at her ear, whispering her name.

He kissed her again, his tongue urging her to open to him. Neither of them seemed capable of fulfilling their hunger for the other. Lucy had known a man's kisses—Reggie had certainly made sure of that—but this was so different. Jeremy's kisses were as much about giving pleasure as taking it—whether that was deliberate or simply born of the discovery that the more pleasure he gave, the more he was likely to get in return, she could not have said. At the moment, she certainly didn't care what his motives might be. She only hoped he would keep on kissing her.

And then, he pulled away. He gently eased both straps back into place and then arranged wisps of her hair back into her chignon. "It's late," he said softly as he pulled her back into his embrace. "You need your rest."

She looked up at him, still caught up in the spiral of passion he had ignited. He smiled and bent to kiss her once again, although everything in his eyes and action told her that he meant for this to be a more chaste kiss of good night. But the moment their lips met, he seemed to reconsider his decision and once again, he was kissing her with all the passion that he had forced himself to repress a moment earlier.

Eight

"Mr. Barrington? Jeremy?"

Someone calling Jeremy's name penetrated the fog that had obliterated everything. Jeremy dragged his mouth from Lucy's and held her close to his chest as he willed his breathing to resume some semblance of normalcy.

"Mr. Barrington, are you here?"

They both recognized the slightly nasal voice of Karl Oglethorpe, the company's bookkeeper.

"Stay here," Jeremy whispered as he tenderly skimmed her now swollen lip with the tip of his finger. "It's Karl—no doubt he has some worry about tomorrow's engagement."

Lucy felt bereft of his embrace the moment Jeremy was gone. She turned her face to the open window, hoping to cool the flush of passion that she knew must bloom on her cheeks and throat. With shaky hands she readjusted her gown and could not help but notice how her breasts strained against the fabric. If anything, the dress seemed to have shrunk.

How long had it been since the others had left? Who might have taken notice of her absence? She touched one hand to her hair, checking it for needed repairs, then trailed her fingers over her kiss-swollen lips. How on earth could she possibly face anyone?

She tiptoed along the narrow passage to one of the bedrooms. The room itself was surprisingly spacious. It boasted a full bed with brass headboard on one wall. Opposite that was a mirrored dresser lighted by two small gas lamps. She rushed toward the mirror to study her reflection and groaned.

The woman staring back at her from the mirror might have been a total stranger. Her eyes were dilated with remembered desire, her lips bore the mark of his kisses, and her hair fell around her face and down her neck as if she had just come from bed. The cut of her gown had suddenly become more scandalous than provocative, the white of her breasts obvious against the deep red of the satin.

What had she been thinking of to permit such liberties? Especially with this man. She had been a willing, even an eager participant in an assignation that bordered on ravishment. She could find no blame to place on him. She had not once resisted. No, she had welcomed . . . encouraged . . . relished his every move. He had very nearly succeeded in accomplishing what a man like Evan Gilchrist only dreamed of achieving.

Tears welled and overflowed as she tried to rearrange her hair into some semblance of the intricate upsweep she had worn at the outset of the evening. The feather adornment that Trixie had insisted was just the thing to accent her beauty was missing. She took a step away from the mirror and forced herself to take a deep breath.

She spotted a washbasin in the corner of the room and was relieved to see that there was still water in the pitcher. She poured some into the bowl and began to wash her face and arms and shoulders. The cool water was soothing, and the action of washing herself calmed her. She dried herself with the crisp linen towel that hung on the washstand. She needed to consider her next move.

She would take her leave as politely and quickly as possible, making sure to keep her distance from Jeremy. Then, she would slip along the side of Jeremy's railroad car, her presence concealed by darkness until she reached the path along the river. She would take that path back to her own car, and if she encountered anyone along the way—and she sincerely hoped that she would—she would say that it had been such an exciting day that she had decided to take a walk to calm herself before retiring. She folded the damp towel and hung it back on the towel bar, then waited by the door until she heard Karl leave. Satisfied that her plan would work, she checked her appearance one final time and started down the hallway toward the light of the drawing room.

Jeremy knew the minute that Lucy entered the room that everything had changed—something that he had thought they had found had been lost in the brief time it had taken him to calm Karl's concerns and send him on his way.

"Lucy, I . . ."

"It was a lovely evening, Jeremy," she said, with her stage smile firmly in place. "Thank you so much. Everyone had such a wonderful time." She continued to move toward the door as she chattered on. "It's always such fun to dress up in our finery, and we so seldom have the opportunity to do so."

He remained where he was, aware that nothing was to be salvaged from the interruption. Obviously, she had had time to regret what had occurred in the intimacy of the observation room. "Lucy . . ."

Her dark eyes widened, as did the fake smile. "It's late, Jeremy. I'll see you tomorrow." Her hand was turning the door handle even as she spoke.

"Lucy, what happened before—"

"Good night, Jeremy," she said as the smile faltered. She hurried out the door before he could say anything more, and he saw her walking quickly across the grounds toward the river.

On their way to the engagement in Springfield, the itinerary still had them playing two performances a day in each town. The timetable was grueling, and it was monotonous. Every day was the same, except Sundays, when there were no shows: arrive at dawn, set up, bathe the stock, wash and polish the wagons, parade, afternoon performance, supper, evening performance, breakdown, travel through the night, and start all over the following day.

The novelty of being on the road had worn off, and if members of the company gathered in the pie car at all, it was only to find a quiet place to read or write a letter or perhaps to join a card game. Most of them were content to stay to themselves, catching up on sleep or nursing aches and pains brought on by the ceaseless demands of performing two shows a day and trying to improve their acts in between with new and more daring feats.

Jeremy often traveled ahead of the group, his private car linked to a regularly scheduled train. He preferred to double-check arrangements rather than leaving everything to their advance man. His absence should have made life easier for her. And yet, even when she had awakened that morning after the party to see his car gone, she had felt only abandonment rather than the relief she told herself she should feel.

During this time, Lucy knew that he had made at least two trips to Chicago. The idea of him in a large city, surrounded by the culture and luxury that he clearly loved, was maddening. She imagined him at society parties and dinners where there would be any number of proper young ladies vying for his attention. She told herself that she didn't care, that the kisses they had shared that night had meant nothing. Still, her mood blackened with each day that passed without seeing the now-familiar private car attached to the train.

It certainly didn't help matters that Trixie and Ian were blatantly in love and that neither of them seemed capable of normal conversation. Ever since the night of Jeremy's party, they had been quite open about their feelings. Lucy thought that she far preferred the days when the two of them were only dancing around the possibility of a romance. If she heard one more rapturous description of her brother's charm and talent, she thought she might actually throw something.

Ian was no better. At every rehearsal he would find some way to bring Trixie into the conversation. The woman was constantly on his mind—much as Jeremy seemed to constantly invade Lucy's thoughts and dreams. Yet, it was hardly the same. Ian and Trixie were in love, and their devotion ran both ways. Lucy was riding a one-way ticket to heartbreak if she didn't get a grip on herself.

On the morning that the train rolled into Springfield, Lucy was standing on the rear platform. She'd spent another restless night, and she was feeling tired and out of sorts. The weather was of little help. It was hot and muggy and raining in a steady drizzle that permeated everything and offered no relief at all from the oppressive heat. If it was this hot at five in the morning, what on earth would it be like later, under the canvas? She leaned out from under the canopy that covered the open platform to scan the skies for signs of clearing. She saw only unremitting gray.

The train rolled slowly past the station and switched onto a siding that they would follow to the edge of the river. She barely registered the station house or the small cluster of people gathered under the shelter of the station's overhang. A woman holding a large umbrella waved to her, and Lucy automatically lifted her hand in response as the woman started to walk quickly along the platform following the train. A man in a wheelchair called to the woman.

Lucy blinked, then rubbed her eyes.

"Lucy!" The woman called, running now as the train gathered speed after switching onto the side track. "Lucy!" The umbrella tipped to one side, revealing Shirley's uplifted, laughing face.

"Mama!" Lucy leaned out over the railing, her arms outstretched toward her mother. "Mama!" And suddenly, the rain became a balm, a welcome washing away of her ill spirits.

"Stay there," Shirley shouted. "We're hooking up with you."

And sure enough, the train paused, wheezing and snorting as Jeremy's private car edged toward her.

He was back, and he had brought Harry and Shirley in their Pullman with him. Her heart took flight, and she took advantage of the train's momentary pause to swing down from the platform. She ran the short distance back to her mother. The two women embraced, laughing and talking at the same time.

"You'll get soaked," Shirley said, wrapping an arm around Lucy's waist and drawing her under the shelter of the umbrella as they walked back toward the station's covered platform.

As soon as they were at the station, Lucy broke free and ran to her father. "Papa," she said hoarsely as she fell to her knees next to his wheelchair. She studied his face to assure herself that he was indeed real, as she started to cry.

"Now, stop this," he groused, placing one weathered palm on her cheek. "You didn't think they could keep me away forever, did you?"

"Oh, Papa, I'm so glad to see you."

"And I you, little girl," Harry replied softly. Then he cleared his throat and looked around. "I think we can get rid of this contraption now," he said to Shirley, pushing himself forward as if to stand. "Get me my cane before the others see me sitting here like some old codger."

"You *are* an old codger," Shirley said affectionately. She unhooked the cane from the back of the chair and handed it to him. Lucy hovered nearby, her hand out, ready to catch her father should he collapse again as he had that terrible night at the winter quarters.

He brushed her away. "Stop that, little girl. You're worse than your mother. Let a fella have a little pneumonia and the womenfolk in his life act like he's at death's door. Where's Jeremy?"

"Right here, sir."

Jeremy emerged from the station house. He was holding a telegram and he looked more dashing and handsome than ever. Lucy felt suddenly shy in his presence. He looked at her, and for what seemed like a long time, neither of them spoke . . . and neither did anyone else.

"Well," Shirley said softly after a moment. Lucy looked away from Jeremy and saw her mother glance at her father in a knowing way.

"I have so much to tell you," Lucy said, focusing all of her attention on her parents as she walked between them arm in arm toward their private car, now hooked to the rest of the train. "I'm doing the neck spin, and—"

"Jeremy told us all about how everyone counts your spins, Lucy," Shirley said as they walked. "Are you very sure that it's safe to keep trying to top your last number?"

"Now, Mama, stop worrying. You know that I don't take unnecessary risks."

"Your definition of 'unnecessary' may differ from ours, little girl," Harry said. "We'll be the judge of just how much risk you're taking when we see you perform tonight."

Lucy grinned. "How long can you stay?"

"This isn't a visit, Luce. We're back," Harry said firmly.

Lucy felt as if a great weight had been lifted from her chest—a weight she hadn't even known she carried until it was gone. Things would return to normal now. Harry and Shirley would take charge. Jeremy was there as well, but no longer necessary as the person she would depend upon, for surely that was what had started to happen. Her attraction to him had been to s someone who would guide and protect her, who would assume the role that her parents had always played. There was no romance in it—only security. It was a relief to finally have some rational explanation for her sleepless nights and restless spirit over the past several days.

"So, Jeremy is going back to New York?"

"Heavens, no," Harry said. "He's in charge—doing a hell of a job here, don't you know? I'm not one to change something that's working—you oughta know that, little girl."

"Now that Jeremy has found us Otto to handle the ringmaster duties, your father and I will concentrate on the day-to-day operations," Shirley said. "Harry will oversee the setup and teardown. I'll manage the ticket and concession sales. It'll be like old times, all of us together again—only better."

"Where's your brother?" Harry asked, glancing around. "I hear he finally had the good sense to stop pussyfooting around and make his move with Trixie. Have they set a date yet?"

"Now, Harry, don't try to rush things," Shirley admonished him.

"Rush things! Why, if that boy takes any longer—"

"Hush," Shirley scolded as she looked up and saw Ian waiting for them.

Lucy watched the reunion of her brother and parents from her position on the platform. She was all too aware that Jeremy was standing just behind her.

"Hello," he said softly. "I've missed you."

She turned and glanced up at him, then immediately turned her attention back to her parents. "We've all missed you, too," she replied pleasantly. If in looking at him she had seen even a hint of the torture she had endured over the past several days, she might have convinced herself that there was genuine intimacy in his remark. But the devil had been smiling at her—that cocky smile that he knew full well set feminine hearts aflutter.

"I wasn't talking about everyone, Lucy," he said irritably.

She raised her eyes to him and batted her lashes the way she imagined one of his society coquettes might do. "Why, Jeremy, what a sweet thing to say."

He scowled at her with disapproval. "We need to . . ."

She mounted the stairs and followed her parents and Ian back inside the train. When she looked out the window, Jeremy was still standing there watching her, and he was smiling again. *Arrogant cad.*

The morning flew by. Everyone was energized by the arrival of Harry and Shirley and the news that they were to travel with the company for the remainder of the season. The parade came off without a hitch, if one didn't count the fact that Lucy had looked down from her perch on the swing at one point to see Jeremy standing along the parade route looking up at her. With him were two men in business suits who did not look as if they were local town fathers. She had got used to his being at the head of the parade or, more recently, not there at all. It was disconcerting to have him watching her and pointing her out to others, as he did now to the two men at his side.

Unable to stop herself, she looked back at him and immediately felt a rush of regret. Like most circus folk, Lucy was superstitious. She quickly faced forward once again, hoping that perhaps the fates had failed to note her lapse, but not before she had caught a glimpse of Trixie riding behind her and frowning up at her.

They had barely made it back to the circus grounds when Trixie reined her horse in next to Lucy's wagon. "What on earth were you thinking?" she demanded. "You know better."

If Lucy was as superstitious as the next person, Trixie was downright fanatical when it came to charms and omens—both bad and good.

"I—I'm sorry," Lucy replied as she climbed down off the wagon and headed for wardrobe to change for the afternoon performance.

Trixie caught up to her and coached her horse to keep pace. "You'll need to be careful today—we all will, but especially you. Bad luck surrounds you," Trixie said ominously.

"I'll be careful," Lucy snapped.

"I mean it, Luce." Trixie had halted her horse and let Lucy keep walking, but she called after her. "You watch yourself today. Don't take any unnecessary chances."

Lucy waved a hand in acknowledgment without turning around. She didn't need for Trixie to see that she was upset with herself. It had been a stupid thing to do—a first-of-May mistake. It was high time she let Harry and Shirley worry about what Jeremy Barrington might be planning to do next. After all, so far his ideas had worked out pretty well. Still, there had been something familiar about one of the two men. That's why she'd looked back. She could swear that she'd seen him before, and whatever the association with that faint memory was, it wasn't a pleasant one.

She didn't have to wait long to solve the mystery.

Several people were already in the dressing area, and they were buzzing with curiosity. She saw Wally and knew that he would know exactly what was going on.

"Parnelli is shutting down, selling out—to us," he replied with a gleeful smile. "The man has burned so many territories that he can't put together a decent schedule to even get him through the rest of the season."

Lucy had heard the same stories as the others about how Parnelli had sometimes left town before settling up with his creditors. Burning a territory meant his outfit would not be welcomed back—ever. "But how?"

"Jeremy's stepsister—I guess she's married to Porterfield, but something of the independent sort—has her own business and all?"

Lucy nodded, impatient for him to get on with the news.

"Well, she sent Jeremy money and told him to invest it for her in the Conroy Cavalcade. Jeremy used it—with Porterfield's blessing—to buy Parnelli out."

"But, what does that mean . . . I mean, for us?"

"Well, for starters it means that we have much better traveling accommodations. The Parnelli train is first class. Of course, we have to share it with their acts, but there's always a dark side of the moon, isn't there?"

"Their acts . . . with us?" *Reggie? Eleanore?* "All of them?"

"Yep, 'fraid so." Wally studied her. "You all right with that?"

"Of course." She would never look back in a parade again. Bad luck sure didn't waste any time collecting on a momentary slip. "When are they joining us?"

"They're already here. Jeremy and Harry are finalizing the contracts for the rest of the season right now. They've called a combined company meeting for right after the performance this afternoon."

Lucy swallowed and wondered if it might be possible to fake illness. *Oh, for heaven's sake, get hold of yourself.*

"Hey, you're still gonna be the star of this thing, you know," Wally assured her.

"Oh, I'm not worried about that, Wally," she replied with a grin. "After all, that's *my* family name up there." She pointed to the broadside pasted on the side of a fence.

"That's not the reason and you know it," Wally said. "You're the star, because you *are* the star and don't you forget that."

Lucy bent and kissed the little man's balding forehead. "What would I do without you, my friend?"

The afternoon performance was rough. It was clear to everyone in the company that the news of the acquisition of the Parnelli circus had affected performances. Thankfully, the audience seemed to be oblivious to the small mistakes and minor mishaps, and they applauded enthusiastically at the close of the show.

"What the devil's going on with you folks?" Harry demanded after the finale, when everyone had gathered in the backyard of the lot. "If this is an example of the level of work you've been showing him, no wonder Jeremy went out and got Parnelli's people."

"It was just one of—" Ian began, but Harry cut him off with an impatient wave of his cane.

"We don't have shows like this one—*ever*," he said, and his voice had softened to barely a whisper so that everyone had to lean forward to hear his words. "Now, you hear me well, folks. There's not an act in this company that isn't far and away better than anything Parnelli was offering, but if you don't watch yourselves, you're gonna find those acts taking top billing right from under your noses."

He glared at each of the lead performers in turn.

"Do you get my meaning?" he asked.

Every head was already bowed, and as one they all nodded.

"Now, you hold those heads up high and get yourselves together before that meeting Jeremy has scheduled. I want to see every one of you walking into that tent like you own the place—you got that?"

"Yes, sir," they replied in unison and then quickly dispersed in all directions.

"Lucinda, I need a word with you."

Lucy knew that tone in her father's voice—it meant she was in trouble. "Yes, Papa."

"Are you hurt?"

"No, sir."

"Sick, then?"

"No, sir."

"Well, from what I heard you're doing at least fifty turns at every performance—and that's on your off days. This afternoon you barely made thirty."

"But . . ."

Harry looked at her evenly. "If you want to hold your own against the likes of Eleanore Wilson, Lucy, you're gonna have to put your whole heart into it every day—every show. Understood?"

He was right, of course. She had permitted the

news of the union with Parnelli's outfit to distract her. "It won't happen again, Harry," she said.

Her father nodded once. "That's what I thought."

The day did not get any easier. Lucy knew Reggie was on the premises and, therefore, that she was bound to run into him sooner or later. Even so, her first encounter with him affected her more than she would have expected. On the one hand, it surprised her to realize that any romantic feelings she might once have held for him simply were no longer there. On the other, he still held the power to elicit feelings of uncertainty and insecurity about her talent.

"And, there's my Lucy-girl," he announced as he strode into the big top during her warmup for the evening show. He completely ignored Ian and moved to the center of the ring to look up at her. "No net, sweetheart? But then, with the level of risk your father permits, a net was always more for show than necessity, wasn't it?"

He looked at Ian for the first time. "Eleanore will need the safety of a net for her performance," he instructed. "Her feats are truly daring, and we cannot take a chance that—"

"I'm not her spotter," Ian replied as Lucy descended the rope ladder he held for her. "Luce, I promised to meet Trixie for supper, but if you . . ." He glanced sideways at Reggie.

"You go ahead," Lucy said and placed her hand on his arm to reassure him. When he had gone, she turned to Reggie. "Well, look who's come home to roost," she said as she toweled off and covered herself with her cape.

Reggie gave her a cold smile and then made a slow

perusal of her body. "You know, Lucy, with a body like that, you're really not suited to acrobatics. Harry should have had the good sense to keep you on the ground, where you could be seen . . . and appreciated." He trailed the back of his finger over her cheek.

Lucy stepped away. "How is Eleanore?" she asked.

"She's not you," he replied with a sexy huskiness to his voice that she remembered and now recognized as a device he used for seduction. He took a step toward her, his eyes half lowered and focused on her mouth. "I've missed you, babe."

Lucy laughed, and his eyes widened immediately. "Well, I've been far too busy to miss you, and now here you are back again. Do you happen to have any of my money left?"

His smile froze, but his eyes darted over her face as if he expected her to be joking. "Your money? I don't know any—"

"Oh, I've no doubt that your memory has conveniently slipped on this matter, Reggie, and you know what? It doesn't matter. You see, your leaving me might have been the best thing that ever happened to me."

He chuckled and placed one hand against a support pole, effectively holding her there. "Moved on to someone new, have you? Perhaps it's that English dandy. Is he the one? You always were a sucker for the blue-blooded types. A fella like that, though, ain't gonna settle for a couple of stolen kisses here and there. How far have you let him get, Lucy?"

She felt her fists clench and fought the urge to strike him. She wouldn't give him the satisfaction. "Excuse me," she said tightly and tried to move past him, but he caught her and held her, his large hands tightening around her upper arms, his breath hot on her face.

"I'd have never left if you'd been willing to . . ."

"Then leaving was the right thing to do," she replied, refusing to struggle, knowing that it was what he wanted. "Now, let me go."

He loosened his grip slightly, but not enough to free her. "You know, Eleanore has no such reservations when it comes to satisfying her man. I think it might be what makes her such an outstanding performer—she takes risks and she doesn't care how high the stakes might go." He drew her closer, and Lucy could not help stiffening. "Better watch out, little girl, or she'll steal the spotlight from you just like she—"

With a mighty wrench of her body, Lucy pulled herself free of his grip. "If you are about to imply that she stole you, then it might interest her to know that you've barely been back half a day and here you are trying to seduce me."

His tone changed. "Lucy," he said pleadingly, "I've been half out of my head missing you. Forgive me, darling, won't you?"

"And take you back?"

He ducked his head in mock shyness and grinned. "All I'm asking is a chance. I made a mistake. Eleanore is . . . well, she's not you."

She was shocked at her recognition of the ploy he had always used to try and get around her temper. It was in that moment that she realized how her feelings had changed and saw them for the youthful infatuation that they had been. She stood tall and looked up at him.

"I need a man that I can trust," she replied.

Now the grin became cruel again. "Well, little girl,

take some advice from me: if you're banking on hooking up with the dandy, don't. Word has it that he's here for one reason—he got in a scrape back in New York and was sent here to cool his heels while things were set right back there. The minute he gets the word, he's on the first train outta here—and you, my sweet, will be the last thing on his mind. A man like him has got some rich man's daughter waiting back there; you can be sure of that."

"I know all about what happened with Jeremy in New York," she shot back with bravado.

"Then you know that he's got his back against the wall to turn this dog-and-pony show into a money-maker. Word has it that he's been doing a pretty good job of convincing folks that he can do just that." He moved closer and Lucy stepped out of his range. He laughed. "Ask yourself one thing, Lucy. Ask yourself why we're here—me and Eleanore and the others. It's because Parnelli had a successful troupe—the best. He made mistakes with money, but he knew talent—and so does your English duke. He brought Eleanore here for one reason, my sweet. You aren't good enough."

She couldn't take any more. She felt the threat of tears, hot and burning against her lashes. Refusing to let him see how his words hurt her, she stalked out of the tent and into the rain and coming storm.

Nine

Jeremy heard distant thunder as he paced his office after the meeting. Things had not gone well at all. Oh, the members of both companies had been on their best behavior, but the tension between the two groups reminded him of the animosity that had often charged the room when he and his stepsister, Olivia, had sparred in their younger days. If looks had been physical blows, Lucy and Eleanore Wilson might both be showing some bruising on their fair complexions.

Still, the more immediate concern was the approaching storm. He stepped outside and studied the sky. The dark clouds rolled topsy-turvy across the horizon, gathering speed as the thunder echoed and a hint of lightning flickered in the dark sky.

"Harry?" he called as he strode across the grounds toward the ticket wagon.

Harry and Shirley were inside the wagon, sharing a cold supper. They looked up as the wind caught the door and Jeremy joined them. He shook the rain from his straw hat and brushed it from his shoulders.

"I think we should cancel."

"But we've sold over seven hundred tickets already," Shirley protested. "How can we refund all that money with all the bills we have coming due?"

She tapped her pencil against the ledger. "What am I saying? Of course we should cancel."

"Or we could do a John Robinson," Harry said.

"I beg your pardon?" Jeremy asked.

"A John Robinson—a shorter show. Robinson was a promoter who got a reputation for always cheating his patrons on length of the performance. Over the years though, it's become a way of saying that we'll do the show but only what we can do safely under the conditions. Folks will understand the need for a shorter show—if they show up at all."

"What if we postpone?" Jeremy asked.

"Postpone? Jeremy, we have to be in Edwardston in two days, and the day after tomorrow is the governor's gala and . . ."

"I just meant postpone a few hours—until the storm blows over."

"You mean perform at—what, nine o'clock? Ten?"

"Why not?"

Shirley's eyes grew large with disbelief. "Because there are children to consider," she said as if talking to a two-year-old.

Jeremy shrugged. "It's not as if they have school tomorrow. It won't harm them to stay up a bit later," he replied. "Suppose we send out the crew to spread the word . . . we'll make it something special. . . ." He snapped his fingers and smiled. "We'll tell everyone to bring a guest."

"A guest? You're gonna give out hundreds of Annie Oakleys at one performance?" Shirley exclaimed.

Harry started to explain the term.

"That one I know—free tickets—and yes, that is precisely what we are going to do."

Harry and Shirley looked at each other and rolled their eyes.

"But that means that half our audience might not pay," Shirley protested.

"No, lovely lady. Don't you see? By essentially cutting the price in half, we double the number of people and quadruple the amount of publicity that those people will garner us when they tell the tale far and wide. For the two remaining performances tomorrow, we will pack the house. I'll wager that some people who attend tonight's performance will return to be sure that they have seen every act. By the time we do the performance for the governor day after tomorrow, we'll be the talk of the state."

Harry began to smile, then he clapped Jeremy on the shoulder. "What did I tell you about this boy, Shirl? He's got the master touch for this business. The kid is a natural showman."

Shirley just grinned and shook her head.

"I'll go get things started," Harry said. "Send the boys out to let folks know to come right after the storm blows through, right?"

"That's the ticket," Jeremy said. "Tell them to listen for the bugle call. I'll go and tell the company our plan." He walked back across the lot feeling measurably better than he had earlier, and then he saw Lucy.

She was striding across the lot, as much as one could under the conditions of mud and ankle-deep puddles. Her fists were clenched and her mouth worked as if she were talking to someone, but no one else was around.

"Lucy?"

She whipped her braided hair back from one

shoulder and glared at him. Then she kept right on walking, oblivious to the wind and rain.

He hurried after her. "Lucy, is there a problem?"

"It's none of your business."

"You're crying."

"It's raining." She swiped at both eyes with the backs of her hands. "Did you want something?"

"We're postponing the show—until after the storm."

"Nobody will come," she said, looking up at him as the rain pelted them both.

"Yes, I believe they will, and so do Harry and Shirley. In fact, we believe that it will be quite the topic of conversation by morning." The words were spoken in a monotone because his attention was completely on her: the dark eyes in that alabaster face, the soaked fabric of her costume clinging to her.

They were alone in the rain; every sane person had taken shelter as the sky came alive with lightning and a lion's roar of thunder. He reached over and tucked a sodden lock of her hair behind her ear. Her chin quivered slightly. He cupped the back of her head and pulled her toward him.

"No," she said as she jerked away and ran toward the dressing tent.

She was crying. He started after her.

"Sir Jeremy!"

Jeremy turned and saw a man standing in the entrance to the big top. He was wearing tight pants tucked into knee-high black boots, and he was carrying a whip.

It was the lion tamer—the one backstage gossip had it that Lucy once loved. Lucy had been coming from the big top. Jeremy cast one final look after Lucy and then headed toward Reginald Dunworthy.

"I believe that I told everyone to skip the 'Sir,' Reggie. What is it that you want?"

"It's about Eleanore. She's . . . disappointed with her billing."

"She doesn't have billing at this point. We just brought the two companies together."

Reggie smiled. "Nevertheless . . ." He slapped the whip stem idly against one thigh.

"Eleanore will have to prove herself with this outfit, as will you."

The smile faltered slightly. "Nevertheless . . . compared to Miss Conroy . . ."

"Let me make one thing very clear to you, sir," Jeremy said as he stepped closer to Reggie and put his hand on the handle of the whip, stilling it. "This outfit belongs to Miss Conroy's family, but even if it did not—even if it were your name on all those broadsides around town—Miss Conroy would maintain her position as the star of this circus. It is her daring that has consistently put people in those seats on this tour, and until you or Miss Wilson can prove otherwise, Miss Conroy will remain the star of this show."

Jeremy could see that Reggie was weighing his response. On the one hand, the lion tamer really wanted badly to strike him. On the other hand, he was prudent enough to understand that Jeremy was the man with the money and the power.

"I only meant to say that Miss Conroy—while she is very good at her craft . . . well, you haven't seen Eleanore perform, and she—"

"Fair enough. I shall review her performance—and yours—as soon as we arrive in Edwardston in two days. For now, we have a performance to do tonight. There is a storm coming. We need to make sure that everything is secure and that our animals are kept calm. There is a great deal of work to be done, Mr. Dunworthy, and in this outfit, everyone pulls his own weight. I do believe that those are your lions I can hear calling. May I suggest that you attend to them?"

Reggie glared at him with undisguised loathing. Then, he smiled. "Sure," he said as he turned on one booted heel and strolled out into the night.

Jeremy considered following him and then decided to drop the matter for now. Harry had given the man high marks on his ability as an animal handler. To Jeremy it was crystal clear that he had the potential to be as dangerous as the cats he trained. Jeremy decided that it was high time he had a chat with the other half of this duo, and went to find Miss Eleanore Wilson.

"Could you please sit down?" Trixie moaned as Lucy paced past the dressing table for the twentieth time. "You are making me nervous, and I never get nervous; but if I do, Bucko smells it and it affects the performance, so *sit.*"

"Why, Lucy, this is so unlike you," Eleanore gushed, having joined them at the long dressing table, even though she was not scheduled to perform and would be watching from a seat in the front row. "The one thing I used to admire the most about you were those nerves of steel. Honestly, if I could have found some way to steal that from you, nothing would have stopped me." She focused her attention on her reflection, leaning close to apply her trademark fake eyelashes.

"But you just thought stealing her man and half her act would do," Trixie muttered under her breath just loud enough for Lucy to hear.

In spite of her foul mood, Lucy felt the beginnings of a smile, and then uncontrollable giggles consumed her. Trixie tried hard to suppress her own mirth. "Sh-h-h," she begged.

"What's so funny?" Eleanore asked with a tight little smile.

"Nothing," Trixie replied and broke into full-blown gales of laughter.

"Well, really!" Eleanore huffed and headed for the exit. "Oh, hello there," she said in the syrupy sweet tone she seemed to have adopted for addressing anyone of the male gender.

Lucy and Trixie looked up. Jeremy was standing at the door, and that sobered both of them instantly. They glanced at each other, then back at him. He seemed to have all of his attention focused on Eleanore. Lucy turned her back on both of them and began brushing her hair with more energy than was normal.

"Easy, sweetie," Trixie whispered. "Don't want to pull it out by the roots."

"I'd like to pull somebody's hair by the roots," Lucy muttered in reply.

"Good evening, Miss Wilson," Jeremy said. "Welcome to the Conroy Cavalcade—but that's right, you were with the company before, is that not correct?"

"I do like a man who does his homework," Eleanore said in a low, husky tone.

Lucy was pretty sure she might throw up.

"Steady," Trixie coached, laying a comforting hand on her shoulder.

"Life is quite interesting, don't you find, Miss Wilson? One starts out in one direction, and then gets distracted and before one knows what has happened, one can find herself right back where she started."

Lucy's hand froze in midbrush. There was something in his tone. . . . She glanced at the mirror, adjusting herself until she caught his reflection. He was smiling at Eleanore, but it was not his usual smile. She knew that smile—it could light up a room. It could make a woman feel as if she were beautiful. This smile was different . . . cold . . . It could . . .

Eleanore giggled and touched his arm. "Oh, you . . ."

His smile did not change. "Miss Wilson—Eleanore, I stopped by this evening to alert you to the fact that in two days, as soon as the train arrives in Edwardston, I'll want to preview your act—and the other acts from the Parnelli company, of course."

"Well, I'm not usually at my best so early in the morning, Jeremy, but for you I am willing."

"Excellent," Jeremy replied, then turned his attention to Trixie and Lucy. "Ladies, I shall send word as soon as the storm has passed and the patrons have gathered." And then he flashed the smile that both women knew to be genuine Jeremy.

"Right, boss," Trixie replied with a mock salute.

The ploy of holding the performance after the storm worked like a charm. There was an extra edge of excitement as the drum-and-bugle corps marched through town in front of Cora, the lead elephant, whose sides had been colorfully painted to herald the start time of the performance. Members of the crew carried flaming torches to light the way and add an extra element of drama and excitement. The people came in droves, anxious to take full advantage of the two-for-one admission price, and more than willing to see less than the full performance.

By the time Lucy was scheduled to perform, however, fresh storm clouds had gathered.

"I don't know, Lucinda," Harry said, with a worried eye on the sky. "Maybe we ought to get right to the grand parade."

On any other night, Lucy would have accepted his advice, but Eleanore was sitting with Reggie in the front row, looking smug and self-important. Eleanore slowly fanned herself with a ridiculously large feather fan, guaranteed to draw attention her way. Lucy wasn't about to give her rival fresh ammunition with which to imply that Lucy was only too willing to bow out when the risk became too great.

"I'll cut the act short, Harry," she promised as she coated her hands with powder. "Fifteen minutes." She looked out at the sky, heard the distant thunder, and saw the hint of lightning on the far horizon. "Let's just go straight to the neck twirl," she said.

"I'll check with Jeremy," Harry said. "You know that if he says you don't go on, then you don't."

"Agreed," Lucy promised and turned her attention to the center ring, where a drumroll announced that Wally was about to make his nightly exit from the mouth of the cannon.

She motioned to Ian and pantomimed her neck twirl. Ian nodded and went to prepare for the stunt.

"Can't find Jeremy," Arnie reported. "Thunder's closer," he added.

Harry considered the sky once again and then looked at his daughter. "You're sure?"

"We'll go straight to it and skip the grand parade. That way the others can secure the animals and get themselves in place to lead everyone to shelter as they exit. We'll announce that the spin is the finale for tonight. Otto will get them to count, and we can end on that note."

Harry nodded. "Okay, get up there and I'll tell Otto the plan."

Lucy ran into the big top just as the audience gasped at the sight of Wally flying through the air. Then they burst into loud applause and cheers, drowning out any hint of the coming storm.

A support pole near the entrance creaked and groaned, and Lucy was aware that the wind was gathering energy. She focused her attention on Eleanore and Reggie for a moment. They were oblivious to Wally, not even applauding as he took his bow. Their heads were bent close together, and Eleanore shielded their faces with her closed fan, whispering something to Reggie that made him laugh.

Lucy frowned and then turned her attention back to her rigging. This was no night to make a mistake. She was going to be perfect. She was going to set a standard for performing excellence that Eleanore would spend the rest of her career trying to match.

"Ready?" Ian asked.

Lucy nodded. Otto introduced her and she made her walk around the perimeter of the ring, waving to the crowd as her cape fluttered around her. Just as she passed Reggie and Eleanore, she saw Eleanore snap the fan, and a single feather floated onto the sawdust at Lucy's feet. It was a peacock's feather— another bad luck omen.

Lucy paused for an instant, then picked up the

feather and handed it back to Eleanore, her eyes blazing with fury. "I believe this is yours, not mine," she said softly, and smiled brightly as she turned and waved once more to the crowd before grasping the rope and starting her climb to the top.

Otto announced that Lady Lucinda, Angel of the Big Top, would close the evening's performance with an abbreviated preview of her original death-defying neck spiral. She would work at the apex of the big top, seventy feet above the ground, and with no net. The audience gasped, and every eye turned to follow her ascent to the top as Otto urged them to return the following day to see the full performance.

Lucy smiled and waved to the crowd as she continued her climb. The tent was quiet now as the drummer began a soft roll and Ian released the neck strap from the top of the tent. She reached the top and looked down. Jeremy had just entered the tent, and his expression told her that he was not at all pleased with seeing her high above him. He went to Ian and they exchanged words. Then he looked up at her, held up ten fingers, and then made the sign that told her she was to do ten spins and end it there.

Lucy felt the wind buffet the big top, heard the first splatter of huge raindrops on the already soaked and stretched canvas, and knew that only she could hear this, because only she was this close to the top. She knew that Harry had ordered the crew to double-stake the tent, but would it hold?

The orchestra began her music, she placed the strap expertly around her neck, knowing the audience had been watching her, oblivious to the growing danger outside the tent. Jeremy moved around the ring, his eyes on her. He wore a look of panic, and she saw that he was talking with animated hand gestures to Harry and Ian.

Lucy concentrated on her performance. Five more minutes. She positioned herself on the flybar and heard the audience gasp as she released the bar and dropped into her spin. She threw back her head and started into the turns, suspended by her long neck high above the throng of people, with nothing between her and the ground.

She heard Otto announce that she would perform ten spins in the stunt that the Angel herself had created. He invited the audience to count, and they chanted out the numbers.

But when they reached ten, Lucy kept spinning and the audience kept counting, their voices raised in excited anticipation as the number climbed to fifteen and then twenty. She focused on hitting twenty-five.

But, then there was an ear-splitting clap of thunder that even the chants of hundreds of people could not cover. The chanting turned to murmurs of fear and then shrieks as a second clap of thunder followed lightning that split the sky and caused the lighting inside the tent to flicker violently. Instantly, the audience forgot about Lucy and rushed toward the exits.

Feeling the tent sway slightly, she tore the strap from around her neck and clung to it with one hand as she waited for Ian to get her the rope so she could slide to the ground. But the panicked crowds below her had engulfed Ian and everyone else. They had carried him away from her rigging. If there had been a net, she would simply have dropped into it, bounced two or three times before settling enough to work her way to the edge, and then fled with the others. There was no net. She could hear Otto, Harry, and Jeremy shouting out orders, calling for calm, directing the throng to safety.

The socket of her arm ached, and she wasn't sure how much longer she could hang on. Wildly she looked around for an alternative, and seeing none, for the very first time in her life, she was truly frightened.

"Ian! Jeremy!" she screamed.

Below her everyone was caught up in the need to direct patrons to safety and restore order. She saw Ian trying to work his way against the mob back to the post where her exit rope was tied, and then, miraculously, Jeremy was there. He emerged from the throng of terrified people and looked up at her. There was no chance of hearing his words, but his eyes spoke volumes.

Lucy closed her eyes. *Please, hurry,* she prayed as her fingers slipped a little more.

"Lucy!"

She opened her eyes and looked down at Jeremy.

"Catch it," he called as he swung the rope in her direction.

She leaned out but missed. Her fingers slipped a little more and she cried out.

"Now, Lucy," Jeremy shouted as the rope came to her again.

She grabbed it and held on, wrapping her hands around it and sliding toward the ground at a dizzying speed. She felt the rope burn her palms, but she didn't care. Her only thought was to get to Jeremy as quickly as possible.

The wind howled, drowning out her own shriek of terror as the lightning cut multiple jagged cracks in the black sky. After what seemed like an eternity, she felt solid ground under her feet. It came up so suddenly that she twisted her ankle in the landing. In her haste to reach Jeremy, she hobbled forward a few steps and fell.

"I've got you," Jeremy said as he lifted her into his arms and headed for the exit. Still holding her, he barked orders above the roar of the storm. Finally satisfied that the audience was out of the big top and on their way to safety, he carried Lucy to the nearest shelter—his railroad car.

"I'm fine," she yelled above the storm. "Put me down."

"Hush."

He pushed open the door to the drawing room and set her down on a settee.

"I'll ruin it," she protested, seeing the stain of water spread across the silk damask. She tried to get up. "I'm soaked . . . so are you."

"Sit," he ordered as he knelt next to her after first shrugging out of his sodden and mangled linen suit coat. "Let me see your hands."

"They're fine."

He took hold of her hands and turned them palms up, and she could not suppress a grimace of pain as he stretched out her fingers.

"I'll get some salve and bandages. Do not move, and put that ankle up."

Gingerly, she did as she was told. "It'll be fine," she said more to herself than to him.

"I'll be the judge of that," he replied as he returned with a pot of salve and a roll of bandages. "Hold out your hands."

She did as he asked. He sat on the edge of the settee next to her and spread salve on each palm, then wrapped them loosely with the soft gauze. She watched him concentrate on his task. His soft brown hair fell over his forehead in a manner that invited her to comb it back for him with her fingers, but that was impossible. He had already bandaged one hand and was working on the other.

She shifted slightly and he looked up at her. "Are you in pain?"

"I'll be fine."

He smiled. "That is not the answer to my question."

She shrugged. "In this business, you have to expect the occasional injury or mishap. I was stupid coming down the rope that way."

He had moved his attention to her ankle and he was frowning. He removed her shoe. "This is beginning to swell badly."

"I'll be fine by tomorrow afternoon."

"No, you'll stay off it at least until we reach Chicago."

"But . . ."

He concentrated on his examination of her ankle, gently probing the skin. "Eleanore can take your place for a few performances."

"No!" Lucy swung her feet to the floor and attempted to stand. Luckily, Jeremy was there to catch her when the pain shot up her leg.

"Yes," he insisted huskily as he supported her weight and then drew her closer.

She placed one bandaged hand lightly against his chest but did not push him away. "But the governor," she protested more weakly than before.

"We'll manage," he assured her. "Don't you know that I would never jeopardize your welfare for a performance—regardless of the fact that it is a command performance?"

She heard the attempt to tease her a bit, to help her regain her composure. "Nevertheless . . ." She was not going to let Eleanore take her place without a fight.

"Miss Conroy," he said, easing her back down onto the daybed that served as a settee and resuming his position beside her, "must I remind you that I am the person in charge here?"

Their eyes met and his smile faded. He reached up and stroked her cheek. She gently pushed the hair away from his forehead.

The only light came from a small lamp on the side table. The only sounds in the room were the storm battering the windows, and their breathing. She felt as if they were completely alone—the only two people in the world at that moment. She saw in his eyes that he was no longer thinking about Eleanore—nor was she, for that matter.

She dropped her gaze to his mouth as he lowered his face to hers. She closed her eyes and waited for his kiss.

"Open your eyes, Lucy," he said.

She did as he asked.

"I do not know what thoughts you have had about the other evening, but as for myself, I have thought of little else. Do you understand that if we start down this path again, it will only become more difficult to stop—at least for my part?"

She knew that he was speaking only of physical desire, nothing more. It was dangerous territory, but at least he was being honest. He was not like Reggie—trying to win her favors through empty promises. "I understand," she whispered.

"Then . . . you are willing?"

"I am . . . curious," she said honestly.

To her surprise, he smiled and released the low rumble of his laughter. "Curious?"

She squirmed uneasily in his arms, but he did not release her. "I've had little experience with . . . I mean, kissing you that night was very different . . . it aroused . . ." She blushed scarlet. "Oh, for heaven's sake, kiss me or don't," she said.

He chuckled again. "Anything I can do to satisfy your curiosity, Miss Conroy."

He touched her lips gently with his own and she waited for the full passion of his kiss, but instead, she felt the soft flicker of his tongue moistening her lips as well as his own. A knot of white-hot fire seemed to explode at her very core, and she jerked convulsively. In that instant, she knew there would be no turning back. There would be no regrets.

God, I want this woman. Jeremy fought for control and a clearer head. She ignited such conflicting emotions in him. Surely, taking her would resolve them. She was at once impossibly demure and sultry. Her body as spare and lithe as an athlete's, but enhanced by curves that she had to know drove him quite mad. Yet, even as her lips clung to his, he felt her innocence, and that demanded at least a modicum of restraint. But damn, when she reacted as if everything he did was some sort of delightful surprise, what was a man to do? When she pressed her full breasts against him, molded her body to his, was he to be blamed for what he might do?

When he had first swept his tongue through her mouth that night that had haunted him for weeks now, she had gasped, but then she had responded, and in an instant it seemed as if neither of them was capable of satisfaction. Their mouths had moved hungrily against each other, their breaths had been audible, like the pounding cadence of a train in motion. On this night, it was as if they were experiencing that first kiss all over again.

He pressed her back onto the daybed and bent over her. She buried her face in the crook his neck, and he could feel the heat of her breath on his skin. "I want you," he murmured and felt the intake of her breath.

He knelt next to her as he tore at his tie and the buttons of his shirt. She watched him with hooded eyes. Her lips were slightly parted. Her hair spilled over the gold of the settee. He abandoned the tie and ran the tips of his fingers along the neckline of her costume. She shuddered.

"I'm beginning to think that you have cast some sort of spell over me, Miss Conroy," he said softly as he flattened his palm over one breast and began to stroke it with his thumb. The thin, wet gauze of the fabric, supported only by a lacy chemise undergarment, aided him in his task to know the shape of her. Her eyes fluttered shut as she arched to his touch.

Jeremy pressed his mouth to the exposed flesh of her neckline and pulled her costume free of one shoulder. She locked her fingers in his hair, and he felt the involuntary rise of her torso seeking more contact as she repeatedly whispered his name.

He shifted slightly and moved his hand under the hem of the skirt of her costume, bunching the fabric as he ran his fingers lightly along her calf, the back of her knee, her inner thigh. She grew perfectly still but did nothing to stop him.

Jeremy gave her a moment. Without breaking the kiss, he lay next to her on the daybed and pulled her against him. Now his mouth was open, nipping at her, tugging at her lower lip. She shivered. He must be mad. Lucy was not a woman one toyed with. Even were she not the beloved daughter of Harry and Shirley, people whom he deeply respected—even if she were just a woman he had met, something about her demanded respect.

"Lucy," he said, his voice hoarse with desire.

Lucy saw in his eyes that he was no longer thinking about Eleanore or the show or the storm. Nor was she, for that matter. She was thinking about Jeremy and the fact that these days, she found herself thinking of him almost constantly. Somehow, he had infused himself into her life. He wanted to make love to her and she wanted that as well, but the point was that a physical relationship was all he wanted— all he would ever want of her.

If he had not spoken her name, she might have allowed his lovemaking to continue unabated. She already stood on the verge of becoming a willing— even an enthusiastic—participant in the act. Had her experience with Reggie taught her nothing?

She had not one shred of evidence to believe that Jeremy was different from any other man. He wanted her body, not her heart. At the moment, she would have given him both, but something in the way he looked at her, his eyes hungering for more, brought her to her senses. She framed his face with her bandaged hands as if to bring him back to her kiss, then trailed the flats of her palms lightly down his neck to his chest. He released an excited shudder and smiled. She smiled up at him and then gave him a forceful shove, sending him toppling to the floor with a surprised yelp.

Lucy scrambled off the daybed and stood on one foot, holding on to the nearby table for balance. He remained on the floor where she had pushed him.

"The storm has passed," she said, glancing out the window as if they had just been discussing the weather.

He pushed himself to a sitting position and looked up at her.

"Please go and find Ian," she said before he could form the words to speak his mind.

He was taken aback by this new turn of events. "Why?"

"Because it's late and I cannot walk by myself." She used her free hand to check her hair and smooth her costume. "He'll carry me back to my compartment."

"You're not going anywhere on that foot."

She arched one eyebrow and considered him for a moment. "Well, I am most certainly not going to stay here," she said, wincing a little as she eased herself back down to sit gingerly on the very edge of the daybed.

"Oh, yes, you are." He was standing now, looming over her.

"Very well," she replied and saw him relax. Just like a man, thinking all he had to do was loom and automatically a woman would crumble at his feet. She settled herself more comfortably into the cushions. "It's very sweet of you to allow me to recuperate here tonight. And where will *you* be staying?" She batted her eyelids at him.

"I . . . well . . ." He glanced around.

"Because you can't stay here with me. I mean,

you've been so very kind, and of course I know that your motives are above reproach. However, people will talk, you know."

"But . . ."

"I'm sure there's room in the men's car, now that we've added the Parnelli cars to our train, or there's the hotel."

"The hotel . . . here?"

"Springfield is a lovely town," she replied. "Oh, before you go, I wonder if you might have an extra pillow. I do believe that if I prop up my foot, the swelling might not be as great."

"You can't stay here without help. What if you need to . . . you know . . . get up . . ."

"You're absolutely right," she replied, her eyes wide with the acknowledgment that he had hit upon something she hadn't thought of.

He smiled triumphantly. "Well, thank goodness you've decided to be reasonable about this."

"Absolutely." She adjusted the pillow as he prepared to settle into one of the large chairs nearby. "On your way to the hotel, would you ask Shirley to come over and stay with me?"

He was speechless, and Lucy was tempted to laugh. She had never seen him look more at his wit's end. She waited.

He started to say something, then threw up his hands and left.

Ten

What in bloody hell just happened back there? Jeremy wondered as he strode across the muddy lot. They had been on the verge of something passionate. She had been staring up at him with those infernal dark eyes of hers. Her hands had tenderly framed his face. She was responding to his every touch with eagerness and passion. He had not imagined that. Then, out of the blue, he was on the floor and she was settling in for the night—without him.

He shook his head. He'd been working much too hard for much too long. He was losing his touch with the ladies. This simply would not do. Not once in his life had a woman gained the upper hand unless he gave it to her. He had no intention of surrendering that privilege to this guileless young woman from the outback of Wisconsin, of all places. Career or no career, he had a reputation to maintain. He turned on his heel and walked straight back to where he had left Lady Lucinda.

It pleased him to see that he startled her with his quick return.

"Where's Shirley?"

"I did not yet locate your mother." He pulled an oversized ottoman next to the settee. "Why did you change your mind?"

"I haven't. I want my mother to come here and stay the night with me. Clearly, I can't move, and—"

"You changed your mind about making love with me, and I wish to know why."

"I beg your pardon?"

"You heard my question."

"You have a monumental nerve. What on earth makes you think that I was planning to . . . do any such thing?"

"Ha!" Jeremy stood and paced the room like a barrister stating his case—one he had no doubt of winning. "That, fair lady, is not in question. You were planning to participate in the immediate passionate kiss and a great deal more, and you were doing so of your own volition."

"You're ranting," she said with a dismissive wave of one hand. Then she folded her arms across her chest and focused her attention on the darkness outside.

"Do not try and ignore me, Lucy."

She slowly turned back to him. "Oh, so sorry. I did not realize that following your every command was in my contract."

"What has gotten into you?" he demanded.

"I might ask the same of you," she countered.

"I thought—we were very close to . . . you seemed to—no, you did want . . ." He combed his fingers through his thick hair in frustration. "I simply do not understand you, Lucy."

"Well, I understand you quite well, Jeremy."

"Ha!"

She narrowed her eyes at him. "You doubt me?"

"You don't know the first thing about me."

"I know this: you are a man of immense charm. And I know that this charm has worked for you in every situation in which you have found yourself throughout life—especially if a woman was involved."

"You will never convince me that the deed we almost shared was not a matter of mutual intent."

"I had a momentary lapse," she replied offhandedly.

He blanched. "You're impossible."

"And you are angry with me for one reason: I regained my senses and did not permit you to carry through with your little seduction. I expect that this may be your first experience with failure in that particular area. You may take comfort from the fact that it will remain our little secret."

"You flatter yourself."

"Do I? So, your intent was to share a few kisses, some touching, and then . . . what?"

"You know very well that—that night after the party, you did not seem so concerned with . . ." It was unlike him not to be gallant, and he stopped in midsentence as he searched for the appropriate words.

"It's a mistake, Jeremy. You know it as well as I do. You're just upset because I am the first to admit it."

It was clearly a standoff—one neither of them could have explained.

She was right, of course. A romantic entanglement with her could only spell disaster. Hadn't he been thinking the very same thing himself, even as he indulged his need to explore every inch of her?

She saw realization dawn and understood that she had correctly assessed that his interest had been only physical . . . casual. The wonder was that even now as she understood that, she still wanted more.

"I'll go find your mother," he said grudgingly.

"Thank you." As soon as she heard the door close

behind him, she took one of the many small pillows that formed the back of the daybed, and threw it across the room. She'd got what she wanted, so why did she feel so disappointed?

"You have *got* to get back on your feet—more to the point, back in the air," Trixie fumed in an urgent whisper as she and Lucy sat together in the pie car after supper one night. They were back on tour after their successful run in Springfield. "In just a few weeks we'll be in Chicago, and at the moment Eleanore is stealing your place—not to mention your man."

"I really don't begrudge her Reggie," Lucy replied. "She's done me a favor there." Stealing her place in the show's lineup was another matter entirely. It had definitely been uppermost in her mind during the long, monotonous hours she spent alone or helping Shirley with ticket sales while the others performed.

"I'm not talking about Reggie," Trixie said, her whisper hissing with repressed fury. "I'm talking about him." She jerked her head toward the entrance to the club car, where Jeremy stood.

Lucy blushed when she glanced up and saw him looking directly at her. "He is hardly *my* man," she whispered back.

"You could have fooled me—not to mention half the rest of the company," Trixie said and stood.

"Where are you going?" Lucy asked in a panic. If Trixie left, the seat next to her would be vacant. What if Jeremy came and sat with her? What if . . . ?

"I'm going to find Ian. Maybe he can talk some sense into you."

Lucy looked around for a magazine or anything

she might grab to keep from acknowledging Jeremy as he moved through the car, stopping now and then to chat with members of the company or banter with the crew.

"Jeremy, darling," Eleanore's syrupy voice called out from just across the aisle where she and Reggie had been playing cards, "we've saved a place for you." She patted the seat next to her and looked up at Jeremy. Reggie looked as if he was not in agreement with her invitation, but then Lucy observed Eleanore giving Reggie a quick kick in the shins.

"Yes," he said suddenly, leaping to his feet. "Please join our game."

"Game" indeed, Lucy thought as she selected a magazine from the pile on the table and began turning the pages without pausing to read them.

"Good evening, Lucy," Jeremy said politely and then turned his back to her as he slid into the booth next to Reggie and directly across from Eleanore.

Eleanore licked her lips and then pouted. "You've been neglecting me," she whimpered as Reggie dealt a new hand.

"Really? I assure you it was unintentional."

"I wanted to show you my latest stunt—the one I'm prepared to unveil when we perform in Chicago."

"I've been traveling a bit, as you know. I understand that the performances have been going well. Perhaps we should not tamper with success."

Eleanore smiled and laid her hand on top of his. "Now Jeremy, you know as well as I do that the most important thing to staying on top in this business is to give the people something new—something beyond what they anticipated."

Jeremy did not move his hand, and Lucy noticed

that Reggie was casting murderous looks at him, as
if it weren't Eleanore who was initiating the flirtation—not that Jeremy had to be quite so willing to
participate.

"And, what did you have in mind?" Jeremy asked
as he slid his hand free to fan his cards and study
them.

"You'll just have to come and see for yourself," she
replied.

Throughout the playing of several hands,
Eleanore's attempts at seduction were as blatantly
obvious as the tight fit of her high-collared day dress
that seemed strained at the seams to contain her
voluptuous figure. She laughed at everything Jeremy
said, leaning forward to remove a phantom bit of
lint from his jacket and stretching her neck as she
ran her long fingers slowly the length of it in a pretended study of her cards. Every action was
orchestrated to hold his attention on her. Every
movement seemed to offer a promise of more.

Lucy observed all of this from behind the pages of
her magazine. She also observed that Jeremy
seemed not the least bit uncomfortable with
Eleanore's antics. In fact, several times she caught
him glancing at Eleanore's full bosom with a bemused smile. He was indulging a fantasy of opening
that dress one button at a time until Eleanore's
breasts were fully exposed. Lucy just knew that this
was what he was imagining—the cad.

Suddenly, Reggie stood up, jarring the table so
that cards spilled onto the floor. "I gotta get some
air," he grumbled as he pushed past Jeremy and
strode toward the exit.

Jeremy retrieved the cards. Everyone else in the
car had looked around at Reggie's explosive exit and

then gone back to what they'd been doing. Eleanore merely smiled at Jeremy with a knowing look.

"He's upset," she said as she pushed the cards aside. "You see, before he left to join Parnelli, he was always billed as one of the top acts here with Conroy. He knew it would take some time to regain his place, but you do have to admit, Jeremy, that Reggie and his lions are a top draw."

"Are you asking me to reinstate his image on the broadsides, Eleanore?"

Clearly, Eleanore was not used to such a direct approach. For the first time, she seemed to lose her composure. "Oh, Jeremy, darling, what do I know of business matters? You know best, of course." She laughed and reached across the table to push back the hair that had fallen over his forehead, but he leaned back, taking himself out of reach.

"As it happens, I am one step ahead of you. I asked the lithographers to add Reggie's image to the broadsides for the remainder of the tour—assuming, of course, that he doesn't decide to run off with some other company."

"How wonderful . . . for Reggie."

"Perhaps you'd like to go and tell him the good news," Jeremy suggested as he stood in a gesture of courtesy, as if it were she who had decided to leave.

Lucy could not suppress a smile, so she burrowed her face deeper into the pages of the magazine. Her heart felt lighter than it had in the weeks that had passed since that fateful night when she'd rebuffed him. Jeremy obviously understood exactly what Eleanore was up to.

She resumed her study of the magazine, waiting for him to move on through the car.

"Lucy?"

She lowered the magazine just enough to see him standing next to her.

"I understand that your ankle is healing nicely."

"Yes, thank you."

"May I expect that we can put you back on the bill once we reach Chicago?"

"Yes."

"Excellent," he replied. "Then, I'll assume also that you are getting yourself properly prepared for that return."

She knew a reprimand when she heard one, and this was definitely a reprimand. "What are you saying?" She lowered the magazine to her lap and sat tall in her seat.

"I am saying that you seem to have enjoyed your stint as invalid. I'm saying that I have not seen you come near the ring since your unfortunate accident. No stretching. No light work with your equipment. I am simply concerned that such indulgence may not be in your best interests—or mine."

That did it. Her eyes glittered with anger. "I assure you," she replied in a low, even tone, "that you have nothing to worry about. Good day." She opened her magazine and held it high to shield her face from his view. She was aware that he stood there for a moment, then suddenly, he slid the magazine from her fingers and turned it right side up before handing it back to her.

"Have a good evening, Lucy," he said and left.

It pained Lucy in more ways than one to recognize that Jeremy's reprimand had been deserved. The following day, she hobbled over to the big top while everyone else was in the parade. It came as a complete surprise to her to realize just how quickly her strength could ebb with a few weeks of inactivity— not to mention that she had not matched her eating to her reduced activity and had obviously gained a few extra pounds.

"Well, it's good to see you getting yourself back in shape," Trixie announced when she stopped by the tent after the parade and saw Lucy stretching and exercising.

Lucy groaned. "I'm in agony here," she protested. "How could my muscles possibly have tightened so much in such a short time? I can barely touch my toes."

Trixie laughed.

"It's not funny," Lucy protested.

"I know," Trixie replied with genuine sympathy. "Maybe this will give you a little extra incentive," she said and spread out a poster for Lucy to see. "Rudy over in the print shop slipped it to me. Jeremy told them to print some up." Pictured on the announcement were three acts: Wally, Reggie, and Eleanore.

Lucy grabbed the poster away from Trixie. "We'll just see about this," she muttered as she headed directly for Jeremy's car, her tightly taped ankle protesting each step.

He was at his desk, his suit coat off, his shirtsleeves rolled back. He was studying several papers spread out over his desk, and when he looked up, he was clearly annoyed at the interruption. "Yes?" Then he smiled. "Why, Miss Conroy, to what do I owe this singular pleasure?"

She slapped the poster down in front of him. "Would you care to explain this?" she demanded.

"Well, let me see, now. It would appear to be a poster advertising our performances in . . . well, of course, the place has been left blank so that it can serve over a number of stops." He looked up at her. "What would you say it is?"

"An act of betrayal is what it is."

He studied the colorful poster again as if searching for clues. "Truly, I don't see that."

She tapped her finger forcefully on the image of Eleanore. "And what would you call this?"

"I believe that is Miss Eleanore."

"Don't be dense, Jeremy. You have replaced my image with hers."

He stood and moved around the desk. "Actually, if you had been paying attention, I replaced your image with Trixie's just after you injured yourself. I don't believe you had a problem with that. Could it be that you are jealous, Lucy?"

"Trixie is one thing—she deserves billing. This . . ." She tapped the poster again. "This is an insult."

"This is business, Lucy, nothing more and nothing less."

"Oh, really? So you're telling me that her transparent attempts at seduction have not found their mark? Ha! I know you better than that."

He caught her wrist and pulled her close. "You don't know me at all, Lucinda Conroy. You only think you do."

She did not struggle but kept her eyes locked with his. A moment passed.

"I'm going to kiss you now, Lucy," he said. "You want it and I want it and God knows we both need it. When I am done, I will explain this and then we will drop the topic altogether. Is that clear?"

She nodded, never having got beyond his announcement that he was going to kiss her.

He pressed her close and lowered his mouth to

cover hers. This time there was no preliminary test-
ing of mood or willingness. This time their lips and
tongues and teeth engaged in mutual conflict determined to give and gain absolute satisfaction and
fulfillment.

He broke the kiss reluctantly and embraced her,
his voice soft in her ear as he said, "I need for you
to understand that right now every ounce of my energy must be on the business, Lucy."

She pulled away and looked at him. "I know that."

"Do you? Then you will understand that the poster
is business, nothing more. As soon as you are ready,
your image is there, but in the meantime . . . we are
so close to success . . . real success."

She stroked his cheek and saw that his intense
commitment to the business was genuine—more
genuine than she had ever seen. "I understand," she
said. "Forgive me."

He kissed her palm, and the heat of his breath
sent a shiver through her that she could not hide.
"Why, Miss Conroy, I do believe you may be getting
a bit of a chill. Permit me to warm you," he said as he
ran his hands over her body, causing her to shudder with desire.

"Stop that," she protested, but she sounded un-
convincing even to herself.

He pulled her close and they kissed until they
were both breathless. "You need to go," he said
huskily as he nibbled her lower lip.

"I know," she whispered against his ear.

"Your father and I have a meeting in five minutes."

Reluctantly she pulled away.

Jeremy returned to his desk chair and picked up
the poster. "Lucy?"

She glanced back at him from the doorway.

He slowly tore the poster into several pieces and threw them into the wastebasket next to his desk. "We'll use Trixie's image and add yours as soon as you are ready. Welcome back."

It was later that night when Shirley discovered that money was missing. For weeks the circus had been playing to packed houses. In a normal season, they would have placed the money in the safe aboard the train and kept it there until they returned to Delavan for the winter. Then they would have made a deposit at their local bank for the entire season. But with so much cash in the safe already, and knowing that they were heading to Chicago, where the houses would be larger and the take greater, Shirley had become anxious.

"I was thinking that we need to make a deposit before we go to Chicago," she said.

"Sounds like a good idea," Harry said as he and Lucy both looked up from their game of checkers. Although Lucy's hands had healed completely, her ankle would need a few more days, according to the doctor. She had been rehearsing her act when a piece of rigging had slipped and she had reinjured it. The doctor had promised she would be ready for the performances in Chicago. In the meantime, she passed the time playing checkers with Harry in Clown Alley while the show went on without her.

"Yeah, well," Shirley continued, "I thought I would go ahead and prepare a deposit—count the money and all and . . ."

Harry stood and put his arm around his wife. "What's the matter?"

"There's money missing—a lot of money."

The three of them were silent for a long moment.

"There can't be," Harry muttered. "I've tallied it against the books myself."

"We're not the only ones who know the combination to the safe, and you don't go back and count once the money's been put there," Shirley reminded him.

"You're not thinking Jeremy . . ." Lucy objected.

"He's the only one who knows the combination to the safe other than me and Harry," Shirley reminded her gently.

"But the ledgers—I checked them myself. Gus initialed them and so did Karl—every performance."

Gus Walton collected the tickets from patrons as they entered the big top—tickets they had bought at the ticket wagon from Karl Oglethorpe, the accountant that Jeremy had hired in the days before Shirley and Harry returned. The company used pasteboard tickets that Gus collected, counted, and turned in at the ticket wagon once the performance was under way, so they could be used again at the next performance. When he turned them in, he initialed the ledger next to the ticket count.

Karl—and now Shirley—would then count the cash, make sure it tallied with the number of tickets Gus had collected, enter the figure in the ledger, and place tickets, cash, and ledger in a strong box for Jeremy or Harry to place in the safe. It was a foolproof system—or so they had thought.

"Even when I took into account the Annie Oakleys that Jeremy is always handing out to kids and such, the totals still don't add up," Shirley said. She opened the daily ledger and showed it to Harry. "Take a look at this," she said as she pointed to an entry.

Lucy watched her father study the figures. "What's the problem?"

"Now look at this." Shirley handed Harry a handwritten tally. "That's what I found in the safe. Can you get them to match?" she asked her husband.

Harry ran the numbers again. "Get me some paper and a pencil," he said.

Shirley did as he asked and waited while he made his calculations. When he was done, he looked up at his wife.

Lucy watched her parents, her heart hammering.

"Nope. There's no way 'round it," Harry said sadly. "I sure thought we could trust him."

"There's got to be another explanation," Lucy said quietly.

Harry looked up at Shirley. "Does Jeremy know you have the ledger?"

Shirley shook her head. "Neither does Karl. Not that I think he was in on it. There's no way that he could have known."

"It has to be Karl," Lucy insisted.

"Now, Lucy, if he saw Jeremy deposit the cash in the safe every time, there'd be no reason for him to be suspicious. The ledgers haven't been tampered with." Harry held a page up to the light as if to assure himself that no figures had been changed. "Besides, the money's been taken from the safe and Karl doesn't know the combination."

"Well, what are we going to do about it?" Shirley asked.

"Where's the take for tonight?"

"I left Karl over at the ticket wagon tallying the tickets and cash with Gus. I figured I'd go ahead and start preparing the deposit and then add tonight's take in."

"Did you say anything about making a deposit?"

"No, just that I was going over to the office to do a little work. Karl said he'd be by directly with tonight's money."

"Where's Jeremy?"

"He was watching the performance, last I saw of him. We have to do something, Harry," Shirley urged.

Harry stroked his chin. "You go on back over so that you're there when Karl comes by. Let me study on this a bit."

"I know you don't want to believe—none of us do, Harry—but he's the only one who could have, and he has a history," Shirley said.

"Go on. I'll handle it," Harry assured her.

Shirley left and Harry returned his gaze to the checkerboard.

"Papa, what was it that Jeremy did in New York that got him sent to us in the first place?"

"That's not for you to concern yourself with," he said evenly.

"But if—"

"It's your move, Luce."

When Shirley returned a short time later, she told them that she had not encountered Jeremy and had returned the ledger to the office and placed the cash in the safe. Harry gave Shirley a look and a brief nod in Lucy's direction, and Shirley changed the subject. It was clear that neither parent intended to discuss their plans in front of her, so Lucy feigned exhaustion and said good night. But instead of heading back to her compartment, she hung around outside the performers' entrance and waited for the show to end.

Everyone gathered just outside the exit, and the

scene was reminiscent of that night when she had made sure that Jeremy was accepted as a full member of the company. Now it appeared that she was the outsider.

Jeremy was once again the center of attention as he praised various performers and gave his notes to others. It had become his routine when he was on site—watch the performance and give notes afterward.

"I also have some good news," he told them. "I received word today that our run in Chicago will be extended for an additional week."

The entire company erupted into cheers of approval. Lucy saw Eleanore take Jeremy's hands in hers and look up at him with tears glistening as she mouthed a dramatic "Thank you" and rose on tiptoe to kiss him lightly on the lips.

Jeremy accepted the kiss and smiled at her. Lucy could not hear his words—his actions were enough. She turned to leave and ran straight into Karl Oglethorpe. The small, balding man made no apology as he brushed past her with the intense expression that he commonly wore—one that made one think twice about approaching him. He headed directly for the car that held his office, the safe, and his sleeping quarters.

"Karl?"

When he turned, she mustered her most charming smile. "My, you seem to be intent on your destination. I don't think you even saw me just now." She kept her tone light and teasing.

He blinked behind his thick glasses. "I'm sorry," he mumbled. "Was there something you needed, Miss Conroy?"

Lucy staged a light tinkle of laughter. "Not really.

I'm afraid that I'm just at loose ends. Ever since I injured my ankle," she added when he looked at her blankly.

He nodded slowly but said nothing.

"So, how did the show go tonight? And did you hear the good news? We're to perform an extra week in Chicago." She took his arm and felt him stiffen slightly in surprise. "You don't mind if I lean on you a bit, do you, Karl? I seem to have mislaid my cane, as usual."

He relaxed and even mustered what she assumed passed for a smile. "Not at all, Miss Conroy."

"Oh, for heaven's sake, Karl, it's *Lucy.*"

The company celebration had ended and they found themselves surrounded by activity. She glanced up to see Jeremy walking toward her with Eleanore clinging to his arm. She tightened her hold on Karl's arm, and to her surprise the book-keeper actually patted her hand. "As you wish, my dear," he said loudly just as Jeremy and Eleanore passed by.

Lucy saw that both Jeremy and Eleanore had overhead the comment, for they were looking at her curiously. Eleanore wore a smile of contempt, while Jeremy seemed genuinely puzzled. She also realized that for whatever reason, Karl had meant to be overheard.

Eleanore clutched Jeremy's sleeve to reclaim his attention. "What do you think of my new idea, Jeremy?" she asked in a voice that dripped with sweetness.

Lucy did not hear Jeremy's response as she and Karl continued on their way. She turned her attention back to him.

"We had a good crowd tonight," she said.

"Full house," Karl replied.

"In the circus, we call that a 'straw house'—don't ask me why." Lucy released a sigh. "Well, at least that's one good thing—a sellout means extra money coming in, and heaven knows, we need that."

Karl's mind seemed to have wandered.

"Your work must be especially tedious on a night like this—trying to match exactly the number of patrons to the receipts. Does it ever just not match?" She was certain that Karl knew something about the missing money. After all, he'd been the one handling things when Jeremy was acting as the advance man and was not even in residence with the company.

Karl glanced at her. They were about the same height, and his eyes met hers. "There are always factors beyond the simple that can affect the tally, Lucy."

"Really?" Her eyes were wide with the pretense of fascination, and she saw that indeed he relished the opportunity to discuss his work. Maybe the two men were in cahoots. She had to learn everything she could about how Karl operated and whether or not it was strictly on Jeremy's orders.

"Absolutely. For example, there are those patrons who come through the gate at no charge. Then there is sometimes the need to use petty cash for emergencies of one sort or another."

"But surely, you factor those circumstances into the final count?"

"Of course but . . ." He seemed befuddled at her sudden interest. "Lucy, I would very much enjoy explaining the finer points of accounting to you at another time, but at the moment I really must get to my work. May I call someone to assist you back to your compartment?"

"Oh, I can make it from here, Karl. You go ahead and work your magic on those numbers." She smiled at him and patted his arm as she disengaged her hand from the crook of his elbow. "Good night."

"Good night," he replied.

Lucy heard him rummaging through his ring of keys to locate the one to the locked train car as she moved off into the darkness. She planned to circle back around to see what would happen next. Would Jeremy come to meet with him? Were the two men working together, or did Jeremy wait until the little bookkeeper had gone to bed and then go in and remove funds from the safe? And either way, why would he think he could get away with it indefinitely?

Because he knows that there is usually only one deposit made each season, and by the time Harry makes that, Jeremy will be back in New York, and Karl—if he's involved—will be long gone as well.

She found a place in the shadows with a clear view of the railroad car and waited.

"What are we waiting for?" Jeremy whispered loudly close to her ear.

Lucy jumped to her feet and winced in pain. "What are you doing here?" she asked irritably. "I thought you and Eleanore were headed back to your car to discuss her career."

"It was a brief discussion, so going all the way to my car was unnecessary. What are you doing here?"

"Nothing," she lied. "Just getting a bit of fresh air before retiring for the night."

"I see. Or is it that you think perhaps that Karl is stepping out on you?"

"What?" She saw that he was perfectly serious. "That's ridiculous and you know it."

"I know nothing of the kind. The two of you seemed quite oblivious to anyone else when we passed earlier."

I am always aware of you, she thought. "You have this habit of assuming that your interpretation of what you see is the absolute way of things, Jeremy. It really is annoying."

"My apologies." He leaned against the wagon.

Lucy ran through her options. She couldn't very well stay here indefinitely, and it was clear that he was prepared to wait her out. She stretched and yawned. "Well, it's late and I should get some rest."

He did not move. "Giving up so soon? There's still the possibility that Karl might . . . what? Have a visitor? Sneak off into the night? Why are you spying on Karl Oglethorpe?"

He had folded his arms across his chest, and it was apparent that he expected an answer.

"You're crazy," she said and turned to go.

He caught her arm; his touch was gentle but firm. "Am I? I'm not so daft that I would seriously consider the possibility of a romantic entanglement between you and Karl despite evidence to the contrary earlier. What's going on, Lucy?"

"Nothing."

"Very well. I shall escort you back to your compartment. I see that as usual you have abandoned your cane." He held out his arm to her and she had little choice but to take it.

They strolled along the river in silence.

"I understand that the doctor has agreed that you can return to performing in another week."

"Yes. I do hope there is still a place for me," she replied with sarcastic sweetness.

Jeremy took a deep breath and deliberately changed the subject. "There's a hint of autumn in the air tonight, don't you agree, Lucy?"

"It's August," she replied, accepting the shift in conversation.

"Nevertheless, there's something there. It seems quite impossible that the season has passed so quickly."

"And, successfully," Lucy added. "Mr. Porterfield must be delighted with the work you've done here. We've taken in a great deal of money this season already, and there's still Chicago."

"Adam is not a man who measures the value of a job until it is completed," Jeremy replied. "We shall see where things stand when the season closes."

They reached the juncture where the path met the street. Lucy knew that she should be satisfied with discussing the weather and other such matters, but she had never been one not to say exactly what was uppermost in her mind.

"What happened back in New York, Jeremy? I mean, what really happened?" For weeks, she had wondered about the circumstances that might have brought him to them. Now, she needed to know— wanted to reassure herself that what she and her parents were thinking could not possibly be true.

"I told you," he replied evasively. "I made a mistake."

"A mistake that got you banished to the wilds of Wisconsin must have been quite a blunder."

He chuckled. "Those were my very thoughts at the outset. I dreaded the trip and even more so the idea of enduring weeks and months here. The truth is, I have found the whole experience enormously rewarding."

"But, your . . . mistake . . ."

He halted, and since her arm was in his, so did she. "Will that make a difference, Lucy? If I tell you every sordid detail, will it change the way things are between us?"

Yes. No. I don't know, she thought, her mind racing. She tried to keep her voice calm. "That isn't the question."

He tightened his hold on her arm a fraction, forcing her to look at him. "I believe that it is the only question," he said softly.

They were standing in a pool of light cast by a street lamp. Half of his face was in shadow, the other half revealed by the golden glow of the light.

He looked at her and then up the street. He spotted a passing carriage for hire and hailed it.

"Jeremy . . ."

"We need to talk, Lucy, and we need a place where we will not be interrupted. If you want an answer to your question, you'll come with me."

Without another word, she climbed into the carriage. Jeremy handed the driver several bills. "Drive until I tell you otherwise, and then bring us back here," he instructed and then climbed in behind her and shut the carriage door.

Eleven

Jeremy sat across from her and gathered his thoughts. Finally, he took a deep breath and sat forward on the edge of the seat, his knees only a fraction of an inch from touching hers.

"The blunt fact is that I stole from others—including my own stepsister," he said, his eyes holding hers, forcing her to let him observe her reactions. "I could dress the facts up in language that would make the deed more palatable, but that is the real truth of it." He looked down for a moment and then back at her. "The wonder is that when I left New York and for some time thereafter, I truly believed that I was the wronged party."

"What has changed?" she asked.

"I'm not sure." He took her hand in his and looked deeply into her eyes. "What I do know is that it is very important to me that you have no doubts about me. For that reason I am going to tell you the whole story—every detail, details that even your father does not know."

She swallowed hard. Suddenly, she felt the urge to stop him, to tell him it didn't matter, for suddenly her worst fear was that once he had told her, it would matter a great deal. "Go on," she said finally.

It took nearly an hour for him to tell her the entire story. How he had determined to come to America to make a life for himself away from the control of his father. How he had first tricked Adam into believing that he had the skills to bring new business to Adam's firm. How he had also tricked Olivia and taken charge of her inheritance of a fine collection of jewelry at the same time—an inheritance that he would surely have squandered had he not later been duped by his own father into believing that the jewels were counterfeit. And finally, how he had moved money from one client's account to cover his investment in an operation that proved to be nothing more than a con man's talk. "The irony is that I was duped by my own kind—a fast-talker who had his own best interests at heart."

With each revelation, Lucy's heart sank. The pattern was there, and the shame of it was that he had done each of these things, thinking that he was not harming anyone—not really. His intentions had always been to make good. He would prove to his father that he could succeed on his own. His stepsister would reap the greater benefits of her jewels turned into a larger fortune, one that would allow them both to live lives of comfort in New York. Even in the last venture — the one that had ended with Adam Porterfield banishing him to Wisconsin—Jeremy's intentions had been virtuous. He had wanted to prove himself to Adam by increasing the man's fortune and success. How small a step was it from those actions to one in which he became convinced that it was his turn?

"Why?" she asked, knowing she was really asking about more than facts. It was motive she needed.

He shrugged. "I should like to be able to chalk it

up to immaturity, but I was a grown man well past the time for taking responsibility for my actions."

"And how did you view your assignment with my father?"

"In the beginning, it was a trial to be endured. I knew what I needed to achieve in order to redeem myself and get back to New York. Frankly, my initial intent was to prove to Adam that the circus was beyond redemption and needed to be sold."

"You miss New York a great deal, don't you?"

"Ah, Lucy, it's a wonderful place." His eyes shone.

"So, you would take whatever steps might be necessary to . . ."

He frowned and looked puzzled. "At the outset, yes, that was the way things were. But now . . ."

Her heart leaped. "Now?"

He touched her face with his fingertips. "I did not know your fine parents or your gifted brother then. I did not know you then," he replied. "*You* have made a difference, Lucy. It is your family who have made me appreciate the others and the work they do. But it is in *your* eyes that I aspire to shine—to prove myself truly worthy."

He signaled the driver to take them back, then leaned back in the seat. "And what do you think of me now, Lucy?"

Lucy did not know what to say. "I really need more time to digest all of this," she said finally.

"Very well," he replied softly, but he seemed saddened by her response.

When they returned to the circus grounds, he helped her down from the carriage but did not see her to the car that held her compartment. "I have a meeting and I fear I am already late," he explained. Then he smiled a little wistfully. "And you have all that thinking to do," he added as he lifted her hand to his lips and kissed it as a knight might a lady's.

There was not a single reason why she shouldn't accept that he was the culprit, Lucy told herself that Sunday as she sat at lunch with her parents and listened to them discussing the missing money. After all, the pattern of taking money and believing that he was doing so for the good of others was there in his past behavior. He had more access than anyone, even Harry.

Once Lucy told her parents that Jeremy had told her all about his problems in New York, Shirley saw no reason not to examine the background of Jeremy's banishment to the Conroy Cavalcade—and came to one conclusion.

"He had a choice," she explained. "He could make as much money as possible, then pour it all back into the circus to build the financial success of the business and its investors—including Adam Porterfield."

"Well, that way he would redeem his reputation with Adam and be welcomed back into the fold of the millionaire's business," Harry countered. "He could return to New York."

"On the other hand," Shirley continued, "if Jeremy made money and then took it for himself, he could establish his own business and build his *own* fortune. We've seen it all before, Harry, and let's don't forget what Lucy said about his wanting to prove himself to his father."

"I can't deny that Jeremy strikes me as the independent sort of man," Harry agreed with obvious reluctance. "Maybe he has seen his chance to go off on his own. It wouldn't be the first time that he went down that path. He walked out on a sure thing with his father, and if it hadn't been for Adam's forgiveness—would have repeated the mistake there—that's for sure."

"Exactly," Lucy insisted. "It's what got him into hot water before and that's just the reason I don't think he'd risk it again."

Shirley remained unconvinced. "You're not saying that he *didn't* take the money," she argued.

"No." Lucy felt cornered. "No, I can't say that . . . yet."

"There's no getting 'round the fact that Jeremy had the best chance," Harry reminded her gently.

"But he didn't do it," Lucy said. "I just know he didn't." Her voice caught. "He . . . he couldn't. . . ." She looked from her mother to her father for verification.

"Now, honey, we'd all like to be wrong, but . . ."

"I'll prove you wrong," she vowed quietly and left the room.

She walked the river path to the far end of the train, where Jeremy could be found every day including Sundays when he wasn't off on some advance trip. She wondered how she could be so certain of Jeremy's innocence. After all, the evidence did point squarely in his direction. Shirley and Harry were always willing to give a person the benefit of the doubt. That's why they hadn't called in the police yet. If they were sure, then who was she to think that she knew better?

She suddenly thought about their very first performance of the season, when they had succeeded beyond his highest expectations. Then there was that night when she had drawn him into the group. She had seen his face—seen his delight at being one of them. And what about the night of the storm? No one had been more concerned about the safety of the audience and performers. If he'd been making money to take money, wouldn't he be upset about *losing* money because of the storm? They had paid out refunds that night to every person. No one had asked for a refund, but Jeremy had insisted. She had seen him take the money box to town himself.

Her confidence faltered for the first time. Had he taken that money and pocketed it? No one would have been the wiser, for the train had already moved on. Jeremy had stayed behind and caught up to them later. They really wouldn't know if he'd refunded money or not.

"No," she whispered firmly to herself, refusing to believe the evidence she had just produced. "Well, there's nothing to do but go to the source," she said aloud.

She passed the animal corrals and several unoccupied cars until she reached his. She opened the door and stepped inside as he looked up from a pile of papers scattered across his elegant desk.

"You have a problem," she said.

"And good afternoon to you, Miss Conroy," he replied with a wry smile. He pushed the leather swivel chair away from his desk and stretched without rising. "As much as I always look forward to seeing you, Lucy, I have a great deal of work to attend to before we arrive in Chicago, and Sundays are—"

"That can wait." She was growing exasperated with his calm appraisal of her. She folded her arms and tapped her foot impatiently.

"I take note that you have indicated that I have a problem—not *we* as in the entire company?"

"This is nothing to joke about," she said.

"Very well, why don't you take a seat and tell me about this problem that I seem to have and yet of which I know nothing." He indicated a chair and folded his hands behind his head as he continued to smile at her. "Might I assume that this has something to do with your need to think about my explanation of my past?"

She sat on the edge of a low-backed leather chair across from him and took a deep breath. "Money is missing from the till. A lot of money. Shirley is certain that you have taken it. Harry is less certain but not convinced that you didn't."

He arched one eyebrow but, other than that, made no move. "And what do you believe, Lucy?"

She swallowed and then met his gaze directly. "I think that you are innocent, but I also think that if you don't act quickly, it will not matter what I think."

"Why would you believe in me when your parents do not?"

"I . . . *Did* you take the money?"

"Absolutely not." He picked up his pen and pulled a stack of papers closer. He began signing papers, then glanced up. "Was there something more?"

She was staring at him openmouthed. "Have you heard a word of this? People—people who are quite close to Adam Porterfield—believe that you are stealing money from this operation."

He nodded. "I heard you and I shall handle it. Now, if there is nothing more . . ."

The only clue that what she had told him had affected him in any way was the way he was gripping that pen. A pool of ink spread out from the point, soiling the pristine white paper. His knuckles were white and the pen shook from the force of his grip.

"Jeremy," she said softly. Then she moved around

the desk and gripped his shoulders. "Jeremy, we'll find out what's happening," she promised him.

He released the pen and then covered her hand on his shoulder. "I've known about this for a week or more now. I thought I could uncover the thief and no one would be the wiser. Lucy, I cannot . . . Adam will never believe me . . . if it happens again, he'll think . . ." He shook his head slowly from side to side. "How did your parents discover it?"

"They were worried about how much cash we have accumulated. I think they were especially concerned about going into Chicago with so much in the safe. They decided it would be wise to deposit the money on hand before we reached Chicago. How did you discover it?"

"I was thinking along those same lines. I was actually going to suggest to Harry that it would make sense, so I counted the cash one night and something seemed off so I checked it against the books, and . . ." He threw up his hands. "I would do anything not to have Harry doubt me, Lucy. His respect—his trust—they've been everything to me."

"Then we'll just have to find the real thief," she said as she cradled his head against her and stroked his hair.

"Why would you do that, Lucy? Why would you believe me above your parents?"

Because I love you. "Because, even though you can be incredibly dense one moment and arrogant the next, you have worked hard and you have made a difference—for all of us."

He looked up at her, his eyes full of a mixture of hope, disbelief, and gratitude.

"We should get started," she said, easing her hand free of his. "I really am not sure how we should go about this," she said nervously. She turned away from him, unable to look at him. She didn't want his gratitude. "And one more thing, Jeremy," she said.

He lifted his eyebrows expectantly.

"You'd better *not* be the thief." It was her turn to arch an eyebrow as she waited for his response.

"I am innocent."

"Very well. Then we have a thief to find."

Lucy's first action was to go back to her parents. She was relieved to find them together, checking the work of the crew in repairing the canvas as they prepared for the coming week of performances. She begged them not to contact either the authorities or Adam Porterfield.

"But Lucy, if Jeremy is the one . . ." Shirley said.

"He isn't," Lucy insisted.

"Still," Harry said, "we'd be shirking responsibility not to at least let Adam know that there's cause for concern on some front."

"I'm asking you to let Jeremy and me handle it."

Shirley and Harry looked at their daughter for a long moment. She rarely asked for anything. In all the time she had been with them, neither of them could think of a single time when she had stood against them.

"Besides, if it turns out to be Jeremy," Lucy said, thinking she needed to build her case, "then now that he knows we're wise to the missing money, perhaps he'll stop."

"Or perhaps he's smarter than that, Lucy," Harry said. "Perhaps the money will go on missing so that we are led to believe that someone else must be the culprit."

Lucy blinked. She could think of no argument for that except to say quietly and with fierce conviction, "The thief is *not* Jeremy."

Harry and Shirley glanced at each other. "We'll deposit the money we have now and give it a week," Harry said. "If you've identified the thief by that time, then that's that. But if we're no closer to knowing who took the money—regardless of whether or not money continues to disappear—then I will contact Adam . . . and the authorities."

Lucy understood that these were the best terms she could hope to win. She nodded. "Agreed," she said and felt an immediate sense of panic at the thought that they had only seven short days to solve the mystery—less if one counted the fact that neither she nor Jeremy could be expected to work on figuring things out during performances. "If we haven't found the thief by the time we play Chicago, then I'll contact Adam Porterfield myself."

Within minutes she was back in Jeremy's office. "We haven't got much time," she said tersely as she pulled her chair close to his desk. She took up his pen and began to write down what they already knew—which wasn't much. She tapped the pen impatiently, started a list, scribbled through it, and started another.

He placed his hand over hers, effectively stopping her frantic writing. "It's important that you be thoroughly convinced, Lucy—important to me that you not doubt me."

"I don't," she said passionately, knowing that she was doing absolutely nothing to disguise her love and devotion.

"All right then, we will solve this little problem." He stood and came around the desk and offered her his hand. "However, I believe that such serious work should be conducted in a more soothing atmosphere. Will you share a light supper with me in the observation room?"

She sighed with exasperation. "Jeremy, this is very important."

He simply arched one eyebrow.

"Oh, very well, we'll eat, but then we work."

"Yes, ma'am." Jeremy rang for Ezra and ordered for them both. As soon as Ezra left, he turned to Lucy. "Please, Lucy, I wonder if you would excuse me for just a moment. I have an errand to handle. I'll be back shortly."

She watched openmouthed as he left her standing there. She had no idea where he was headed, and he had left so quickly that it had never occurred to her to offer to go with him. She wandered into the observation room. The late-afternoon sun cast a golden glow over the plush surroundings. Lucy settled into one large overstuffed chair. She could not help but recall the last time she had been with Jeremy in this room.

"Concentrate," she admonished herself. She forced herself to consider who else might have had the opportunity to take money. She needed to look beyond the obvious. Perhaps if she made a chart of every member of the company and their movements over the past several weeks . . . She hurried back to Jeremy's desk and rummaged through the drawer for a pencil.

She reached far into the back of the drawer for the pencil that had rolled away, and pulled the contents toward her. There was the pencil. And there was also a lavender envelope with Jeremy's name written across it in flowery script.

Curious, she pulled the envelope out and caught a

whiff of the scent of it. There could be no mistaking that perfume. *Eleanore.* What possible reason might Eleanore have to write a personal note to Jeremy?

Lucy slid the single tissue-thin sheet from the envelope.

> *My darling Jeremy,*
>   *You cannot possibly understand what your special attentiveness and kindness have meant to me these last few weeks. I hope it will not embarrass you to know that the times we have spent together have made my life not only bearable but thrilling. Is it too much to say that you have brought me alive? That your plans for the future have touched me deeply? I know that you must take care not to upset others, but please know that I remain willing to accept whatever favors you choose to impart . . . whenever you may choose to impart them.*
>   *Always, E*

Lucy felt sick with doubt. Had Shirley been right? Had he indeed fooled her? Fooled all of them? She cast about for memories of Jeremy and Eleanore together: the shared looks, the seemingly innocent touch of a hand or shoulder. Had his avoiding Eleanore's gesture to smooth back his hair that day in the pie car been merely a warning to her that she was becoming too obvious? And last night when he had left Lucy after their carriage ride, saying he was late for an appointment, was that to meet Eleanore?

"Damn," she muttered as she stuffed the letter inside its scented envelope and laid it back inside the drawer. Then, immediately, she retrieved it. Perhaps she should confront him with it, demand an explanation. But on what basis?

A light knock at the door decided the matter for

her. She dropped the letter as if it had burned her fingers, and slammed the drawer shut just as Ezra opened the door and smiled.

"I have your supper here, miss."

"Yes, thank you, Ezra. We'll take it in there." She indicated the observation room. The steward nodded and rolled the cart down the hallway.

Alone again, she studied the pencil and blank paper she'd left on the desk. For one instant, she couldn't recall why she had wanted them in the first place. The only item of interest was that lavender note. Even if she looked upon it as another of Eleanore's ploys to endear herself to Jeremy, why had he kept it?

"Everything's all laid out, miss," Ezra said as he rolled the cart back toward the door. "Will you be wanting me to serve?"

"No, thank you." She smiled and kept smiling until the man had left the room.

"So awfully sorry to have left you alone like that, Lucy," Jeremy said as he came through the door and shut it behind him.

She shrugged. "I managed." She saw that he was confused at the change in her demeanor, and chastised herself for being unable to disguise her feelings.

"Are you upset because I did not tell you my mission?"

"I'm not upset," she replied lightly. "Our supper is waiting. I came in here to find a pencil and some paper. I thought we might want to make a chart."

"A chart?"

"Yes. We could list every member of the company and see who might have had opportunity. By placing everyone on a chart, we would have all of our facts in one place."

Jeremy smiled. "That's a smashingly good idea, Lucy."

She could not help but feel a tug of pleasure at his praise, but forced herself to suppress it. "Well, we'd best get started."

"Shall we?" He relieved her of the paper and pencil and offered her his arm to escort her to the other room.

"Really, Jeremy, it's completely . . ."

"Necessary," he said firmly. "Chivalry in the presence of a lady is always required. Ah, doesn't this look inviting?" He pulled out a chair for her and sat opposite her at the small table set with white linen and fine silver and china. "Wine?" he offered, holding the bottle over her crystal goblet.

"Sure." Eleanore would surely take wine, wouldn't she? There was no way that Lucy was going to play the Wisconsin hayseed to Eleanore's worldly woman.

"I went to see your parents," he said after they had filled their plates and started to eat.

"Why?"

"Because I wanted to thank them for allowing us this opportunity to clear my name, and I wanted to assure them that your faith in me is not misplaced."

She continued eating. It was a very kind thing to do . . . or perhaps a very clever one.

"Are you having second thoughts?" he asked after several minutes had passed with no comment from her.

"Not at all."

"It's just that when you arrived here earlier you seemed quite intent on getting our plan in order as quickly as possible. Yet suddenly . . ."

"You were the one who wanted a delay," she reminded him. "To have supper?"

"Ah, yes." He took a swallow of his wine. "Lucy, I am not quite as in the dark as you seem to think I am."

Lucy knew that he was waiting for her to comment, but she remained silent.

Jeremy rose and began placing their dishes onto the serving tray. "As I mentioned, I have known about the stolen funds. At first, I thought that I must be missing something in the figures. I'm afraid that my pride would not permit me to go to Harry with any question, so I continued to try and account for the discrepancy myself."

"But you know now that the money has been stolen," Lucy said. "Then you must have some idea about who . . ."

Jeremy smiled. "I have my theories, but they make no sense and I have been unable to verify any of them."

Lucy brushed the crumbs from the tablecloth and deposited them onto the stacked plates. "Well, if we're to get any work done, we should begin," she said.

Jeremy nodded. "I'll just take these to the other room and get the ledger for the season."

When he had taken the tray and left, Lucy felt the train move. They were on their way to the next stop. She let out a deep sigh. The shift of the train from the side track to the main one was executed with barely a pause in motion. The familiar rhythm of the train traversing each section of track seemed to remind her over and over again that their week had begun—by this time next week, they would be in Chicago. Would they also have uncovered the real thief?

Twelve

Lucy remained lost in thought as she stood facing the windows and absorbing the beauty of the pinks and purples that streaked the clouds as the sun sank below the horizon.

"It is quite magnificent, isn't it?" Jeremy commented as he came to stand next to her. "I especially love being in here at night when the train is in motion. Something about the movement increases the magic." He placed his hands on her shoulders. "Lucy," he said, his mouth close and warm to her ear.

She did not move or speak.

"Are you upset with me because you found the note from Eleanore?"

"I don't . . ."

"The drawer to my desk was not closed all the way—her note was caught in the opening."

"I was just unaware that you and Eleanore shared a correspondence," she replied. "It seemed unnecessary, given her inclination to be wherever you are. And, of course, a relationship with her could make things awkward for you, since at this point no one can be above suspicion."

"I have a relationship with *you*, Lucy—one that I am very much in favor of deepening. Eleanore is . . . an employee."

"I think she might disagree."

Jeremy chuckled. "You don't deny reading the note, then?"

Lucy shrugged. "I'm not in the habit of lying."

"And that is one of the many attributes about you that I admire, Lucy." His face was even closer to hers now. His breath was a breeze tickling her temple. She made a move to step away. "Stay," he whispered.

She wanted desperately to do as he asked, and yet she could not get beyond the fact that he had turned the conversation to complimenting her rather than denying that Eleanore meant more to him than he was willing to admit.

She made the mistake of turning toward him when he wouldn't release her. "Jeremy, if we are to work on this together, then there is—"

"Eleanore is nothing to me, Lucy. She has tried various techniques—crude as they are. The fact is that there was a time when I would have found her thinly veiled attempts at seducing me amusing. There was a time when I would have thought nothing of taking whatever she might be willing to offer and doing so with no regrets and no thought of who else might be hurt in the process."

He held her with his gaze as well as his hands lightly touching her shoulders. He steadied her as the train navigated a turn.

"What has changed you?" she asked.

"You," he replied and swept her fully into his embrace. "Let me show you, Lucy, that you have no rival . . . you have no equal. It is you who has captured my heart completely."

"We have work . . ."

He shushed her and drew her a fraction of an inch closer. "Ah, Lucy, I learned long ago that problems keep very well until tomorrow in most cases. Of far more importance at the moment is that I erase any doubt you may have about my feelings for you."

"I accept that Eleanore—"

"Eleanore be damned," he growled and lowered his mouth to hers.

With that kiss, the reservoir of her resistance broke. Whatever would come—whether she had him only for tonight or for this week or longer—in this moment he was hers to love, and she would seize that moment.

As soon as she returned his kiss, it was as if the world and its cares evaporated. There was only the two of them. The movements of their mouths and hands and bodies were uncoordinated, even awkward. They halfwaltzed and halfstumbled the short distance to the window seat. By the time they reached it, he had pulled free the combs holding her hair and she had pushed his suit coat free of his shoulders. He allowed it to fall to the floor and turned his attention to opening the tiny pearl buttons that held her shirtwaist closed at her throat.

As he reached the lowest buttons, he tugged the blouse free of her waistband and spread the fabric open as he bent to kiss the tops of her breasts pressed tight against the neckline of her chemise. When she wove her fingers into his hair and pressed him closer, he shuddered and she felt a sense of power and confidence like as none she had ever known.

She moved her hands to his shoulders and hooked her thumbs under his braces. When she pushed them off, he looked at her.

"You're playing a dangerous game, Lucy," he warned, and there was no levity in his tone.

"I enjoy danger," she reminded him.

He sat back and pulled his arms free of his suspenders, then removed his tie and collar and unfastened his cuffs. All the time, he watched her. She did not avert her eyes. He pulled his shirt free of his trousers, and still she only watched. Slowly he opened his shirt, and as he did she placed her palms against his bare skin and ran her fingers over the planes of his chest, around to his back.

"Stop that," he said when she thumbed his nipples as he had done hers.

She smiled and did not stop.

"There's no net, Lucy," he warned as he reached below the hem of her skirt and ran his palm hard over her inner thigh and up to just below the flat of her stomach. "You'll have to see it through."

She arched. "I've been working without a net for some time now," she reminded him.

"Not at this height," he reminded her as he found the opening of her undergarment.

When he touched her damp center, Lucy sucked in her breath even as she cast about for some way to make him feel the same thrill and danger she was experiencing. She moved her flattened palm down his chest, stroking him again and again, each time moving closer to the waist of his trousers, allowing just the tips of her fingers to breach that barrier before moving her hand up again.

His eyes glittered with passion. "Come here," he growled as he pulled her to him. In a few expert moves, he had stripped her of her blouse and opened her chemise until she was fully exposed to him. He took his time then, ravishing first one breast and then the other with his open mouth and tongue and teeth, suckling, nibbling, and generally driving her to the edge of ecstasy before pulling away and standing.

He kicked off his shoes and opened the waist of his trousers but did not completely undress. Instead, he pulled her to her feet and began opening her skirt and the hooks and eyes of her petticoat.

"You're very good at this," she said breathlessly.

"Yes, I am," he replied as he pushed the garments past her hips. "Does that alarm you, Miss Conroy?"

"A little," she managed through ragged breaths. "I'll get past it." She took a step toward him, kicking free of her clothing, and pressing the length of her body to his.

She could feel his arousal through the only remaining barriers—his trousers and the thin cotton of her drawers. Her naked breasts were flattened against the hardness of his muscular chest. Their mouths collided and melded. She felt him pressing her hips to his. She ran her palms over his bare back and down until she plunged them beneath the waist of his trousers to urge him closer still.

He pulled his mouth free of hers and stared at her. "You're sure?"

I love you, she wanted to scream, but she only said, "I want you to make love to me."

He lifted her and instinctively she wrapped her legs around his waist and hips as he carried her down the passageway to his bedroom, where he paused only to close and lock the door.

Perhaps it was abstinence and the frustrations of those times when they had resisted consummation that drove them. Perhaps it was longing to know each other to the very core. Neither of them thought about motive as they tore at each remaining item of clothing and then fell across the bed, their arms and legs entwined. They uttered no words, using only their hands and mouths to communicate. Jeremy straddled her, and only then did their frantic thrashing cease.

"Last chance," he whispered.

She reached up and cupped his face with both hands. "Or maybe it's only the first chance," she said as she pulled him down to meet her kiss.

Lucy had been witness to the couplings of enough circus livestock and had been privy to enough dressing room gossip to know the rudiments of the act. She bent her knees, opening herself to him. She knew what he would do next, but nothing could have possibly prepared her for what she would feel when he did it.

First came the sensation of probing, and her body voluntarily lifted to his. Then he pushed, but nothing seemed to fit. He made a move to pull away, but she dug her nails into his hips, demanding that he stay.

"Lucy!" His voice was raspy, and she opened her eyes to find him staring at her with a look of surprise. "You're . . . you've never . . ."

She wondered if it mattered to him. Did it work better with a more experienced woman? *Well, of course it does. Don't be an idiot.* "I'm sorry," she whispered and turned her face away.

"Sorry for giving yourself to me when you could have . . . when you must have had every opportunity to . . ." He kissed her with a passion that she would never have thought possible, given what they had already shared. "You must be absolutely certain that this is what you want, love. That it is I on whom you wish to bestow this gift." He was actually frowning to impress upon her the seriousness of the occasion and his genuine sincerity in asking the question.

"I'm certain," she replied.

"I shall not be able to manage gentleness," he warned, "for I fear we passed that point some time ago."

"I don't care."

"It will hurt—at first, it might hurt a great deal, but only for an instant."

She nodded, her eyes wide with anxiety. "Please, don't hold back on my account," she said. "I want to please you."

His expression softened to the point that she thought he might actually weep. "Oh, my lovely Lucinda, you please me more than I can begin to say."

He kissed her with a slow, agonizing thoroughness while massaging her entire body with his large, warm hands. Lightly he skimmed his hands over her breasts and down to her hips, then around to her inner thighs and up and inside her. She did not know when the probing tip of his penis replaced his fingers, for she had relaxed and begun to enjoy his pleasuring her with nothing more than his fingers.

He rolled with her until she sat astride him, and in that moment the entire length of him slid past the tight barrier nature had armed her with, and claimed her for his own.

Jeremy knew the exact second that he had torn her, saw the look of shock widen her dark eyes as she straddled him, saw her mouth—swollen by his kisses—form the startled gasp. He ran his palms up her thighs and on to her breasts, forcing her concentration away from the pain and back to pleasure.

He remained still, filling her and throbbing with a need for release that bordered on agony.

When he saw her eyes dilate with pleasure, heard her soft murmuring of need, he began to move. She tried to bend to him, her hair falling over them both like a canopy, but he wanted to watch her, to see her reaction as he moved her to the next level of desire.

"Tell me what to do," she whimpered. "I . . ." She flailed her hands about in frustration.

"Sh-h-h." He pushed her hair back from her face. "Trust me."

He placed his hands on her waist and pushed the last distance inside her, pulled almost free, and smiled as she tightened to hold him inside. "That's it," he whispered and then gave up on words as his traitorous body declared a will of its own and he thrust up and in harder and faster, until he felt the coming at last of the release he sought. He tried pulling free of her in that last instant, but she thwarted his intention by falling over him, stretching her legs, and moving them inside his to hold him there. "Lucy, no," he whispered, but even as he spoke the words, he knew that it was too late.

He understood that her move had been pure instinct and without guile. Knew that she had little inkling of what might result from her rash action.

She was crying silently. No sound, but he could feel her tears on his chest.

"I'm sorry," she said when he stroked her hair. "I only thought . . . I wanted so to . . ."

He chuckled, a deep rumbling in his chest, which had the effect he expected. She raised herself onto her elbow and stared at him. She was furious.

"Well, it's not as if . . ." Her eyes widened again. "Oh my stars!" she whispered and turned away from him. She sat up suddenly and moved to the edge of the bed. "Oh, no . . ."

He touched her shoulder. Now she was crying in earnest. "Lie down."

"There's blood, but it's not that time . . . I mean . . ."

He could hear in her voice her feeling of complete embarrassment and mortification.

"It's not that, Lucy," he assured her. "There's always a little bleeding the first time. It will heal quickly. Now, lie down."

She flopped back onto the pillows while he went to the small toilet and turned on the water. Returning to the bed, he sat beside her and began to wash her.

"I can do it," she protested and tried to sit up.

"Be still," he ordered and continued to gently clean away her blood mingled with his semen. He dried her with a soft towel and then set the linens on the floor.

"Come here," he urged, pulling her into his arms as he settled back into the bed with her. He pulled the covers high enough for her to cover her breasts. "Now, you listen to me, my little angel of the big top. Making love is not a performance. It is two people giving pleasure to each other. With any luck at all, it results in both of them giving and receiving that pleasure. In our case, I fear that I have been the recipient of a great deal of pleasure while neglecting you."

"Oh, no, Jeremy." She looked up at him. "It was quite . . ."

"It can be better," he said tenderly and knew the minute their eyes met that he was far from ready to say that this particular session of lovemaking had reached its end. "Shall I demonstrate?" he whispered against her ear.

She shivered with anticipation and he smiled. "I

promise you won't regret it," he added, eliciting the response he had anticipated. Lucy curled more tightly against him.

"I'm not sure that we should."

"Suppose we begin, and at any point you may simply say that I am to stop . . . or push ever so gently against me, and I will cease. All right?"

She smiled and gave him a playful punch to his side. "You know how I love to try daring new things. You are only trying to serve your own needs by playing upon my weakness."

"You are in complete control," he vowed. "You have my word."

"Show me the start of it," she said, curious in spite of herself.

"These matters usually begin with a kiss." He kissed her so tenderly that when he pulled away, she clung to him.

"And then?"

"Touching and abstinence—the combination assures a certain level of titillation."

"Like this?" she said playfully as she ran her palm over his chest and down across the flat of his stomach.

He caught her hand just before she reached her target, and held it firmly. "No, love. In this particular situation, I touch—you abstain."

"All right," she agreed and lay back on the pillows, her hands folded behind her head, the covers fallen to expose her breasts.

He smiled, pulled the covers away entirely, and moved over her. He captured her hands in his and held them above her head. "Just a precaution," he assured her. Then, with his free hand he began an erotic massage designed to have her writhing beneath him within a matter of moments.

"Jeremy . . . Jeremy . . ." She repeated his name as she flailed her head from side to side.

"Shall I stop?" he asked as he bent and took one nipple into his mouth. At that moment he released her hands and felt them immediately entwine in his hair, holding him to her.

He moved his other hand down her side, around and across her hipbone until he felt the soft down of her hair at the juncture of her thighs. Her lower body bolted upward to receive his touch.

He moved his attention to the other breast and slid his fingers inside her. In no time at all, she was chanting now a single plea.

"Please . . . please . . ."

He had brought her to the very edge of her passion. Normally, he would have smiled at his expertise in such matters. Hers had been achieved in record time, but there was one unanticipated problem.

For the very first time in his experience, she—using nothing more than her fingers in his hair and her chanted plea—had also succeeded in bringing him back to the verge in that same record time.

He redoubled his efforts as he expertly manipulated the core of her passion, driving her ever closer to the edge.

"Come. Let it go," he urged her as he looked up at her lidded eyes watching him with undisguised adoration.

"I want you with me," she replied.

"It doesn't work that way, love," he assured her with an attempt at a laugh. But, his body had betrayed him completely. It would work that way. With Lucy it could only work that way.

She tenderly brushed back his hair and all was lost. In a motion as smooth as any he had ever seen

her perform in midair, he was covering her, filling
her, holding her as they both surrendered at the
same moment.

When Lucy woke, she was alone. The room was
dark and she had no idea what time it was. She sat
up and saw Jeremy's silk dressing gown spread across
the chair next to the bed, along with fresh linens and
a bar of sandalwood soap. She took everything with
her into the small toilet.

Perhaps there was time for her to dress and return
to her compartment, as if she'd simply fallen asleep
while reading in the pie car. Of course, no one
would have seen her there, and Trixie would know.

As she washed herself and considered her predica-
ment, she could not help but take stock of the marks
of Jeremy's lovemaking. Marks that were both physical and emotional. There on her breasts were the
marks, red as ripe strawberries, from his sucking
kisses that had left her breathless. There on the insides of her thighs was the beginning of bruising
where he had tried to pull away and she had held
him. When she moved, she ached as she might ache
after a long period without performing. And, when
she looked into the mirror, she saw an indefinable
difference. Her lips reminded her only of his kiss.
Just before sashing the robe, she studied her naked
body. Even if her skin had remained unblemished,
she knew that he had claimed her in a way that no
man would ever be able to fully banish.

She pulled the robe closed and tied the sash
tightly, and the fabric sliding against itself produced
the faint scent of tobacco and a spicy cologne that
was uniquely Jeremy.

He was sitting on the bed when she emerged from the toilet. He wore only his trousers, still unbuttoned at the waist. His naked torso and bare feet made him seem more vulnerable than she might have anticipated. He kept his head slightly lowered as he looked up at her.

"Are you all right?" he asked.

"Yes."

He kept his eyes averted. "I brought your clothes. They're just there, on the chair." He stood and started toward the door. "I've prepared tea in the galley if you'd like some."

"Yes, please." Her heart sank. He regretted it—all of it.

"Jeremy, look at me."

"I can't," he said and then stood tall and straight, his hand on the doorknob, his back to her. "If I look at you, I shall want you all over again, and I have to go." He opened the door without giving her any opportunity to respond and closed it behind him.

Lucy dressed with a heart full of joy and delight. He wanted her. She pulled on her undergarments and swept her hair high into a chignon. He desired her. She donned her skirt and shirtwaist and fastened the buttons all the way to her throat. And then, she paused. But he did not love her. A man like him would not love a woman like her. He was, after all, nobility in his native England, and even if he spent the rest of his days in his adopted America, he would want to spend them in New York or some other city where he could take his rightful place in society.

Lucy sat on the edge of the bed and fingered his robe. Then she clutched it to her breast and buried her face in it. An affair would be the best she could manage. And now, Lucy knew that it would never be enough.

By the time she had dressed and worked up her courage to face him, Jeremy was also fully dressed. He had set up her tea in the compact galley kitchen.

"Lucy, there was a message under the door. It seems that one of the elephants has taken quite ill. Your parents have been in attendance, and now that we've arrived, they've called for the local veterinarian. I . . ."

"Of course. Go," she urged.

He nodded and took his hat from the carved stand near the door. He glanced back at her, then in three strides covered the distance necessary to reach her, and swept her into his arms for a searing kiss. "I shall see you later, love," he promised and was gone.

If only he would not call her that: *love*. It made things so much more difficult. Lucy gulped down the hot tea and tore off pieces of the roll he'd left for her. She heard the familiar sounds of the crew managing the livestock and setting up for the day's parade. Then it hit her: a sick elephant—it might be Cora; it could only be Cora. Jeremy would have named any of the others, but he had spared her. Uncaring of who saw her coming from Jeremy's car at such an hour, she raced outside and ran alongside the cars until she reached the point where they were unloading the livestock.

"Where's Cora?" she asked everyone she passed.

Most professed not to know, with a shrug of shoulders as they hurried on their way. A few looked away and became suspiciously involved in waving or calling out to another roustabout. Lucy quickened her step as her heart raced. Soon she was running toward the open door of the car that she knew carried Cora.

"Hey, Corabelle," she said softly as she reached the car and saw the gigantic pachyderm lying on her side. Harry and the vet looked up at her entrance. Shirley stood in a corner, wiping her nose and eyes with a wadded handkerchief. Jeremy moved to intercept Lucy.

"She's gone, Luce," Harry said. His hand was resting on Cora's flank. The tanned, weathered skin of the man not all that different from the leathery hide of the animal.

"No," Lucy whispered and sank to her knees next to Cora's head. "What happened?"

"Not sure," the vet replied. "Could have just been her time. She was getting up there, you know, and the stress of traveling and performing—well, it might just have finally been too much for the old girl." He, too, patted Cora's side, then began packing his equipment into his black leather satchel. "Should I make arrangements?" he asked Harry after he had accepted his coat and hat from Shirley with a nod.

"Give us a bit of time, if you please," Jeremy replied before Harry could say anything. He remained standing protectively near Lucy.

"Oh, Cora," Lucy said softly. "I'm going to miss you so." She stroked Cora's huge, flat ear. "I can't imagine the show without you. I can't imagine my life . . ." She broke down and sobbed.

"Cora's been her favorite from the day we brought her home from the orphanage," Harry explained.

"Well, folks, you let me know if there's anything I can do," the vet said as he prepared to leave.

"Do you know an excellent taxidermist?" Jeremy asked.

There was a long moment of silence—incredulous silence.

"You're thinking of having this beast stuffed?" the vet finally said.

"You're joking," Lucy said, showing a hint of the anger she had tried to suppress—anger that Jeremy would think this was the right time or place for levity.

Jeremy shook his head. "Just hear me out, Lucy. What if Cora could be with you—always? What if at every performance, she was there?"

Lucy looked from her father to her mother. Shirley nodded. "Cora has always been the star of the menagerie, Lucy, and this way she would still be the star."

"Makes sense to me," the vet said. "She's one of the finest specimens I've ever seen. Keeping her in the show will give folks the chance to see just how big these babies can get. Why, they'll be able to walk right up to her, touch her—makes a lot of sense." He picked up his bag and turned to go. "I'll do some checking and get back to you." He tipped his hat to the women and left.

Lucy barely heard or saw him. She was staring at her beloved Cora. The elephant was the closest thing she'd ever had to a household pet. Cora had been there every day of her life with the Conroys. As a child she'd ridden Cora around the grounds, stood on her back, performed some of her first tricks with Cora. She had confided all of her secrets, all of her longings to Cora. She had even been trying to imag-

ine how she might take Cora with her when she left
the show for that little country place on Lake Michigan.

"Does Ian know?" she asked.

"Yeah." Harry knelt next to her and laid his hand
on her shoulder. "You okay with this idea, Lucy?"

She shrugged and stroked Cora's fan-shaped ear.
"I guess in a way she'll still be with us," she said.

"'Cause the final decision is yours—this ain't
about business," Shirley told her.

Jeremy also knelt next to her. "Lucy, if you'd
rather, we can have Cora shipped back to Delavan to
be buried there. We'll order a proper marker and
hold services the minute we return at the end of the
season."

"On the other hand," Harry continued, "if having Cora along helps . . ."

Lucy mustered a smile. "Cora has always been one
of our main attractions," she said. "I see no reason
for that to change if we can help it. She did so love
being the center of attention."

"If you're sure," Jeremy said, touching her shoulder.

"Just go find the taxidermist," she replied without
looking at him.

She was pretty sure that both parents had
breathed a sigh of relief, or maybe it was just exhaustion from trying to save Cora all night. "You two
should get some rest," she said, standing and brushing the straw from her skirt. "Go on. I'll stay here
until Jeremy gets back. I don't want to see either one
of you until this afternoon, okay?"

Harry grinned. "Bossy little thing, aren't you?
Wonder where she gets that?" he asked Shirley.

Shirley just smiled and then hugged Lucy. "I'm so

sorry, honey. She was like one of the family, and it'll take some time, but you're doing the right thing letting Jeremy have her stuffed."

"You two go on, now, and get some rest."

Harry nodded to Shirley, who left, and then he turned to Lucy. "Any progress in this missing-money matter when you met with Jeremy last night?"

Lucy's heart sank. Did her father know what she and Jeremy had done? What she had permitted? What she had *enjoyed*? "We talked about it and we're working on a plan to catch the thief," she assured him. "Remember, you promised me a week."

"I know, but . . ."

"Papa, you promised."

Harry nodded reluctantly. "It's just that this last sum was pretty substantial. We can't afford that kind of loss, Lucy. If it is Jeremy . . ."

"It isn't," she said firmly. *It can't be.*

Thirteen

Jeremy barely saw Lucy for the next two days. He was well aware of the urgency to identify the thief in their midst, but getting the troupe prepared for Chicago was more important at the moment. Cora's death had been a major setback for the company. She was the largest elephant in any circus of their size, and they had relied on that fact for years as a way to sell tickets. The idea of stuffing the beast had come to him as much out of sheer instinct to survive as from any sort of ingenious plan. He and Ian had managed to locate an expert in the field of taxidermy, and Ian assured him that the man was working day and night to complete the transformation by their opening performance.

"Got a minute, boss?"

Wally Wiggins stood looking up at him, his trademark cigar unlit and firmly ensconced in the corner of his mouth.

"Is there a problem?"

"Nope. Got an idea." He pulled a crumpled and soiled piece of paper from his coat pocket and spread it out for Jeremy to see.

In the center was a crude drawing of an elephant. Jeremy guessed the genus of the beast by the evidence of a long, disproportionate trunk. Next to it was an equally crude rendering of a cannon.

"I'm at a loss, old boy," Jeremy admitted after studying the drawing for a long moment.

"This is me," Wally said pointing to a stick figure half in and half out of the cannon. "This is Cora." He punched the cannon and then Cora and then repeated the action.

Jeremy began to smile. "It's bloody inspired!" he said.

Wally grinned up at him. "My thoughts exactly, Jeremy. Can I do it?"

"The ability to do it is a question I must ask of you."

Wally looked confused.

"That is," Jeremy continued, "*can* you do it? Can you actually make the leap from your cannon to Cora's back?"

"Well, sure," Wally replied. "I wouldn't be talking about it if I couldn't do it."

"Then you may do it."

Wally began to squirm uncomfortably. "There ain't a lot of time here for 'may' or 'might.' I gotta know one way or another, Jeremy. Can I or can't I?"

To Wally's obvious astonishment, his boss laughed. "Wally Wiggins, you have my complete permission to proceed with your brilliant plan. As a matter of fact, let's open the show with it. That way we can already have Cora in place with a spotlight. Then you come bursting forth and announce the opening from high atop our beloved Cora. Yes, that's the ticket."

Wally beamed. "Do you mean it? Me—opening the show? Me?"

Jeremy nodded.

Wally grabbed his hand and pumped it heartily.

"Thank you, sir. Thank you." He hurried off in the direction of the dressing area and then turned again. "Thank you."

Jeremy was still standing there smiling long after Wally had disappeared. He felt something he had been distantly aware of feeling for some time now, but here it was full-force. He was happy.

He really could not recall ever having experienced that unique combination of satisfaction with the present along with anticipation of the future. Oh, there were complications to be sure, but they simply added to the sense of wholeness in his life.

Quite by accident he had been thrust into a career that suited him beyond anything he might have dreamed for himself. On top of that, he had met the one woman capable of making him actually consider the benefits to be had in the sort of conventional life that included a wife and children. Of course, the idea had only come to mind because he understood that Lucy was not a woman to be trifled with. From that very first day of their meeting, he had found her impervious to any attempt he might make to charm her in the usual manner that he had used so successfully for years. On top of that, he had been dumbfounded by an innate need to care for her, protect her, provide for her.

Blimey, half the time when he was worrying over the books or how they might make it through this season and on to the next, it had been Lucy's future he had considered—not his own and not Adam's investment. If he failed in his mission to salvage Conroy Cavalcade, what would become of her?

As always when he thought of her, he felt his blood run hot with wanting her. His need for her had reached the level of obsession, especially since he had not had a moment alone with her since that incredible night they had spent making love. All he had to do was catch a glimpse of her as he went about attending to the thousand and one details of getting things ready for their Chicago opening. With a smile or a wave of her hand, every detail of that night came flooding back in such graphic imagery that more than once he had been forced to change his course rather than risk being close enough to actually face her, touch her, kiss her.

Initially, his reaction had startled him so that he had vowed to keep his distance until he could get a grip on himself. It simply would not do for her to know the power she held over him. But he had finally admitted defeat.

After three sleepless nights spent in a chair in his office because he could not bear to occupy either his bed or the daybed in the observation room without imagining her there with him, he had been forced to surrender his pride. He had sent her a message by way of Shirley to join him for supper that very evening. He had told Shirley that they needed to compare notes on what each of them had managed to discover about the missing money.

The fact was that indeed they did need to discuss progress on that front. But his true motive was far less pure. That very morning, he had stood unobserved in a quiet corner of the tent as she had rehearsed her act. Her rehearsal costume left little to the imagination, especially for one who had come to know every inch of her in that enchanted night. Every movement stirred a memory that left him reeling: Lucy with her legs wrapped around his waist as he carried her to his bed; Lucy stretched taut to hold him inside her; Lucy driving him to ever riskier acts just for the reward of pleasing her.

Above him, she had held tight to the bar, her head thrown back, her throat exposed, her breasts flattened against the force of her movement as she soared through the air. In that moment, he had vowed to himself that he would have her back in his bed before the night ended.

Lucy knew that she and Jeremy did indeed need to meet and discuss a plan for revealing the true thief. Since that night in his bed, she had found ways to avoid him, leaving him notes and a copy of the chart she had put together to show who might have been around on those occasions when money was missed. Unable to talk directly to her due to his own schedule and her intentional avoidance, he had returned messages by talking to Harry or Shirley. But now, the moment she had been dreading had come.

"Tell him I'll see him in the morning—first thing," she said lightly when Shirley delivered his message.

"He can't see you then, honey," Shirley reminded her. "Tomorrow is our first performance. He has that breakfast with the mayor and all the dignitaries to attend, and then there's the parade and the afternoon show and then getting things ready for the evening and . . ."

"All right. You're right, but I can't possibly stay for supper. I have a thousand things to do myself."

"You have to eat," Shirley reminded her. "Why not kill two birds with one stone, so to speak? Besides, the days are running out for you to find the true thief."

"I thought you believed me to be on a fool's mission," Lucy said irritably.

Shirley touched her daughter's shoulders. "No one wants you to succeed in finding another suspect more than your father and I do, Lucy."

There was no way out. "I'll be back early," she promised. She had taken to staying in her parents' car, telling herself that it was more convenient for getting Shirley's help with her costumes and with a new stunt she planned to add to her act.

Shirley nodded. "You'll have the place to yourself, I'm afraid." She smiled dreamily. "Jeremy asked Adam to get your father and me a suite at the Drake Hotel. Can you imagine? He said we deserved a special night for just the two of us. Isn't he the most romantic man?"

Damn!

"Now, what should I wear?" Shirley asked. "Jeremy made reservations for Harry and me to dine at the hotel restaurant. It's very posh, according to Jeremy. He suggested that red gown of yours."

Red doesn't suit you.

"I'll get it," Lucy said, glad for some excuse to leave the room and avoid any more talk of Jeremy.

Once she had gotten her parents off for their night on the town, Lucy considered her own plans. She did need to talk to Jeremy. After studying the list of all those they had rejected as possible suspects, she had moved one name to the list of prime suspects—a list that up to then had only included Karl's name and Reggie's with a question mark. This new entry was a name that Jeremy had dismissed early on, and Lucy could not debate his logic. There was no reason to suspect this individual who had no apparent motive or opportunity. But the name had

stayed with her, haunting her until now she thought
she had the answer.

With deliberate care, she selected her plainest
dress. She pulled her hair back into a tight bun at
the nape of her neck. She put on the heavy, sensi-
ble shoes and thick cotton stockings that she wore
when working with the animals. She even wore a
corset, thinking that the more barriers she placed
before him in terms of disrobing her, the more discouraged he was likely to become. In the end, she
pulled a heavy, shapeless sweater on over the whole
costume and surveyed the results in her mirror.

"That should do," she decided and trudged off toward his car like a condemned woman.

He greeted her with that bemused smile that was
guaranteed to turn her insides to jelly.

"Has there been a sudden onset of cold weather?"
he asked lightly. He had removed his coat and tie
and was dressed in a shirt open at the throat with
sleeves turned back to reveal the sinewy muscles of
his forearms. "You are not ill, are you?" He reached
to touch her cheek with his palm.

She stepped out of range and deposited on his
desk the pile of notes she'd carried clutched to her
chest as she had waited for him to answer her knock.
She breathed a little easier when she saw that their
supper had been left in his office rather than in the
more intimate setting of the observation room.

"I thought we could eat while we go over our strategy," he said, catching her notice of the food. "Do
you mind?"

"Not at all." She reached to pull a chair closer to
the desk, but he was there first, his hand covering
hers, sending his damnable heat straight through
her.

"Lucy," he said softly and touched her shoulder. "I've missed you, love." He started to draw her closer.

Despite every bit of her intent, she could not bring herself to turn away. "We must work," she replied, but his mouth was so close and tempting. She moistened her suddenly parched lips.

"Don't do that, then," he said in a husky whisper, "or I shall have no choice but to . . ."

Their lips met, tasted, opened. In a stunningly brief moment, Lucy found herself braced against the wall, the shapeless sweater pulled off her shoulders to pin her arms, her carefully arranged hair coming undone as he pressed his length to hers and she pressed back.

The kiss might have lasted forever had he not made clear his intent to carry her to his bed.

"No," she protested, resisting his move to lift her into his arms. "We must work, remember?" she said more calmly when he looked at her with a hurt and confused expression. "Harry gave us the week, and regardless of how much he wants to believe you, he will expect proof."

He remained pressed against her for a moment, then smiled. "You're right, of course." He moved half a step away and finished taking the pins from her hair, using his fingers to comb it over one shoulder. "Work before pleasure—see, you are a good influence. I am beginning to be a thoroughly responsible person."

She smiled in spite of herself. He was utterly charming—of that there could never be any doubt. And she was totally in love with him, and therein lay the problem.

"Shall I serve?" he asked lightly.

"No, let me. You sit over there and tell me what you've been able to discover."

He did as she asked, and she calmed her frayed nerves by turning to the familiar and routine tasks of filling plates for each of them, pouring wine, and buttering rolls.

"I can't seem to put it together," he admitted, fingering the stack of papers she'd left on his desk. "Everything would indicate that Karl is the culprit, but the man is as skittish as a mouse. I can't believe him capable of such audacity as it would take to pull this off once, much less repeatedly."

"Have there been any new incidents?"

"Yes, just today I discovered a cache of bills that I had placed inside the safe missing. But to accomplish that, someone would have to know the combination to the safe."

"And that would be . . . ?"

"You know already. Only your father and myself."

"Not Karl?"

"I thought of him, for he has been in the office on occasions when either Harry or I have had to open the safe. It is conceivable that he could be keen enough to have observed the combination over our shoulder. But he wears those glasses and they are quite thick, and his desk is all the way across the room from the safe, and—"

"Jeremy, is the combination to the safe right to one, left past one to five, then back right again to nine and left all the way round to nine again?"

"Harry told you?"

"No—even Shirley doesn't know."

"Then, how . . . ?"

"First of May," she said softly.

"And the nines?"

"The year."

"Of course. But, Karl would never guess . . ."

"But Eleanore would."

"Eleanore?" He was incredulous. "Love, we discussed this. Eleanore was never even close to the vicinity. She was performing. And even if she had made a move after hours, someone would have noticed her hanging around the office."

"She had an accomplice—a willing one—in Karl. Don't you see? She seduced him into believing that she cared for him, and that with enough money, they would be able to run away and make a life together."

Jeremy frowned. "I suspect that you are giving her far too much credit, Lucy. Eleanore does not strike me as possessing the sort of complex thinking that it would take to plot such a scheme, and Karl is no fool."

"Men can be remarkable fools when a woman who seems beyond their reach pays them some attention. As for Eleanore, I know her very well, Jeremy. She and I were students of Shirley's together. She even lived with us for a time, and I agree that outwardly, one would peg her as a simple woman whose thoughts go no further than how to arrange her hair or what gown to choose."

"Precisely. I know her type as well, Lucy. There is little difference between her and women I've known in New York and London. She is self-centered to a fault, but hardly an inspired conspirator."

"That's where you're wrong," Lucy replied. "Working the trapeze and high wire takes a great deal of mental as well as physical skill, Jeremy. It is necessary to think through every move—even the seemingly insignificant ones. The placement of a foot this way or that by a mere fraction of an inch can spell the difference between magnificence and tragedy." She saw that she had his full attention.

"Go on."

"When Reggie left and my savings was also missing, my first thought was of him. He was the culprit—I had no doubt of it. But that first meeting after he and Eleanore rejoined us, I flung the accusation at him in a moment of anger."

"And he denied it, of course. You could hardly expect that—"

"But it was the look on his face *before* he denied it. It was the pause *before* he spoke. Looking back, I see now that my accusation came as a complete surprise to him. Reggie did not take my savings."

"Then who did? Karl wasn't even—"

"Eleanore."

Jeremy laughed. "Lucy, love, she wasn't with this outfit then. She didn't simply walk into the place and . . ."

"That is precisely what she did. You know that she went with Parnelli several weeks before Reggie ran off to join her. One evening she stopped by on the pretense of making amends to Harry and Shirley for leaving our company. She said that they had always been kind to her and she would never forget all they had done, but that she was not as young as I was and she wouldn't try and compete."

"But that hardly explains . . ."

"Shirley invited her to stay for supper like old times, and that evening it was really quite lovely. We all sat around the table reminiscing and laughing. Sometime after dessert, she complained of not feeling well. Shirley insisted that she go upstairs and lie down while we cleared the dishes. She accepted."

"And that's when she took your money," Jeremy

said quietly. "But how did she know it was even there?"

"That would have been Reggie. I'm certain that he told her all about my 'dream savings,' as I used to call it."

Jeremy glanced at her with interest. "And what, pray tell, is a 'dream savings'?"

"It's foolish, I know. But, well, a girl can't spend her whole life flying through the air. After a while she needs to land on solid ground. I thought that would be in this little house I once saw overlooking Lake Michigan." Her voice took on a whimsical tone. "I thought that Reggie and I would settle there and raise our children and grow apples or cherries . . . or maybe both. They have the most wonderful cherries there."

"It sounds quite lovely," Jeremy said as he covered her hand with his. "It's a wonderful dream."

Lucy pulled her hand away and shrugged. "Nevertheless, we're moving off the point. Eleanore is our thief and we must find a way to stop her."

"You do seem to have this all worked out, but I haven't invited her to supper, and as far as I know she does not have access to the combination to the safe."

"That was the toughest piece of the puzzle, for I was certain that somehow she had provided Karl with that information."

"And you have the solution?"

Lucy nodded. "When Eleanore was training with my mother, she lived with us. She was privy to family discussions at supper and casual conversations we might have as we traveled on the road. She was a member of the family. The day that Harry got the safe, we were all very excited, and I recall a lively discussion about coming up with a secret combination—I'm sure that Eleanore remembered that day as well, for Shirley made quite a celebration of it."

"Of getting a safe?"

"Of *needing* a safe—it meant that Conroy Cavalcade had flourished to the point where we could no longer manage to carry our proceeds around in a simple box. The safe actually came with the second-hand train car Harry bought to use as an office during the season."

"But how could Eleanore possibly have guessed that the combination he settled upon would be *first of May*?"

"She probably wasn't certain at all, but she did know that it had something to do with the circus—Ian had suggested that."

Jeremy blinked as understanding dawned. "So, she had Karl try that specific combination. If it hadn't worked, then she would have tried something else."

Lucy nodded. "Like perhaps the anniversary of our founding—always a day of celebration—or the day we first laid claim to the world's largest elephant herd. She was there for each of them. She would not have forgotten."

"How clever. And knowing the combination, she could have Karl take funds whenever she wanted. There did not have to be a specific time or day."

"Exactly. That's why she was able to take smaller amounts along the way. There was no reason to imagine that there would be a reckoning of cash against the ledger until we got back to Delavan for the winter and Harry prepared the deposit for the season. By then she would be long gone."

"But why not make one large hit and leave?"

"Eleanore is not a person who leaves anything to

chance—in her act or in her life. What if they planned a single theft and something prevented it? Perhaps you walked in or Karl got cold feet or . . ." Lucy guessed.

"So on the theory that something was better than nothing, she continued to build her nest egg. Where would she have kept the money? Surely she would not entrust it to Karl."

Lucy laughed. "Hardly. Especially since she never intended to take Karl with her. My guess is that the money is somewhere in her compartment."

Jeremy stood and paced the length of the room and back again.

Lucy knew that he was thinking through what she had revealed, looking for any possible faults in her logic. When he had run through all of it and found nothing, he returned to the desk and sat on its edge near her chair. "So, Detective, how do we proceed?"

"Heavens, that's for you to decide. I haven't the slightest idea."

"But, you will assist me, will you not? I cannot do this alone, Lucy, and I truly do not wish to involve anyone else if it is not necessary." He touched her cheek.

She would have walked over a wire of fire at eighty feet in the air if he'd asked her to do so. "Of course I'll help you," she replied. "How about this? You tell her that I can't perform quite yet and she must take my place. Then I'll search . . ."

"You'll do no such thing. In the first place, you will perform because you are our top draw and because I will not give our Chicago audiences less than our best. I will handle Miss Eleanore Wilson."

He pulled her to her feet. "But enough of work and dreary things like thieves and scoundrels," he announced. Holding her hand tightly in his own, he headed for the door.

"Where are we going?"

"We are going to see the sights of this great city of Chicago, love. I need a bit of pleasure in my life and I plan to seize this singular opportunity to have that. Are you with me?"

He was impossible to resist as he drew an imaginary sword and struck a pose like that of a general leading his troops. He charged forward a few strides and then looked back. "Well, come along," he ordered with mock sternness. "The night is young but ages quickly."

Lucy ran the distance that separated them, and she was laughing as he wrapped his arm around her shoulders and hailed a passing carriage for hire.

Fourteen

It was well past midnight by the time they ended the night at a small tavern, where Jeremy persuaded Lucy to entertain the patrons with several songs while he paid for rounds of drinks. Outside, the carriage driver waited to take them back to the circus grounds. Lucy climbed sleepily into the enclosed carriage while Jeremy gave the driver directions. Jeremy had given the driver ample incentive to take the long route back to the circus grounds. He had plans—plans that required privacy. But when he climbed into the carriage, Lucy was fast asleep and he did not have the heart to wake her.

Instead, he eased her into his arms until her face rested against his chest. She stirred slightly but did not wake. He settled himself more comfortably into the corner of the seat and smiled when she snuggled against him.

For a time, he simply enjoyed the sensation of the steady clop of the horse's hooves on the pavement, the creak of the carriage wheels, and Lucy's soft, steady breathing. He stroked her hair absently as he recalled the pleasure of the evening they had shared. It had been the first time they had gone out in public together, and he had thoroughly enjoyed showing her the wonders of the city.

He thought of business, as he usually did these days. The next engagement, the next box office, the possibility of some new act he might add to their slate to enthrall new audiences and bring back the experienced ones. Next season they would need to . . .

When had he begun to see himself still there after a year? When had business become such a fascinating topic for him? In New York, he had done what he thought necessary to impress Adam, but from the day of his arrival, he'd focused on the quick and easy way—the way that would leave him the most time for leisure pursuits. *Pursuit* was the operative word in those days for it was the constant pursuit of beautiful women—*wealthy* beautiful women—that had occupied his every waking moment in those days.

It stunned him to realize how very recent *those* days had been. It had been only a matter of a few months since the day he had arrived at what he had considered to be the outpost of Wisconsin. He smiled as he recalled that first day. He'd left the train station with directions for reaching the Conroy outfit—he'd discovered at once that simply requesting directions for reaching the circus winter headquarters was not enough in the town of Delavan. Several small companies made that community their winter home, but it was immediately clear to him that the Conroy outfit was among the most respected.

Unused to the role of directing an operation—not to mention over one hundred employees—on his own, he had determined that he must appear quite stern and forbidding on that first meeting. He had recalled his father's demeanor whenever lesser men than he were before him. Lord Barrington had been a forbidding presence. More often than not, employees—and even some peers—had cowered before his austere look. For reasons Jeremy could not fathom now, he had decided that day to follow his father's example.

He'd actually been doing rather well at it when he'd walked through the enormous open doors of the practice barn. He'd successfully managed to hide his astonishment at finding himself surrounded, not by the usual stalls and hay bales and such, but rather by a large circus ring and rigging for acrobats and props for clowns. He'd been taking it all in when Cora's dung had destroyed any shred of dignity he might have thought he possessed. Not once, but twice, he had landed flat on his bottom in the sawdust. He could still smell the stench of Cora's leavings. He could still see the laughing eyes and very serious mouth of Lucy Conroy after she had flung herself into the safety net and greeted him.

As the carriage rounded a turn, he gently gripped Lucy's shoulder to keep her from falling. She sighed and turned until she was lying on his lap, her legs curled on the seat beside him.

She had changed everything for him. In the beginning, it had been her refusal to hide her skepticism that his presence among them was for good. Her doubt made him all the more determined to prove her wrong. She made no secret of the fact that she suspected that he had come to shut them down. Her perception had startled him. On the long train ride from New York to Wisconsin, he had decided to do whatever it took to sell enough tickets to bring the outfit back into the black. Once he had accomplished that, he would recommend to Adam that he sell it off to one of the larger concerns, who would pay handsomely for the stock and equipment.

When he had discovered that Harry's health was even more frail than Adam had led him to believe, he was mystified that this news did not cheer him. After all, with the owner and founder in failing health, there was all the more reason to salvage the company by selling out. But he had found an instant rapport with the circus veteran and had disguised the seriousness of Harry's health to Adam in his weekly reports. In the meantime, he'd found himself working even longer hours to find ways to increase the stability of the company over the long term.

And always, she had been there. In those early days, he would go into the barn and watch her rehearse, always entering and leaving without her being aware of his presence. At first it had been because she was not only by far the most beautiful woman around, but she would have held her own against any woman he'd ever known. And, of course, his first instinct had been to have her—to bed her and get her out of his system. Then, by the time they were on the road, he would have no entanglements to keep him from selecting from the bevy of females who would no doubt welcome his attentions as the circus came to their towns. He had consoled himself with the fantasy of available women on the trip from New York. In every hamlet there were bound to be women—lonely and starved for a bit of attention. He had envisioned young, buxom milkmaids, farmers' daughters who knew enough of barnyard couplings to know what to do, widows—or even ignored wives who would welcome a brief affair.

But as he watched Lucy stretch and arch and fly, he had found himself mesmerized by her and her alone. The practice costume she wore only enhanced his fantasy, and it had been as easy a leap for him to imagine her body stretched taut under his as it was for her to dangle from her ankles from a height of four stories. He had taken so many cold baths in those early days that he had heard Shirley remark to Harry about their new manager's apparent addiction to cleanliness.

Yet he had been incapable of making his move. Lucy's room was not ten meters from his during those weeks. Her parents slept downstairs and her brother was more often than not out somewhere with Trixie. He could have found some excuse to knock on her door well after she would be in her nightclothes. There was no doubt that he was something of an expert at getting inside a woman's bedroom undetected—that was quite proficient at getting that same woman into bed and having her believe that she was the instigator. Yet this small bundle of desire had left him cowering behind his own door, night after sleepless night.

Lucy murmured something in her sleep and rolled to her back. She had opened the top buttons of her blouse after they'd shared several glasses of beer in the hot stuffy tavern. He could see the edge of her lace chemise in the glow of street lamps they passed. It was that bit of lace that caused the heat to course through him, for he knew what lay beyond— what delights, what pleasure.

He thought of their night of lovemaking. It had been everything and more than he had ever imagined. Her lithe body had responded to his every touch in a way no woman had ever responded before. And yet her innocence had moved him deeply, brought forth a need to assure her pleasure when never before had he ever considered any woman's pleasure. Pleasuring a woman was simply a way of extending his own, for he'd been only a youth when his father's mistress had offered him that bit of advice.

With Lucy, fulfilling her was less a means to his selfish end than its own reward. Ever since that night, he'd found himself dreaming of ever more intricate ways he might surprise and please her. He loved her startled expression when he touched her in places that unnerved her. That wide-eyed look was always followed by a smile, and her eyelids would lower as her breath escaped in little gasps of sheer delight.

Stop this! It was not Lucy's but his own traitorous body that was beginning to react to the memory of making love to her. *I should tell the driver to take us home.* He looked down at her. Her lips were parted and he could not resist running the tip of his finger over them. She closed her mouth around the tip of his finger, and he instantly felt a surge of erotic pleasure. Her action was all the more sensual in its innocence.

Slowly he opened the rest of the buttons of her blouse, pulling it free of her waistband until he could spread the fabric and reveal her chemise. He hesitated. She was wearing a corset. In all the time that he'd known her, he'd never seen her wear a corset. No matter how many layers a woman might have on, the bloody things were as obvious as a straitjacket. How had he missed that? More to the point, why had she worn it tonight of all nights? Tonight, when he had specifically arranged a meeting, handled all the fine details of getting her parents out so that later there would be no questions about when she had returned to her own bed.

He examined the corset as if it might actually

strike him. It had the advantage of pushing her full breasts above the neckline of her chemise. They fairly spilled out as if inviting him to take them, and yet the beastly garment was there like some ancient chastity belt protecting a knight's lady until he could return.

Well, he was no knight in shining armor—more closely related to a knave and rakish scoundrel, if truth be told. Experienced in such matters, he made short work of finding and unhooking the row of fasteners. When he had released the last of them, Lucy let out a deep sigh, as if she could finally breathe comfortably.

"Lucy, love," he whispered as he removed his coat and opened his own shirt. She burrowed her face against his bare skin, her breath teasing him just above his waistband. He sucked in his breath and tried to maintain some control of his manhood, not to mention his sanity.

"You've slept long enough," he said in a husky whisper and lifted her until she was draped across him and her lips were a mere breath away from his own. "Open your eyes, Lucy, for I'll not have you accuse me of ravish you without your knowledge."

Her eyes flickered open, and she gave him a sleepy smile, then wrapped her hand around the nape of his neck and pulled him closer.

As he felt himself pulled under by her kiss, he thanked his lucky stars that he'd had the good sense to tell the driver that they were not to reach their final destination until he had knocked twice on the partition that separated the driver's seat from the cabin.

As the kiss escalated into hands moving over bare skin, and tongues dancing a mad tarantella, he also thanked the fates for his experience with successfully—even romantically—completing the act of lovemaking within the confines of a small hired carriage. In seconds he had positioned Lucy on the facing seat and knelt in the narrow space between the seats. He had stripped off his shirt and was well on his way to completing the removal of hers—and they had not yet broken the kiss. The unwelcome corset had been conquered and cast aside.

Lucy struggled against him, her hands alternately pulling at him and pushing against him.

"Patience, love," he whispered as he slid his mouth to her ear and began caressing it with his tongue. At the same time, he pushed her skirt and petticoats up over her knees. Her breath was coming in heaves as if she had run a great distance, and the sound of it excited him even more.

And then, as suddenly as it had begun, it was over. First she went absolutely still and stiff. He actually thought she might have fainted, but he could feel her clenched fists pressing against his chest and knew that she had to be conscious to exert that kind of force.

He leaned back and tried to see her features in the shadowy confines of the carriage. "What is it, love?"

"Please stop calling me that," she said softly as she took advantage of the opportunity to scramble away from him and curl herself into a protective ball in the corner of the seat.

To say Jeremy was confused was possibly the understatement of the new century—he would certainly hold it up for comparison to anything the next hundred years might bring. They passed a lamp, and he was shocked to see that she was scowling at him.

Blessedly, his surprise had turned his attentions away from fulfilling anyone's needs—his or hers—so he pushed himself off the floor and onto the seat opposite her. They were as separated as the small interior would permit. He held up his hands as if trying to disarm her by professing his intent to leave her alone.

Seemingly satisfied, she uncurled herself enough to snatch her blouse from the seat next to him. He watched as she put it on and concentrated all of her attention on fastening each minute pearl button— something he was fairly certain she could do in the dark with no thought at all.

"I think you owe me some sort of explanation," he said in a normal voice when it became apparent that she did not intend to talk. He shrugged into his own shirt but left it open as he lounged back against the upholstery and folded his arms across his chest.

"This just isn't—I'm just not—I'm still in love with Reggie," she blurted at last, and he knew instantly that it was a lie.

"Indeed? Does Reggie know?"

"Of course not," she snapped.

"Then I shall have to tell him."

He didn't need to see her face to know that her eyes had just gone huge. "You wouldn't!" she gasped.

He shrugged. "Why not? I want you to be happy. Eleanore is about to go to jail if your theory proves correct. I note that nowhere in putting together your indictment of that lady did you implicate your beloved."

"He isn't involved," she said firmly.

"Love is blind," he shot back. "I'll look into the matter, and if, as you hope, he is only guilty of abject stupidity for involving himself with a common thief, then he'll be free—and no doubt in desperate need of your consoling kisses."

The interior of the carriage was dead silent for several minutes.

"Shouldn't we be back by now?" she asked petulantly.

"Oh, you wish to go to bed—that is, in a real bed where we can be more comfortable?"

"How dare you!"

He smiled. "Because, my love, on at least one occasion you had no difficulty forgetting all about your beloved Reggie for quite some time. Because I know that you are not a loose woman, and therefore, I must assume that you took a certain amount of pleasure in that romp." He swung himself onto the seat next to her until he was as close as he could possibly be without touching her. "Because when you kiss me, you are *not* thinking of Reginald Dunworthy."

There was a long pause during which neither of them stirred, and then she lifted her proud chin and faced him squarely. "I lied."

He was taken aback. He had expected tears or insults or even a slap in the face.

"Really?"

"I don't love Reggie."

"I see."

"I . . ."

She took a deep breath and he waited for, hoped for, prayed for the words he suddenly wanted to hear more than any that had ever been uttered to him.

"It won't work."

"I beg your pardon."

"You . . . me . . . us . . . this!"

She punctuated each word, poking her index finger first at him, then at herself, and then back and forth between them. For a finale, she waved her entire hand to take in the whole carriage.

"I'm a bit confused, love. Precisely what do you mean by *this?*"

She sat back on the seat and folded her arms. "You know very well what I mean. You're only trying to embarrass me."

"Oh," he said slowly as if the light of understanding was dawning, "you mean our physical relationship, that particular pleasure that we *both* take in kissing and touching and . . ."

"You don't have to spell out the details," she grumbled.

"Oh, but I do, love, for you see, the discussion is *in* the details. The details that include the fact that you enjoy these things as much as I do and that neither of us has ever enjoyed them quite so much as we do with each other."

She squirmed as if trying to find a more comfortable place to sit. Jeremy grinned, knowing that he had made his point.

"However," he continued, "as delightful and astonishing as our physical compatibility may be, it is not the whole of it."

The tenderness in his tone got her attention. She looked up at him without really raising her head. He knew exactly what those deep blue eyes revealed. She was curious.

"No," he said as he stretched in such a way that he moved measurably nearer to her. "You see, Lucy, I find that I enjoy your company at any time. I miss you when you are not near. I consider things through your eyes. And I believe that you do the same with me. Are you as surprised as I am to discover that we share so much on so many levels?"

"We are nothing alike," she said firmly. "Our backgrounds are totally different. We do not think alike in the least. Besides, you are educated and cultured and very nearly royalty, for heaven's sake." Her voice gained strength and conviction as she stated her case. She turned and looked directly at him. "There is very little you could say or do to convince me that there is any possibility that you will not grow weary of me once the thrill of the conquest has passed. You mistake your feelings, Jeremy. They are not based in genuine . . . affection."

He felt impatience and annoyance blossom into outright anger. How dare she presume to tell him how he felt? Did she not understand that he had already wrestled those particular demons? "For one who professes to be uneducated, you certainly have no problem lecturing," he said and tapped twice on the partition between them and the driver.

"It will do no good at all to get angry with me just because I have realized the truth of it before you."

"You have done nothing of the sort. Furthermore, when I wish for you to explain my feelings to me, I shall ask you. Until that time, I would suggest that you examine your own feelings in this matter. Ask yourself what lies you have concocted to persuade yourself that you—that *we* do not share an extraordinary passion."

She pulled herself away from him and pretended an interest in the passing scenery, which she certainly could not see.

"Ask yourself," he whispered as he moved quickly next to her, effectively pinning her in the corner of the seat, with no escape. "Ask yourself, Lucy, if you don't hunger for this as much as I do." He kissed her then and was triumphant in his realization that before she pushed him away, she surrendered to the kiss, savored it . . . returned it.

"As I suspected . . ." he said with a chuckle when she had finally found the will to turn her mouth away from his. "The only question we need discuss, Lucinda, is where we go from here."

She did not reply, and he could fairly feel the heat of her rage as she sat forward on the edge of the seat, her hand on the door handle, ready to spring from the carriage the moment it came to a halt.

"Have a care, my love. I can't have you injuring yourself anew just when I am about to make you my Angel of the Big Top for all of Chicago to see."

She wheeled on him then, and it was he who was forced to retreat as she poked his chest with her forefinger, emphasizing her points. "It is *you* who live in some fantasy world of your own making, sir. And I will thank you to not go around town—any town— taking the credit for my stardom. Until it is you hanging seventy or eighty feet in the air by your throat, do not dare take one instant's credit for my being there. Is that quite clear?"

He managed a nod.

"And another thing," she continued just when he thought it might be safe to draw a normal breath, "I will not deny that our physical . . . contact . . . has been something of a—something that I have—that it has been pleasurable. However, unlike you, I am unwilling to settle for only physical contact or the promise of such and call it anything that even hints of permanence. It is a momentary and fleeting delight and we both know that, so do not play me for one of your society fools who might think for one moment that you have more serious intent at heart."

"I . . ."

"You do *not* want to say another word, Jeremy. You have said quite enough to hang yourself in my eyes for weeks to come."

"But . . ."

She held up her finger and he swallowed his protest. The carriage stopped as if on her cue, and she calmly gathered her discarded corset and climbed out. On her way to her parents' Pullman, she did not look back once.

Jeremy sank back onto the seat and watched her go. He was as pleasantly exhausted as he might have been had they completed the lovemaking he had planned. *What a woman!*

Fifteen

By morning, Lucy had managed to regain control of herself. She had passed the rest of the night in her parents' car, alternating between restless pacing and heartrending sobbing. The one thing she was thankful to Jeremy for was the fact that her parents were not there to witness any of it.

However, when they returned the following morning, giggling and snuggling against each other, it was quite evident how they had spent the night. Lucy fought against the jealousy she felt. If she'd kept her wits about her and played the sophisticate that she would never be, she too might have enjoyed one final night of passion.

"You look awful, Lucy," Shirley said as the two of them walked across the circus grounds together. She placed a nurturing hand on Lucy's cheek. "No fever that I can detect."

"I'm fine," Lucy assured her. "It's just nerves, I'm sure."

Shirley nodded but it was clear that she remained unconvinced. "Did you and Jeremy quarrel?"

"Mother, you ask that as if Jeremy were my beau or something."

"Well, isn't he?"

"Heavens, no, and please don't let him hear you

say anything of the sort. I'm sure he thinks all the females in the company are half in love with him. I prefer not to be added to his list of conquests."

"Because you are not half in love with him like the others," Shirley said, as if mulling over the reasoning.

"Exactly."

"You are *totally* in love with him, then?"

Lucy's heart lurched. Shirley knew, and if she knew, then others must think the same thing. What an absolute fool she must seem to them all. "I am not."

She saw in her mother's smile that her denial had been seen for the lie that it was. "All right, dear, if you say so."

"I have to rehearse," Lucy said, kissing her mother's cheek.

"But wait," Shirley said. "You haven't told me if you and Jeremy have uncovered our thief."

The thief. Eleanore. Lucy had forgotten all about her, and she had to know how Jeremy planned to catch her. There might be some detail he had overlooked, some way she could help. Even though the last thing she wanted to do was to face Jeremy again, she had to go to him. They had to be perfectly clear on the details, for there was no telling what Eleanore's next move might be.

"We think we know who it is," she told Shirley. "But I can't explain right now. At the moment I have to find Jeremy."

Shirley smiled. "Well, go along then, dear. You don't want to keep a man like Jeremy waiting."

He was not in his office. One of the roustabouts told her that he'd seen him not half an hour earlier, headed over to the arena where they would perform.

When she reached the arena, she followed a corridor that she thought would lead her to the center ring, but instead found herself entering the seating area where the audience would be. Allowing her eyes to become accustomed to the change from the bright sunlight of the out doors, she leaned against one of the support posts and considered her surroundings.

First, she turned her eyes heavenward, not in supplication but to see where she would be performing later that evening. She imagined the place filled to the rafters with anxious faces turned to hers. From up there she would see their eyes grow wide with wonder, and their mouths would either hang open in astonishment that anyone would be so foolhardy or they would keep their lips tightly drawn as if holding in their own fears. And then she would drop, caught by her neck in the strap they'd never seen her put on. Their gasp of horror would soon turn to cheers of delight as Otto urged them to count her spins. And, on that last spin, just before she caught the trapeze and swung herself to safety, there was one face she would find—his face, watching her, willing her to safety.

She played out the entire scene as she stood alone in the cavernous space. The circus had been her life for as long as she could remember, but one day she would no longer be able to perform, to fly—and before that day came, she intended to walk away. She didn't think she could bear to be a part of the company and not perform. It wasn't that she thought she was too good to sell tickets or work on wardrobe—it just wasn't enough.

In every season she had watched the audience as they had watched her. From her position she envied them as they envied her—envied the mothers with their laughing children, envied the sweethearts who strolled along after the performance, headed to a real house with a yard and a garden. Shaking off her daydream, she started down the aisle toward the ring. But a movement in the dim shadows caught her eye and she paused, then moved closer.

Jeremy was inspecting Eleanore's rigging. *What was he up to? Why would he concern himself with such matters?*

"Ian can do that," she said and took some pleasure in seeing his surprise when he glanced up.

"Come look at this." He held out the ends of two ropes. They had been sliced in half.

"I don't understand."

Jeremy dropped the ropes and brushed his hands on his trousers. "When we returned last night, I received another of Eleanore's lavender missives," he said with a smile. "It seems that she is quite distraught because someone has been tinkering with her equipment, and now she will be unable to perform this evening. She has asked me to see the damage for myself."

"Well, it is clearly sabotage," Lucy replied.

"Self-sabotage, I am sure," Jeremy said with a good-natured smile.

"But why would she do such a thing? What is the purpose?"

"The purpose is to carry out her plan. She has graciously agreed to perform her part in the earlier group acts, but of course, there is no question that she cannot perform her solo, which comes just two acts before your own performance."

"Yes, but . . ."

"I believe that she plans to make herself evident early in the evening and then disappear when everyone is caught up in the finale acts—Wally and his final shot from the cannon, you, the final tableau."

"I still don't understand."

"There is another important activity that transpires just about that time, Lucy. Think."

Mentally Lucy ran through the routine of any performance.

"Think about what is happening out there," he urged, indicating the exterior of the building.

"For the life of me, I—oh, yes, of course, Karl will pick up the night's receipts. He'll count them and . . ."

"Don't you see? We are sold out for tonight in a venue that is three times the size of our own big top. In fact, I have authorized the selling of standing-room tickets for tonight only. With all the excitement of such a large audience and our first performance in the city, they know that everyone will be distracted. The two of them plan to make their biggest hit tonight and then be gone. I must admit I underestimated her. It is quite a clever scheme."

"How do we stop her?"

"*You* do nothing—just go about your usual routine. I will handle this."

"But . . ."

"Lucinda, do not try and thwart me in this. I must do things in such a way that we not only catch Eleanore in the act, but prove once and for all my own innocence beyond the shadow of a doubt."

"Very well." She turned away and then back again. "Nevertheless . . ."

He pressed his finger against her lips—an action

that silenced her even as it sent shivers of pleasure up her spine.

"Did you sleep?" he asked softly.

"Very well," she replied but turned away before he could examine her too closely. The circles under her eyes would tell their own tale.

"I intend to prove myself to you, Lucy."

"I never believed that you were the thief," she replied, turning back to him, confused now with what appeared to be yet another change in subject.

"I am talking about us. I will prove that what I feel for you is not going to change, at least not in the foreseeable future—say, the next ten decades." His words were tender, inviting, seductive.

Lucy knew exactly how to drown the fire he was trying to light. "Jeremy, I am moved more than I can say by your attention and what you think are your true feelings, but uneducated and unsophisticated as I may be, I do know this: you and I . . ."

"Love each other," he said, "and I will prove that to you as soon as I have disposed of Eleanore."

She looked at him with exactly the same expression she had only moments earlier imagined on the audience looking up at her. Her mouth open in awe, her eyes wide with disbelief, and her heart hammering, wanting more than anything to believe that this was possible.

"Jeremy, I will always have feelings for you," she said.

"But?"

"But, I would rather remember our time together as it is now. Please don't toy with that."

He smiled and placed one finger under her chin, lifting her face to his. "I have been a fool, Lucinda, and in the process I have made the mistake of pursuing you as I might have any woman. You are *not* any other woman—you are *the* woman for me, and I will prove that to you." He kissed the tip of her nose. "I must go, love."

She stood rooted to the spot, the light warmth of his kiss lingering on her skin. When she opened her eyes, he was gone.

The cast was more anxious than usual before the evening's performance. The house was packed, and there were no tickets to be had. The advance team had done their best job ever of plastering the city with posters and planting stories in the news that hinted at attractions as yet unrevealed. Jeremy stood at the entrance to the hall and considered his success. Every seat was filled. Seemingly, every father held an excited child on his lap. The sideshows had done a land-office business when patrons had arrived early to assure themselves of a good seat at the main performance. He had asked the security team to see him first before delivering the proceeds of the concession and sideshow sales to Karl. After he'd done a quick count of the money and marked random bills, he'd sent them on their way with instructions not to mention that he had counted the proceeds.

He glanced up and saw Ian across the way. The two men nodded to each other, and Ian continued his task of setting the rigging for the acrobats while Jeremy turned and walked out to Clown Alley, where the performers routinely gathered just before their entrance.

"Standing room only, boss," Wally announced gleefully, having changed from his sideshow costume into his tights and cape for his grand entrance into the cannon. "Cora and me will do you proud."

Jeremy smiled. He noticed that ever since Wally had devised the plan of using the stuffed elephant as a part of his act, he talked about the beast as if she were alive—almost as if she were human. Jeremy glanced up at Cora. Her huge glass eyes reminded him of brown billiard balls, except in Cora's case, they seemed to follow him as he moved past her. Without thinking of what he was doing, he reached up and patted her flank.

He saw Eleanore then. As usual, wherever Eleanore was, Reggie was not far away. At the moment he seemed upset about something. The two of them were having quite a heated conversation. He paused for a moment to observe the dynamics. Reggie appeared to be pleading with her, while Eleanore's antics would indicate that she was responding to him with a sharp retort. Finally, she stormed off and Reggie stood watching her, his expression one of total confusion. Jeremy almost felt sorry for him. He'd been an idiot twice—the first time when he'd jilted Lucy, and the second when he'd had the stupidity to believe that a woman like Eleanore could ever love anyone but herself.

He hurried forward and caught up with her. "Are you all right?" he asked, deliberately keeping his voice soft and tender.

She glanced up and batted her fake lashes at him, trying no doubt to muster a tear or two. "Oh, Jeremy, I think it was Reggie who cut the ropes. He's been crazy with jealousy." She lowered her lashes and placed her fingers on Jeremy's arm. "You see, he believes that . . . you . . . well, he claims that we . . ."

"Sh-h-h," Jeremy said and forced himself to pat her hand. "Can you perform, or would you rather not?"

"Do you want me to?"

"Only if you are up to it," he said.

She took a dramatic breath and let it out slowly, leaning on him so that her breasts brushed his arm. "Will you be there . . . I mean, in case Reggie should . . . ?"

He cupped her cheek with his palm. "I'll be there."

She turned her lips to his palm and kissed it. "Thank you. You are such a gentleman. I just have to run to my room. I forgot something."

"You should hurry, then. The prelude has begun."

She looked up at him and raised her hand to push the lock of hair from his forehead. He caught her wrist before she could touch him. There was only one woman he would allow that particular privilege. Eleanore's doing it would be sacrilege. "Go," he urged. He wanted to give her every chance to stash the money he hoped she had picked up from Karl at the ticket wagon.

"I'll be right back," she promised and hurried on her way. Jeremy took a long breath and returned to the entrance, where he signaled Ian, who nodded and went in search of Reggie Dunworthy.

The show went off without a single mistake. The crowd was on its feet and cheering from the start. When Wally flew from the cannon and landed atop Cora, the roar of surprise and delight was deafening, and from that moment on, every performer seemed determined to outdo any previous performance.

Jeremy watched Reggie with his lions and saw that his anger had translated itself into a performance of daring that inspired his lions and thrilled the audience. He strode about inside the large cage, cracking his whip with more vigor than usual and snapping out orders that the lions obeyed without question. Jeremy smiled. Perhaps something good would come of this after all, for Reggie had long delivered his performance by rote. Perhaps when he heard the crowd's roar of approval, he would remember why he had gone into this business in the first place.

Eleanore completed her part in the tumbling act and lingered over her bows. Jeremy suspected that she was reluctant to admit to herself that this might indeed be her last bow. Someone like Eleanore lived for the adoring audience's ovation. It occurred to him that this, more than anything, might be the difference between Lucy's effortless grace in performing and Eleanore's more studied workmanlike performance. They were equally skilled technically, but Eleanore would never achieve Lucy's inborn elegance.

Finally, Eleanore ran from the ring, her eyes filled with genuine tears now. When she reached the performers' waiting area, she paused a moment as if to regain her composure; then, wrapping her cape around her, she headed for the exit. Jeremy followed.

Outside, she headed straight for Karl's office, no doubt to collect the rest of the cash.

"Eleanore," Jeremy called.

She stopped so suddenly that she almost fell. He covered the distance between them quickly. "I've been looking for you."

"I . . ." She buried her face in her hands and pretended to sob. "Oh, Jeremy, I just . . ." She flung her arms around him and pressed her body to his.

Repulsed as he was, he played his part to perfection. "There, there, my dear," he murmured as he tightened his hold on her and expertly engineered the moves that he knew would take them from consolation to lust. It took less than he'd thought to have her clinging to him, pleading with him.

"I have wanted this," she moaned as she tried desperately to kiss him.

He avoided her kiss by moving his face into the crook of her neck and touching her breasts. "Not here," he said. "Come."

He took hold of her arm and hurried toward the car the women used as a dormitory.

"No," she protested. "Couldn't—wouldn't your car be more discreet?"

He fixed her with a look that he had practically patented. A look of such heat and desire that it was guaranteed to bring any woman to do his bidding— except for Lucy, of course. The look had not once worked on her. "Your bed is closer," he said and scooped her into his arms to cover the last few yards. "No one will think to look for me here," he assured her. "Which is yours?" he asked as he carried her down the row of compartments. She frowned, but then he smiled. "Or I could take you here on the floor," he suggested.

She laughed then and pressed herself more firmly against him. "There at the end," she said.

He carried her inside and kicked the door shut behind them. He sat her down and began tearing at his tie and lowering the blinds. "Undress," he ordered as he turned on the single lamp.

"Couldn't we . . . ?"

"I like to watch," he said with an arched eyebrow as he perused her body from head to toe. "I find it enormously erotic to see a woman undress herself, especially when you choose to wear those high-necked costumes that can be even more tantalizing than exposure."

She giggled. "Darling, patience." She started to unfasten his shirtfront, and he used the opportunity to glance around her cabin.

He spotted a small trunk and saw that it was locked with a flimsy padlock. He knew instinctively what he would find there. She had finished opening his shirt and was about to start on his trousers. He covered her hand with his own. "Not so fast. If you refuse to do it yourself, than I shall have the pleasure."

He lightly skimmed his fingertips over her. Her costume, of course, was sheer enough to reveal a great deal, and he had to swallow the revulsion he felt at touching her at all. *Where the hell is Ian?* he wondered as he fingered the chain at her throat. A small key hung from the cheap gold necklace.

"What's this?" he asked lightly as he pulled the chain outside the ruffled neckline and fingered the key.

"It's yours—I'm yours," she said in a husky whisper. She was trembling with excitement. "Touch me, darling. Take me, please." She tore at the fastenings of her costume, tugging the fabric lower, seeming to tease him without quite exposing herself to him.

Jeremy prayed that Ian was on his way. He wasn't sure how much more of this he could handle. He tugged sharply at the key and the chain broke.

Eleanore gasped and made a grasp for the key, but he held it above her head out of reach. "I have the key to your heart, then," he said. She reached for it. Jeremy moved away. "Ah, so this is important to you.

What could it open?" He looked around the cabin, still pretending to tease her.

"It's nothing," she said lightly.

"This?" he asked, fingering a small makeup kit. "Or perhaps . . ."

"Two can play your teasing game, darling," she said with a pout as she pressed herself against him and cupped the front of his trousers.

He froze and so did she. He knew that she had expected to find him fully aroused. He knew that never in his dealings with any woman had he been less aroused than he was now. "Sorry, Eleanore," he said lightly. "I'm afraid it just isn't there for me."

Her eyes glittered in the dim light of the cabin. "How dare you!" She backed away a step and began to pull her costume back into place. "How dare you! Get out!"

Jeremy sat down on one of the narrow seats and crossed his legs. "I think the more pressing question here, my dear Eleanore, is how dare *you*? And we're not going anywhere until we have resolved this little matter."

He had heard Ian's approach and knew that in a few moments it would all be over.

"Jeremy?"

Eleanore jumped at the sound of Ian's call. Jeremy reached around her and opened the door to the cabin. "In here."

Ian pushed Karl into the cabin ahead of him. The bookkeeper looked first at Eleanore, who had not quite succeeded in redressing herself, and then at Jeremy, whose open shirt and unfastened button at the waist of his trousers seemed to tell their own tale.

"You Jezebel," the man roared at Eleanore with a

fury that no one in the cabin would have thought him capable of managing. Ian restrained him.

"As Reggie and I both tried to tell you," Ian said "she's played you for the fool."

Karl looked at Ian and then collapsed onto the seat next to Jeremy. He seemed totally deflated, and Jeremy thought for a moment that the man might actually faint. Instead, he removed his wire-rimmed glasses and pinched the bridge of his nose.

"What is it you want to know?"

"Shut up, you fool," Eleanore screamed.

Ian stepped between her and the bookkeeper. "Jeremy?"

Jeremy sat up and put a hand on Karl's shoulder. "First things first. I want you to know that I regret the measures to which I had to go here. Nothing happened, I assure you, but in spite of the pain you are experiencing, believe me, she would never have taken you with her."

"You used me," Karl muttered, but his eyes were on Eleanore and they were so filled with fury that Jeremy saw Eleanore actually cower behind Ian for protection.

"Just be quiet, darling," she crooned. "They are bluffing. The truth is that Karl and I are deeply in love, and yes, we planned to run away tonight and . . ."

"And you just thought you'd stop for an hour in the sack with me, is that it?"

"You . . . it was you . . ." She turned to Karl. "You must believe me, darling; he staged the entire thing."

"That I did," Jeremy admitted as he stood up and reached for the locked trunk. "On the other hand, your resistance was weak at best, Eleanore. That was you that I heard not ten minutes ago begging me to—how did you put it?—*take* you?" He swung the trunk down. "Excuse me," he said politely, forcing Eleanore to move out of his way as he placed the trunk on the seat. "Let's just see if this fits . . . ah, look at that," he said with an expression of mock surprise as the lock clicked and opened. Inside were neat stacks of bills and a box filled with coins. "Tell me, Eleanore, how is it that you have bills marked in my hand with today's date?" He rummaged through the contents. "And where is the money you took from Miss Conroy?"

He held up a stack of bills tied carefully with a blue ribbon. "Karl, refresh my memory; have we been in the habit of binding our money with navy grosgrain? I could have sworn I told you to use only green."

"You stole from that sweet Miss Conroy?" Karl asked incredulously. "How could you? She and her folks had so little until Mr. Barrington came along. How could you?"

Eleanore scowled. "Oh, yes, let's all shed a tear for sweet little Lucy. What about what she stole from me? What about the fact that I was supposed to be the star, that her time would come in a year or so when I could no longer perform—when I could no longer find enough makeup to cover . . ." She broke down completely then, rubbing her face savagely with the heels of her hands as she wailed her fury at them all. Jeremy knew that this was no act.

After a long moment, she raised her ravaged, tear-stained face to them, and every man in the cabin gasped. The makeup had been scrubbed away by the dual action of her tears and her hands pawing at her face. Jeremy could not recall ever seeing a woman who carried her years so badly.

"I am thirty-one years old," she said. "How long

could I keep this up? Don't you see I had to? At first I thought that Lucy's stake would be enough. Reggie and I would marry and . . . but he refused to leave the show and I couldn't get him to understand why I *had* to leave without revealing myself to him and then, of course, *he* would have left me—they all did, sooner or later."

"But I loved you," Karl said softly. "All I ever wanted was the chance to take care of you—to take you away from all of this and take care of you."

Her face curdled with revulsion. "I'd rather be alone for the rest of my life," she growled.

"Okay, folks, that about wraps it up from where I'm standing," the detective said as he stepped into the doorway. "Come along, miss." He held out his hand to Eleanore, who stood and draped her cape around herself with a dramatic flare as she left the cabin just ahead of him. "And you, sir," the policeman said to Karl.

Jeremy held up a hand. "I believe you have your thief, Detective."

The detective looked at Karl and then nodded. "Keep yourself available."

Karl nodded, then slumped back against the seat.

Jeremy considered him for a long moment. He realized that he recognized exactly what the man was feeling. He had no doubt that Karl knew that he had done wrong, just as Jeremy himself had known full well that he was committing a crime when he moved the money from one of Adam's accounts into another. But like him, Karl had thought he was doing it all for a good cause. He had loved Eleanore and no doubt convinced himself that she had been badly used all these years by the very company whose funds he was willing to take to assure her future.

"Will you testify?" Jeremy asked him.

Karl nodded without looking up.

Jeremy stood up and stepped around the destroyed man. He reached into the trunk and peeled off several bills from a stack of the cash—one that was not tied with blue ribbon. "Here, take this and get yourself a place to stay until the trial is over."

Both Karl and Ian looked at him as if he must have suddenly gone mad. "Somebody once gave me a second chance," Jeremy said with a shrug and pressed the money into Karl's coat pocket.

Karl accepted the cash, and his lower lip trembled with relief and gratitude.

"Don't thank me," Jeremy said as he stepped into the corridor. "One day you can thank me by doing the same for someone else—giving them the benefit of a second chance. You just might save a life." He started down the corridor.

"Jeremy? I almost forgot. There's someone waiting to see you over in your quarters," Ian said as Jeremy passed him in the corridor.

Lucy. There was no one that Jeremy wanted to see more at the moment than his beautiful Lucinda. She must have decided to skip the finale and come straight to him. He ran the rest of the way to his private railroad car. The lamps were lit, and it felt as if he were going home.

Sixteen

"Luc—" Her name was on Jeremy's lips as he burst through the door and saw Adam Porterfield pouring himself a brandy at the ornate bar.

"Hello, Jeremy," Adam said as if the two of them had seen each other only yesterday. "May I pour you one as well? I understand we have much to celebrate."

"Adam." Jeremy moved to greet his friend and mentor. He offered his handshake, uncertain of the reasons for Adam's unannounced visit. He released a breath of pure relief when Adam pulled him into a welcoming hug.

"It's good to see you again, my friend."

Both men were suddenly uncomfortable with their display of emotion, and Adam turned his attention back to serving their drinks.

"There was no word that you were expected," Jeremy said as he accepted a glass and indicated that Adam should sit with him in one of the wing-backed chairs.

"I wanted to see the performance without anyone knowing I was in the audience."

"Meaning that you did not want *me* to know that you were checking up on me." Jeremy's tone was light, and Adam smiled and raised his glass.

"Exactly."

"And did I pass muster? Did the performance rise to expectations?"

Adam set his glass on the table between them and leaned his elbows on his knees. "It is a magnificent show, Jeremy. I am absolutely stunned with the progress you have made."

Jeremy smiled and sipped his brandy. "Thank you."

"I mean it. When word reached me that you had booked the company into Chicago, I have to admit that I thought you'd completely lost your mind. I was quite prepared for disaster despite the glowing reports I've received from Harry."

Jeremy was actually becoming uneasy with the unadulterated praise. "We have a number of highly talented performers, and then as you well know, Harry Conroy is quite simply a master when it comes to his knowledge of the business and of the competition. I certainly could not have done any of this alone, Adam. Whatever success we may have achieved is due to the people you saw out there tonight."

Adam studied him for a long moment. "You've changed, Jeremy."

"A bit," Jeremy admitted; then he grinned. "I am indeed not at all the same sullen novice you sent out here several months ago. I'm pleased to admit that I have learned a few things, and I am quite surprised to admit that I have enjoyed the experience."

"Are you ready to return to New York?"

Jeremy's reaction came as a surprise to both of them. "We really must complete the season, Adam. You see, when these opportunities arose in Springfield and then here in Chicago, we were forced to postpone performances in some of the smaller communities. I gave those city leaders my word that we would indeed honor our commitment to them."

"I see," Adam said, but it was clear that he didn't see at all. "I must admit that I was so certain that you would leap at the chance to come back that I had not thought much beyond that."

"It's not that I don't appreciate the offer, Adam; it's just that everyone is depending upon me—us."

Adam retrieved his drink and leaned back, crossing his ankle over his knee. "I think Olivia will be quite amazed at the transformation, Jeremy, even though it was she who continued to assure me over the last months that you would prove yourself quite capable of the task I had set for you."

Jeremy smiled. "How is my dear stepsister?"

"She is expecting your step-niece or nephew by early next year. I was assigned the honor of asking if you would agree to be the child's godfather."

"That's bloody wonderful," Jeremy said. "Livvy is having a baby." He shook his head in wonder.

"Well, I did have a thing or two to do with it. She did not accomplish this miracle solely on her own," Adam replied dryly.

Jeremy stood and reached down to shake Adam's hand. "Congratulations, old boy. I can't think of anything more wonderful. How is Sylvia taking the news?"

Adam laughed. "My mother is buying out most of New York, I fear. She has already taken Olivia shopping for furnishings for the nursery, and the two of them are intent upon hiring a proper English nanny for the child."

Jeremy laughed and went to the bar to refill their glasses. "I'm so awfully pleased for all of you."

"And what of you, Jeremy? Olivia will not let me back in the house unless I bring news of you and, hopefully, some young lady. I told her that you were not likely to settle down with—"

"I have found her," Jeremy said quietly as he took his seat again. "You saw her performance tonight. Lady Lucinda, Angel of the Big Top."

"Conroy's daughter?"

Jeremy nodded.

"The old man must be delighted."

Jeremy shifted in his chair. "Lucy and I haven't exactly worked out the details yet, so at this moment . . . while I am sure her parents suspect that we have feelings . . . nothing formal . . ."

"Now, Jeremy, if you are stalling, I must warn you that I cannot have you trifling with a woman like Lucy."

"I wouldn't," Jeremy assured him and sank back in his chair. "I am hardly the problem."

"Are you saying that she . . . that it is her reluctance . . . ?"

Jeremy nodded and Adam exploded with laughter.

"Wait until Olivia hears this," he gasped.

"She'll say that it serves me right," Jeremy replied miserably.

"And what is at the root of her reluctance?"

"I haven't a clue—well, I have. She thinks I'll grow bored and wish to move on and such, but Adam, I have never in all my experience felt what I feel for her."

The two men were silent for several moments as they sipped their brandy and pondered the dilemma of Jeremy's love life.

"It's possible that I may have a solution," Adam said finally.

"I shall go to any lengths," Jeremy vowed.

"Olivia is planning a charity ball for late November. She has had this idea that a circus theme might be just the thing to set the entire evening off. What if you were to bring several of your best acts to New York and perform at the ball?"

"That would be fantastic."

"I will admit to ulterior motives. As you no doubt know, some of the larger outfits are planning European tours in the coming year. When I continued to hear of the success you've made of Conroy's outfit, it occurred to me that we might wish to explore that possibility ourselves."

"Europe?"

Adam smiled and nodded. "How do you think your father might react to seeing your company performing for his peers in Parliament and members of the royal family?"

It was almost too delicious to contemplate. The idea of returning to England as a successful entrepreneur—one who had not relied upon either his father's social position or fortune—was something he had never thought to achieve.

"You are serious?"

"Now, Jeremy, if you know nothing else about me, you know that when it comes to business I am always serious. May I let Olivia know that you've agreed to entertain at the charity event? And that you will bring Miss Conroy and her parents with you?"

"Of course."

"Good. Once I have you in New York we can talk more in depth about Europe—as well as your engagement to Lucy." Adam set down his empty glass and stood. "Now, tell me how you resolved this business of the missing funds."

Jeremy blinked. "You knew?"

"I met with Harry earlier this evening. It was quite apparent that he had some concerns regarding my seeing the books, and that there were some shenanigans going on tonight at the ticket wagon."

"It was I who persuaded him to withhold . . ."

"He was quite your champion in our talk. There was certainly no doubt in his mind of your innocence and your ability to resolve the situation with no loss to the company or its investors. Now, tell me, is my investment still secure?"

"Oh my stars, wait till you hear this," Trixie announced as she burst into the dressing room where Lucy had lingered after the others had changed and left.

"Ian just told me the whole story." She pulled a stool close to Lucy's. "Apparently, Eleanore had tricked poor Karl into believing that she loved him and that they were going to run away together after tonight's performance."

"I know," Lucy said softly.

"Oh, yeah? Well, I bet what you don't know is how Jeremy and Ian hatched this plan to trap the two of them and get the goods on them."

Lucy glanced at her friend. Was it possible that when she had caught sight of Jeremy carrying Eleanore onto the train . . . ?

"Are you listening to me?" Trixie demanded impatiently. "Jeremy got Eleanore to believe that he was attracted to her and got her to take him to her compartment on the train so he could look for the missing money. Meanwhile, Ian showed up at the office, and of course, poor Karl was expecting to see Eleanore, but instead Ian walks in and—"

"But if Eleanore wasn't there," Lucy protested, "how could she be implicated?'

"Jeremy took care of all that. Meanwhile, it gets better. Ian told Karl all about Eleanore's plan to take the money and dump him just like she'd done once before when she took up with Reggie. And then— get this—in walks Reggie of all people, and he tells Karl all about how Eleanore must have taken money from you based on information she'd wheedled out of him while playing the same game."

In spite of her fears about just how much Jeremy might have enjoyed the opportunity for a love tryst with the beautiful and oh-so-willing Eleanore, she couldn't help wanting to hear every detail. "Then what?"

"Karl started singing like a bird, told them everything including where she hid the money. And how Eleanore promised him her undying love, not to mention some physical contortions in the bedroom that Ian wouldn't tell me about. Reggie was practically finishing the man's sentences because, of course, she'd sung the same song with him when she got him to run off with her so she could get top billing with Parnelli."

"Why did she need Reggie for that?"

"Ian says that apparently Parnelli wanted her to perform certain private acts, and so she told him that Reggie had threatened him and that if he was smart he'd take Reggie on so he could keep an eye on him."

"And then?"

"Then Ian called in the detective who'd been waiting outside and hearing everything, and they all marched over to the train and back to Eleanore's compartment."

"Jeremy was there?"

Trixie nodded. "According to Ian, he looked like he might hug your brother, so relieved was he to see him. He'd let Eleanore get close enough that he discovered that little gold key she always wears—I myself never thought much about it, what with her giggling and calling it the key to her cage given her by Reggie. The woman is downright coarse if you ask me, and what any man would ever see in her is—"

"But what happened?"

"Oh, Ian says that Jeremy was magnificent. In a matter of minutes he had her admitting the whole thing *and* he found the money—all of it, including what she took from you."

"How could he know that?"

"Did you tie it up with a navy blue ribbon?"

Lucy's heart hammered. "Yes."

"Then he found it right there in Eleanore's trunk—the lock that the key opened. The sheriff hauled her off and then . . ." Trixie took a deep breath and a dramatic pause.

"Well?"

"Ian says that Jeremy talked real nice to Karl, told him that once upon a time somebody had given him a second chance, and he gave Karl money to live on while he waits to testify. Isn't that incredible?"

Lucy stood up. Her heart was so full of love that she thought it might burst. "I have to go."

"Not yet—I haven't finished." Trixie tugged at her arm, urging her to sit down again.

"There's more?"

"Adam Porterfield was in the audience tonight

and nobody even knew he was coming to town, much less coming to see the show. He came walking up to the ticket window like any other patron and laid down his money. When Shirley looked up and saw it was him, she pretty near passed out. Then she called Harry over from where he had just finished the ballyhoo for the sideshow and the three of them were hugging and laughing and stuff, but Adam made them promise not to let on that he was there—not even to Jeremy."

"Jeremy didn't know?"

"Nope. He and Adam are over there in Jeremy's private car now. Harry says that Adam was downright thrilled with the show. Said he saw him standing and whistling through his teeth and cheering just like any regular townie might."

"Where are my parents now—are they in the meeting?"

"No. They went back to their car. I promised to come find you and then I've got to meet Ian and some of the others—we're taking Reggie out for a beer. The poor guy needs to drown his sorrows. You wanna come along?"

"No, you go. I want to see Harry and Shirley."

"And Jeremy—don't forget Jeremy," Trixie said with a teasing smile. "The man has earned a great big kiss right smack on those gorgeous English lips."

Lucy felt the color rise to her cheeks, but she could not deny that she was thinking exactly the same thing. "I'm sure that Mr. Porterfield will see that he's amply rewarded for his good work," she replied primly, and then she and Trixie both burst into giggles as they wrapped their arms around each other and left the dressing area.

Harry and Shirley were fairly bursting with excitement when Lucy finally located them.

"Right after we leave Chicago, we're heading back to pick up those dates we missed earlier," Harry told her.

"Meanwhile, Jeremy will be in New York—we'll let him tell you why. It's all so exciting!" Shirley gushed.

"Tell me," Lucy pleaded.

"We can't. We promised Jeremy. He's gone to see Adam off and then he'll stop by."

"He left you a present," Harry added, handing her a package.

Lucy was uncertain of the nature of the gift. Knowing Jeremy, it could be something intimate—something she would not particularly want to open with her parents standing nearby. "Do you know what it is?" she asked, stalling by pretending to examine the wrapping.

"Yes. Go on, open it," Shirley urged.

Carefully Lucy untied the string and folded back the paper. Then she gasped. Inside were two bundles of cash wrapped in navy grosgrain ribbon. "It's my savings," she whispered, fingering the bills.

"He recovered it all. Eleanore had it in hiding along with everything she'd gotten Karl to take for her from the safe."

Lifting the edge of the wide ribbon, Lucy saw the corner of a small calling card—*his* calling card. In his strong script was written: *Now you can buy that dream house. J*

Lucy read the note and wondered why it didn't make her happy. He was right. She could at least manage a down payment on a place of her very own. It might not be the little house with the orchards, but she could manage a house of her very own. At one time in her life, it had seemed as if fulfilling that dream was her reason for being. Now it wasn't nearly enough.

Harry put his arms around Lucy. "No need to cry, honey. It's all over now and Jeremy has set everything to rights again—for all of us."

Shirley wiped at her own tears with the cuff of her sleeve. "I'm embarrassed to have ever doubted him. He's been so good to us. Like I told Adam, sending us Jeremy was the best thing he could have done. He had good reason to shut us down or sell us off, but he didn't. Clay would have been real proud of the way he handled this whole thing."

"I understand that Adam enjoyed the show," Lucy said.

"Enjoyed it? He thought it was grand—that was his very word: *grand.*"

"Honey, why don't you let me take that cash and keep it in the safe for you until we get home," Harry suggested.

"Thanks, Papa." She knew they had both read Jeremy's note over her shoulder. "I guess you're wondering about what Jeremy meant about . . ."

"Oh, hush now," Shirley said. "It's none of our business, and even if it was, there isn't a woman in the circus who hasn't at one time or another dreamed about making a normal life for herself. Why should you be any different? The good news is that most of us outgrow it." She peered at Lucy for a long moment.

"Maybe she will and maybe she won't," Harry said softly. "We brought you up to follow *your* dreams, Luce, not ours. You're a grown woman and independent, financially speaking. You do what suits you, and your mother and me will be happy for you."

Lucy felt a fresh wave of tears building and knew she'd best get out of there before they were all bawling. She handed the money to Harry and turned. "I'd better go freshen up if Jeremy is stopping by," she mumbled as she fled out the door.

To her surprise, there was a knock on her compartment door about a quarter of an hour later. She had just finished changing into a peach-colored shirtwaist and apricot cotton skirt. "Come in," she called, certain that it was Shirley.

She sat on the seat and tried in vain to see her reflection in the small mirror well enough to put up her hair.

"Leave it down."

Jeremy stood just inside the door. He was dressed in a brown serge suit and held his fedora in one hand. "Leave it down," he repeated. "I prefer it down."

Lucy pulled a length of peach satin ribbon from her makeup box and tied her hair back at the nape of her neck. "I thought I was to meet you at—"

"I finished early and . . ."

They spoke over each other and then smiled.

"Would you go for a walk with me?" he asked.

The night air was refreshingly crisp. She took his arm after he had helped her down from the train.

"Jeremy, I am so grateful to you for retrieving my savings," she said when they had walked for more than a block without saying a word.

He shrugged. "It was a lucky bonus. You were the one who solved the mystery. I simply—"

"No, you were quite the hero. Just ask anyone."

He stopped and peered down at her, his hat casting his handsome features in shadow. "And shall I ask you, Lucy?"

She tried to laugh it off, but it was clear that he was quite serious. "You're in a strange mood this evening," she countered.

"And you are not answering the question," he replied mildly.

She needed a moment to consider her words. Left to her own devices, she was quite certain that she would frighten him half to death with the declaration of her undying love. "You have been quite wonderful to my family and to me, Jeremy. All of us hold you in the highest esteem."

"That wasn't always the case, was it?"

She could hear in his tone that he was smiling, teasing her.

"No," she admitted.

"But . . ." he coached.

"But I was wrong," she said.

"Well said."

"Are you laughing at me, Sir Jeremy?" She was relieved that they had made the transition from his earlier solemnity to a lighter tone. She locked her hand more firmly in the crook of his arm. He covered her fingers with his.

"Come sit with me a minute." He led the way to a park bench near a street lamp. "I don't know how much Harry and Shirley told you, but . . ."

"Practically nothing, and they were behaving very mysteriously."

He smiled and placed his hat on the bench beside him as he leaned back and spread his arm behind her. "It has indeed been a most rewarding evening."

"Is that all you're going to tell me?"

"Have you ever been to New York, Lucy?"

"You know that I haven't."

"Well, in November, you are—we are—the whole company."

"New York, but . . ."

"My dear stepsister is chair of some charity ball, and in her wisdom she has decided to build the theme around a circus—our circus." He wrapped his arm around her shoulders, pulling her close. "We are going to perform in New York, love."

"I . . . but . . ."

"And there is more. Following that, Adam wishes to discuss the possibility of a European tour. All the major producers are performing over there these days, and Adam sees no reason why we can't compete with them."

"Europe?"

"Ah, Lucy, just wait until you see England and France—we may even play Italy."

His face was bathed in the glow of the street lamp, and she saw that he was relishing the dream of traveling throughout the capitals of the world, being acclaimed by all. "Kings and queens and their courts all clamoring for the opportunity to see our Angel of the Big Top for themselves. Adam is more excited about this venture than any other I have seen him handle."

Up until that moment, Lucy had thrilled to his words. She had imagined the two of them together in New York, traveling throughout Europe. She had imagined their romance growing stronger with every success. She had soared through the imagery he painted. But in an instant she found herself falling back to reality. For Jeremy, New York and Europe were exciting because they were the evidence that he had redeemed himself fully. Adam's name was the one he invoked. She was his star, not his love.

"That's quite wonderful, Jeremy. I'm so happy for you," she said, trying hard to keep her tone light.

"You are a part of it, Lucy," he said as he sat forward and grasped her hands in his. "You are at the very core of it."

"You exaggerate."

He looked totally confused. "Lucy, do you not understand what this means for us?"

She understood that if she permitted this charade of pretending to be thrilled that he had achieved everything he had set out to attain, without speaking her mind, her heart was in danger of shattering. Self-preservation was her only recourse.

She took a deep breath. "I understand completely, Jeremy. You have succeeded beyond your wildest dreams, and in the bargain you have created success for all of us—my family is eternally grateful. And now, the time has come for all of us to move forward with our lives."

"What on earth are you talking about?"

"We have six weeks before the engagement you propose in New York. That is ample time for you to work with my father and Ian to put together a program that will please your stepsister and her friends. You know very well what my dream has been for some time, and having recovered my money, you have made that come true as well. I shall play the remaining dates we have scheduled, and then I plan to—"

"No."

The lone word was short, vehement, and unequivocal.

"No?" Her ire flared.

"No. I am not going to New York or to Europe without you." He folded his arms across his chest and looked away.

"You overestimate my appeal. Your audiences have no expectations . . . the larger companies have long focused on their equestrian acts, and Trixie is quite capable of . . ."

In an instant she was in his arms and on the receiving end of a kiss that began with the intent of shutting her up and continued with the intent of driving her insane.

"Really, Jeremy," she gasped when at last he broke the kiss. "That's hardly . . ."

He kissed her again. This time the message was undeniable hunger and desire.

"Are you getting this?" he asked in a raspy, breathless voice when he pulled back a fraction.

"It will do absolutely no . . ."

He took a deep breath, as if he were about to leap into the ocean, and kissed her again. By the time he pulled back, she was having a great deal of trouble remembering what the issue was.

"Now, then, it occurs to me that I have gone about this badly," he announced, resuming his position of long legs stretched and crossed at the ankles and one arm draped along the back of the bench. He frowned as if considering his next move while Lucy tried desperately to get her breathing under control.

"The problem is that I must leave tonight for New York, and I will be there working with Adam while Harry and Shirley and Ian manage our remaining time in Chicago and the other dates."

Lucy opened her mouth and immediately closed it when he shot her a look that was anything but casual.

"Therefore, a traditional courtship is probably out of the question, but then there has been little that has been traditional about our union from the start."

"Our . . ."

"Therefore, I shall require you to remain openminded about my techniques and to keep in mind that conventional courtship is not really among my repertoire of skills. Still, I shall make a go of it."

"I do not wish to be courted," she said very quickly before he could silence her with a look.

"Nevertheless, I shall. Every lady deserves that courtesy before—well, of course, in our case, we have already . . ."

"And therefore, the entire matter is ludicrous," Lucy said, certain that she had finally gained the better of him.

"Not at all. No mother of my children will ever—"

"Mother of your children! Your arrogance is astonishing."

"Oh, for heaven's sake, Lucy, we are meant for each other. Any fool can see that."

"I notice there is no mention of love in this; it is strictly business."

He frowned and tried to take her hand, but she jerked it away. "I told you I was quite bad at this, Lucy."

Nearby, a clock chimed the hour. "Damn, I have to go," he said. "I am taking a conventional train to New York, leaving my car for use as Harry sees fit for the remainder of the circuit." He stood and pulled her to her feet.

"Stop mauling me," she ordered as he pulled her against him.

"No," he replied and kissed her once again until her knees threatened to buckle from under her.

"Oh, for heaven's sake, go," she said, pushing him away.

He hailed a passing cab and helped her inside, giving the driver instructions to take her the few blocks back to the circus grounds.

"I shall be in touch—daily," he promised as he kissed her once more. "Until then, this should ward off any bad luck that might befall you."

He removed a small velvet box from his pocket and pressed it into her hand, then shut the carriage door and signaled the driver to leave.

Seventeen

Lucy waited until she arrived back at the circus grounds before opening the box. As expected, Trixie was out with Ian and she had the privacy of their compartment. She studied the blue velvet box tied with a white satin ribbon for a long moment, then slid the small envelope from beneath the bow and took out the note inside.

To my Lucy, my love . . .
    Cora and I both thought that this would keep you safe while I must be away and would serve as a reminder that in a few short months I have learned a great deal of circus lore and tradition. Cora has made her contribution to this talisman and here is mine . . . you are with me every moment of every hour of every day. I cannot wait to have you at my side in New York. Until then . . .

                                 Jeremy

She could not help but smile at his mention of Cora. Since having the huge elephant stuffed and making her even more of a draw than she had been in life, Jeremy seemed to have become as attached to the pachyderm as Lucy had been her whole life. Curious how he might have come up with a gift that would remind her not only of him but also of her beloved Cora, she untied the ribbon and lifted the stiff, hinged lid of the box.

"Oh, Jeremy," she murmured as she stared at the delicate gold bracelet nestled against a bed of silk. "It's so lovely."

She held the bracelet up to the light to examine it more closely. A series of small gold filigree hearts were linked together, and entwined with them like a ribbon was a dark-brown braid. Only she realized immediately that it was no ordinary twine. The braid was woven from the hair of an elephant's tail—a symbol of good luck to circus people everywhere. With an excited little shriek, Lucy dropped the box and fastened the bracelet around her wrist. The fit was perfect. "I shall never take it off," she vowed. "No matter what happens."

Throughout the rest of the run in Chicago and beyond, not a day went by without a gift or surprise from Jeremy. Sometimes there were massive flower bouquets, so huge that they barely fit inside her compartment or dressing room. Other days there would be a single rose placed on her pillow or left on the tiny aerial platform seventy feet above the crowd, for her to discover as she did her act. On another occasion, she stepped off the train at dawn to find a lone violinist waiting to serenade her. When the troupe neared the town where once she had seen her dream house, she received a bushel basket of apples and a note telling her that there were also orchards and houses in New York.

Trixie and Ian both denied any role in the delivery of these gifts, as did her parents. In fact, the entire company seemed as anxious as she was to see what the new day might bring. It was all incredibly wonderful, and Lucy could not for the life of her understand why she became increasingly panicky as the time approached for them to travel to New York.

On the trip out, she felt nervous and apprehensive, which made her irritable.

"What's the matter with you?" Wally asked with little attempt to conceal his exasperation. "You've got the world by the tail and you're acting like doomsday is just over the next horizon."

"I'm just a little nervous—about the performance for the charity event. After all, this audience will be quite a bit different. They . . ."

"High-society folks?" Wally huffed derisively. "Why, they ain't all that different from us. And what if they don't like us? So what? The one thing you can count on there is that they'll be too polite to show it in front of Adam and his missus."

"I suppose," Lucy reluctantly agreed.

"But that ain't it, is it?"

"I don't know what you mean," she declared, trying to keep her voice light.

"It's Jeremy that's got you scared. It was one thing when you thought loving him was a one-way thing. You were in charge then—you've got this streak in you, girl, that likes being in charge."

"That's preposterous."

Wally shrugged. "Even so, now that he's told you and the rest of us that loving runs both ways, you're scared."

"He has never actually said that he . . ."

Wally laughed so hard that he doubled over. "You think a man's gonna go to this kind of expense and trouble if he doesn't love you?"

Lucy straightened to her full height and gave the little man a look from on high. "Has it not occurred to you that he is only trying to—that what he wants is something more . . ."

"To get you in the sack?" Wally said and snorted another laugh. "Honey, a man like that don't have to spend money like he's spending to get a woman in his bed. A man like that is beating them off even as we sit here talking."

"There's no need to be crude," Lucy groused.

"Yeah, I think there might be. I think the only way you're likely to wake up to the truth is to have it laid out plain for you. Jeremy Barrington is one good-looking son of a gun. Add to that the fact that he's got a lot of money, not to mention a title, and how does that tally up? I'll tell you. It adds up to the fact that there ain't an eligible dolly in the whole New York Social Register who isn't setting her cap for him—probably a few ineligible women as well. The chance to be a duchess or whatever the woman would be? You think they aren't pulling out all the stops?"

"And what if they are? Why on earth wouldn't Jeremy be drawn to that—to them? What can I possibly offer him to compete with them?" Lucy moaned.

Wally blinked. "My stars in heaven, you're serious. Honey, you have the greatest prize of all: the man is head over heels for you—has been since the first day I met him and probably before that. Now, I'll admit that a fella like that probably thought at first that it was just the challenge of . . . well, having you, so to speak, but then . . ."

Lucy's face flamed red as she realized that Wally knew or had guessed that she and Jeremy had slept together—had made love. "Oh, my God," she moaned and buried her face in her hands.

"Now, you listen to me, girl. What's gone on between you and Jeremy is nobody's business but yours. The fact is, he loves you and you love him and you're bound and determined to find some way to ruin it. I can see it plain as day. You are staying up nights figuring out how to make sure that you end it before he does—or convincing yourself that he will end it so that you can say 'told you so.'"

"I am not," she argued.

"You just think you're not. I'm here to tell you that from where I'm standing that's exactly what you're doing."

"But . . ."

"Do you love the guy?"

Lucy nodded.

"Then get yourself together, honey, because he's gonna meet this train tomorrow and he's gonna want to see you more than he's gonna want to take his next breath. Now, get yourself back to your berth and let Trixie figure out what you should be wearing when he sees you that first moment."

"Peach," Lucy murmured after a moment. "He likes me in peach."

Wally grinned and bit down on his cigar. "Then peach it'll be."

Jeremy looked at the giant bouquet of roses he was carrying and frowned. He had overdone it. They were too much. He should have brought a single rose or a small nosegay.

"What about the balloons?" he asked Olivia, who

was waiting on the platform with him. "Too much, right?" he said miserably.

He had ordered bouquets of brightly colored balloons placed on every possible column at the gate where the train would arrive.

"They're quite festive," Olivia said. "I think that they will be delighted with your efforts to make them welcome."

"How do I look?"

Olivia suppressed a smile behind a gloved hand, as if considering his appearance. "Quite handsome as always," she assured him.

"I shouldn't have brought the flowers," he muttered more to himself than to her.

"Perhaps if I presented them to Miss Conroy it would seem less . . ."

Jeremy thrust them into her hands. "Thank you, Livvy. I mean, I don't want to cause a scene or anything."

"No, one would not wish to do that. Ah, here's Adam." She waved as Adam hurried toward them.

Jeremy was struck anew by the way a single look passing between them could say more than words, more than a passionate embrace. He felt—as he often did in their presence—like an intruder. And, as always when he observed the love that they shared, he missed Lucy all the more.

Her letters had been filled with news of the troupe. Details of the performances and the audiences, stories about Trixie and Ian or other members of the company. Only once had she come close to anything more intimate, and that had been her first letter, thanking him for the bracelet. Clearly, that gift had touched her heart beyond anything he had done since. He just hoped that what he had planned for her now would be equally well received.

In the distance he heard the train whistle and then watched as the beast lumbered into the station at a snail's pace. He scanned the windows for a glimpse of her, waving to members of the company who leaned out of windows and doors to greet him.

With a long hissing sigh, the train came to a halt and people spilled out of the cars. Jeremy began to walk the length of the train. Where was she?

"Jeremy, we made it," Harry called out to him as he helped Shirley down from the train and then grasped Jeremy's hand between both of his.

"Where's Lucy?"

Harry smiled and jerked his head toward the last doorway. "My little girl does know the importance of an entrance," Shirley said quietly and then took Harry's arm as the two of them moved forward to greet Adam and Olivia.

Lucy.

He felt momentarily paralyzed when he saw her poised on the threshold of the last car. She was dressed in a suit of peach serge with a short amber cape over her shoulders and a plumed hat that set off her beautiful face to perfection. She had left her hair partially down, long fat curls draped over her shoulders inviting his touch.

She hesitated as their eyes met, searching his face for something that he desperately wanted her to find, even if he didn't understand what it might be.

And then he was running the last few yards to her, encircling her tiny waist with his hands, lifting her and holding her there in midair. "Lucy, my love," he said, and it came out in an awed whisper.

"Jeremy, you must put me down," she said gently. "People are beginning to stare."

"Let them."

That made her laugh, and he smiled and set her on her feet but immediately grasped her hand and placed it firmly in the crook of his arm. "Come. I want you to meet Olivia."

The moment Lucy saw Olivia Porterfield, she knew that she had nothing to fear when it came to how Jeremy's stepsister might accept her. Olivia was the most elegant woman that Lucy had ever met, and yet there was no aloofness in that elegance. The minute she saw Jeremy and Lucy start toward her, Olivia excused herself from the others and came to meet them, her hands outstretched to Lucy in welcome.

"At last," she said as she took both of Lucy's hands in hers. "I cannot tell you how much I have been looking forward to meeting you, Lucinda. Adam returned from Chicago positively raving about your performance, of course, but I could tell by the way he spoke of you that there was a great deal more. I am so looking forward to our visit. You will stay at the house, of course," she added as she linked her arm through Lucy's and led her back toward the station. "Adam's mother will be devastated if you don't."

"That would be very kind of you," Lucy managed before Olivia continued.

"Of course, Jeremy is there as well and will no doubt try and monopolize all your time, but he has become quite the businessman during the time he spent with your father. I think that should leave us ample time to get to know one another."

"Her evenings are mine," Jeremy said sternly.

"Sylvia will have some say in that," Olivia replied. "She's already planned a number of entertainments at the house." She turned her attention back to Lucy. "You know that Adam's father and yours were the dearest of friends, and Sylvia is so delighted that Harry and Shirley will be staying with us as well."

Must be some house, Lucy found herself thinking. "Of course, I'll need to rehearse—we all will—for the charity event."

"Yes, of course, although to hear Jeremy tell it, there is nothing that you cannot do and make it seem effortless."

Lucy felt the color rise to her throat and cheeks. "Jeremy exaggerates."

Olivia laughed. "Yes, he does, quite shamelessly, I must say, but in your case I think he may well have understated things."

Within an hour Lucy's head was fairly spinning with all the new experiences she had endured. First, there was the fact that they were to be transported not in the usual horse-drawn carriage but in one of the newfangled motor cars. Harry was thrilled beyond words, especially when Adam insisted that he ride up front with the chauffeur where he could observe firsthand the mechanics of the automobile. Then there were the buildings—Chicago had had its share of tall buildings but nothing on this scale. And that did not even begin to address the added drama of the mansions and tree-lined boulevards, the incredible numbers of people and vehicles on every street, and the fact that seemingly every square foot of the city was occupied by either a residence or a business and sometimes both.

With all of that, Lucy thought that she was pre-

pared for anything once they arrived at the Porterfield mansion, but she was wrong. The house and
grounds were surrounded by an ornate wrought-
iron fence and occupied a full city block. Through
the fence she could see gardens that rivaled anything she had ever seen in picture books of
European castles and their gardens. As they drove
under the portico at the side of the house, servants
hurried forth to greet them and unload the luggage.

Harry and Shirley had seen it all before, of course,
but Lucy never had. When she found herself standing in the front hall of the massive house, all she
could think of was how it might feel to fly on her
trapeze from three stories above her, where a curved
stairway wound its way from a stained-glass skylight
to the place where she stood now with Jeremy.

"Oh, my," she murmured and firmly reminded
herself to close her open mouth.

The week flew by. There were rehearsals during
the day, and then several evenings were occupied
with small dinner parties planned by Sylvia Porterfield to introduce the Conroys to her friends. On
other evenings, the men would closet themselves in
Adam's study to go over the plans for taking the
show to Europe. On those nights Sylvia and Shirley
would amuse themselves by playing cards while
Olivia fitted Lucy with a new costume she had designed especially for the charity performance. Lucy
saw Jeremy at rehearsals and meals, but they were
never alone, and they were both miserable.

Two nights before the gala, Lucy and Olivia were
working together to sew the final beading in place
on her costume when Jeremy entered the room and

announced, "I need to talk to Lucy. Will you ladies please excuse us?" He held out his hand to her.

Lucy glanced at her mother, Olivia, and Sylvia, all of whom seemed to be trying to conceal their amusement at Jeremy's sudden intrusion.

"By all means," Sylvia said, "go, Lucy, or I fear Sir Jeremy shall cause a scene." She played a card from her hand without even glancing at Jeremy.

Lucy crossed the room but did not take Jeremy's hand. Instead she walked out into the grand foyer and turned on him as soon as he had closed the door. "That was rude," she said.

"Perhaps, but if one more day—one more hour passes without my having a moment alone with you, I may be driven to even more desperate actions."

He held her coat for her.

"Where are we going?"

"The Porterfield gardens are quite lovely," he said.

"It's November, Jeremy. I doubt there is much to see."

He smiled. "Never underestimate me, love."

Once outside, Lucy turned her collar up and thrust her hands in the muff that Olivia had insisted on loaning her for her time in New York. They walked in silence along the leaf-strewn paths.

"Lucy, do you recall the idea that you and Wally had for a new ending to your act?"

"The one where I slide down the rope to Cora's back?"

"Yes. I have been giving it some thought. What if, following your spins, you stayed aloft while the grand finale parade began? We could position Cora at the center of the center ring and then, once all the other acts were inside and encircling Cora, you would make that slide down a rope we have covered in white satin to complement the costume Olivia has created for you."

Lucy could feel her excitement building. "We could do trappings for Cora in white as well."

"Yes, Wally thought of that, and we've also come up with the idea of a stairway descending from Cora's back—you would walk down the stairway, where the ringmaster would be waiting—Wally suggested a bit of a Cinderella-and-her-prince angle."

"Oh, Jeremy, I love it. It's inspired, absolutely fabulous."

"Then you'll do it?"

"Of course. We can rehearse it tomorrow before the gala."

"Excellent," Jeremy said and released what sounded like a breath of relief.

"Did you think I wouldn't agree to the change?" she asked.

"I just wanted to be sure." He took her elbow and guided her toward a gazebo. "I have something else to ask you, Lucy."

When they were seated on the bench in the enclosed gazebo, he took her hands in his. "Lucy, I haven't had the chance to tell you what it meant to me for you to believe in my innocence when there was no reason you should have. If it had not been for you, I might—well, none of this would have been possible."

She cupped his cheek with her gloved hand. "Oh, Jeremy, there is no need to . . ."

"Yes," he said fiercely. "Yes, there is. You inspire me, Lucy. You make me worthy of the success I have achieved. Without your presence in my life these past few months, I'm not sure how things might have turned out for me."

"Really, Jeremy, you give me far too much—"

"I love you, Lucy, beyond any level of devotion I would have thought myself capable of. Without you at my side, I am nothing."

Her eyes brimmed with tears of pure joy.

"I know that you have long wanted to leave the circus for a more traditional life, but I am asking you—pleading with you to accompany me to Europe."

In an instant her joy turned to agony. His love was tied to her performance, her talent, her ability to make the show—and therefore, him—a success.

"It's that important to you?"

"It is everything," he vowed.

She smiled. "Then I shall go."

He swept her into his arms and kissed her. She did not resist, for in that moment she had made a decision for herself. She would give him what he needed, but she would also take something for herself. She would cherish every kiss, every caress, every stolen moment of the time they had left.

"I love you," she murmured aloud for the first time, and to her astonishment, he let out a whoop of delight as he lifted her and spun around with her in his arms.

"Ah, Lucy, love, the two of us—we shall set the world afire."

He kissed her again and again until she was quite breathless with wanting him and knew that it was the same for him.

"Jeremy? I really don't think that this is the proper . . ."

He chuckled as he nuzzled her ear. "I can wait, my love. Not long, but I shall wait." He wrapped his arm around her shoulders and held her close as the two of them walked back up to the house, where everyone had retired for the night. Jeremy took advantage of the privacy to kiss her several more times as they stood at the foot of the curved stairway.

"Go," he said finally, giving her a gentle push. "Go now. I am no saint, love, and if you kiss me once more I shall not be responsible."

Eighteen

The following day passed in a frenzy of activity. Lucy, Ian, and Wally spent the day at the hall where the gala would be held that evening. They rehearsed the finale several times, making sure that they had considered every possible contingency. By the time they were satisfied, it was time to dress for the performance.

As she applied her makeup, Lucy could hear the guests gathering in the grand reception hall outside the arena. She heard the firing of Wally's cannon and the gasp of surprise followed by loud applause as she slipped into the exquisite costume Olivia had created for her. She stood in the wings and watched as each act performed.

Trixie was inspired as she thrilled the patrons with her side-stand neck straddle followed by her own version of going under the belly of Bucko as the horse raced full speed around the large ring. Her finale, the Hippodrome stand, brought the audience to its feet. Lucy had to smile at the sight of hundreds of society men and women garbed in elegant evening clothes, cheering wildly and whistling their approval the same way any country audience might.

She did her stretches, warming up for her performance as Babbo and the other clowns teased and delighted the crowd with their antics.

"Lucy?"

She turned and saw Reggie. He was ready for his entrance.

"I just wanted to . . . that is . . . well, I was a damned fool about a lot of things, but I wanted to say that your Jeremy is quite a gentleman. I'm happy for you, Lucy. He's a good man and you deserve only the best."

He bent and kissed her cheek, then strutted into the lights as the band struck up his theme music and Otto announced him.

"Ready?" Ian asked a few minutes later.

Lucy nodded and started to climb the rigging to her platform. She spotted Wally standing near Cora and wondered why he was not yet in his costume. He gave her a wave and rolled his trademark unlit cigar to one side of his mouth as he watched her safely to the perch.

The lights were dimmed, the drumroll rumbled, the audience sat hushed and expectant as Otto bellowed, "Lad-ies and gentlemen. Presenting the most stupendous and daring of aerial acts currently performing across America. Working without the safety of a net, flying over seventy-five feet above you and weighing not much more than that herself. I present to you, the one . . . the only . . . Lady Lucinda, Angel of the Big Top!"

Lucy touched the bracelet that Jeremy had given her for luck. The lights came on and found her as she flew into sight. She executed a flawless twisting somersault and two straight somersaults as she soared from one trapeze to another. The crowd went wild. She performed the classic cat-in-a-cradle and then slid down until she was hanging by her ankles. She released one ankle, holding their attention as she donned the neck strap for the spins.

All the time, she searched the audience for Jeremy. He wasn't there. She saw the Porterfield box, saw the single empty chair where he had sat all evening. Her temper flared. How dare he miss this!

"And now, ladies and gentlemen," Otto said in a stage whisper, "this next trick of Lady Lucinda's requires her full concentration. It is one that will soon thrill the crowned heads of Europe. Please join me in counting as Lady Lucinda performs her own death-defying celestial pirouette!"

On cue, Lucy dropped into her spin.

"One!" Otto said in a hushed voice over the microphone. "Two . . . three . . ."

The audience took up the count, their voices rising with excitement as she passed thirty, then fifty, then seventy.

"Ninety-eight . . . ninety-nine . . ." Otto's voice was almost hoarse with shouting out the count. "One hundred!"

Lucy released the neck strap as she caught the flybar that Ian sent sailing her way. She pumped once, twice, and then flew to the perch where she took her bows. The applause was deafening. Below her she could see Cora positioned in the darkened center ring, ready for the finale.

Jeremy's seat was still vacant.

Lucy concentrated on checking the positioning of the satin rope as the grand finale promenade began below her. She heard the music swell and wrapped the rope around one foot as she prepared to make her slide to Cora's back. Otto was announcing each act, and performers were taking their bows and accepting the thunderous applause as they circled the ring.

"And the star of the Conroy Cavalcade, our very own Angel of the Big Top, Lady Lucinda!" Otto shouted, and the audience came to its feet as Lucinda gracefully slid down the rope and found her footing on the specially disguised platform that was part of Cora's trappings.

She turned to the stairway that led from Cora's back, her smile firmly in place. But instead of Otto, Jeremy was waiting for her at the foot of those stairs. He was resplendent in white formal garb that included a white satin top hat. He was also on one bended knee.

Slowly she traversed the steps, and she noticed that now everyone was applauding—the audience and her fellow performers, all of whom seemed to know something that she did not.

"Lucinda," Jeremy said in a voice meant for only her as he took her hand. "There was one small detail I failed to mention last night when I asked you to accompany me to Europe. Will you accompany me as my wife? Will you marry me?"

She was speechless and felt her smile drop into a shocked, openmouthed gasp. Jeremy was holding the most beautiful emerald-and-diamond ring she had ever seen. "Please?" he mouthed as he stood and, around them, the cheers from her fellow performers escalated.

It was not in the script, but she hardly cared; she catapulted herself into his arms.

"Yes!" she shouted as he caught her and spun her around. "Oh, yes!" She wrapped her arms around his neck and hung on as the music blared to its finale.

Just before Jeremy set her down and kissed her, she caught sight of Wally standing near the bandstand. He was smiling, and for the first time she could ever recall, he was puffing on a fresh, lit cigar.

COMING IN JANUARY 2003 FROM
ZEBRA BALLAD ROMANCES

—BELLE OF THE BALL: The Graces
by Pam McCutcheon   0-8217-7456-5 $5.99US/$7.99CAN
Belle Sullivan is a tomboy—and darn proud of it—until she over-
hears the local swains mocking her and her sisters. Determined to
make the men pay, she vows to become a beauty and ensnare them,
one by one. She then hires handsome Englishman Kit Stanhope to
teach her the art of flirtation. Before long, she is a veritable heart-
breaker. If only she didn't yearn to use her skills on the very man
who taught them to her!

—THE TRUTH ABOUT CASSANDRA: Masquerade
by Laurie Brown   0-8217-7437-9 $5.99US/$7.99CAN
A willing spinster, Anne Weathersby has set aside her own needs to
care for her siblings. But debts and good deeds take their toll. To make
ends meet, Anne embarks on a secret, scandalous career as a novelist.

—THE MOST UNSUITABLE WIFE: The Kincaids
by Caroline Clemmons   0-8217-7443-3 $5.99US/$7.99CAN
Drake Kincaid's parents' will stipulates only that he marry by his thir-
tieth birthday, not that he marry *well*. And no one—including Drake's
grandfather, could possibly think tall, bossy Pearl with her ragtag siblings and questionable "cousin" Belle would make a good wife.

—WHERE THE HEART LEADS: In Love and War
by Marilyn Herr   0-8217-7447-6 $5.99US/$7.99CAN
When Rachel Whitfield's brother is taken by French Canadian ma-
rauders, she persuades brawny trader Jonah Butler to take her north
to rescue him. It's a battle of wills from the beginning, but soon it's
something more—a journey into the secrets of desire . . .

Call toll free **1-888-345-BOOK** to order by phone or use this coupon to order by
mail. *ALL BOOKS AVAILABLE JANUARY 01, 2003*
Name_____
Address_____
City_____State_____Zip_____
Please send me the books that I have checked above.
I am enclosing $_____
Plus postage and handling* $_____
Sales Tax (in NY and TN) $_____
Total amount enclosed $_____
*Add $2.50 for the first book and $.50 for each additional book. Send check or
money order (no cash or CODs) to: **Kensington Publishing Corp., Dept. C.O.,
850 Third Avenue, New York, NY 10022**
Prices and numbers subject to change without notice. Valid only in the U.S. All
orders subject to availablity. **NO ADVANCE ORDERS.**
Visit our website at **www.kensingtonbooks.com.**

Experience the Romances of
Rosanne Bittner